DEATH SWATCH

A SCRAPBOOKING MYSTERY

Death Swatch

LAURA CHILDS

KENNEBEC
CHIVERS

This Large Print edition is published by Kennebec Large Print, Waterville, Maine, USA and by BBC Audiobooks Ltd, Bath, England.
Kennebec Large Print, a part of Gale, Cengage Learning.
Copyright © 2008 by Gerry Schmitt & Associates, Inc.
The moral right of the author has been asserted.
A Scrapbooking Mystery.

The text of this Large Print edition is unabridged.
Other aspects of the book may vary from the original edition.
Set in 16 pt. Plantin.
Printed on permanent paper.

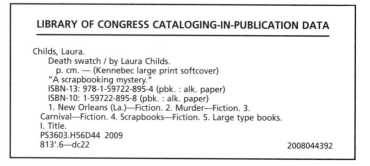

LIBRARY OF CONGRESS CATALOGING-IN-PUBLICATION DATA

Childs, Laura.
    Death swatch / by Laura Childs.
        p. cm. — (Kennebec large print softcover)
    "A scrapbooking mystery."
    ISBN-13: 978-1-59722-895-4 (pbk. : alk. paper)
    ISBN-10: 1-59722-895-8 (pbk. : alk. paper)
    1. New Orleans (La.)—Fiction. 2. Murder—Fiction. 3. Carnival—Fiction. 4. Scrapbooks—Fiction. 5. Large type books.
    I. Title.
    PS3603.H56D44 2009
    813'.6—dc22   2008044392

BRITISH LIBRARY CATALOGUING-IN-PUBLICATION DATA AVAILABLE

Published in 2009 in the U.S. by arrangement with The Berkley Publishing Group, a member of Penguin Group (USA) Inc.
Published in 2009 in the U.K. by arrangement with The Berkley Publishing Group, a division of Penguin Group (USA) Inc.

U.K. Hardcover: 978 1 408 43274 7 (Chivers Large Print)
U.K. Softcover: 978 1 408 43275 4 (Camden Large Print)

Printed in the United States of America
1 2 3 4 5 6 7 13 12 11 10 09

This book is dedicated to
F. Jim Smith,
good friend and advertising "icon."

ACKNOWLEDGMENTS

Thanks to my agent, Sam; my editor, Tom; all the artists, designers, and talented copy department folks at Berkley; Fran in gift sales; Jennie and Elmo; Dan for all his wonderful design work; and, of course, my husband, Dr. Bob, who always believes in me.

CHAPTER 1

It wasn't that Carmela didn't like Mardi Gras. She liked it just fine. Adored it, in fact. Nothing quite set a girl's fur to crackling than those monster-sized floats, festooned and glittering with lights, as they rumbled majestically down Napoleon Avenue.

But all the hoopla leading up to Mardi Gras was enough to drive her bonkers. Like tonight. Jekyl Hardy's party at his elegant, old-world apartment in the French Quarter. Champagne corks were popping, zydeco music was blasting, strands of purple and green beads were being flung from dancing couple to dancing couple. And this was only Tuesday night. A school night at that! Tomorrow morning Carmela's scrapbook shop, Memory Mine, had to be open on the dot of nine. And she had to be primed and ready for the onslaught of customers who would pour in, frantic to grab reams of paper, rubber stamps, and rolls of purple and green ribbon. All the better to create those Mardi Gras menus, party place settings, and scrapbook pages.

Carmela's hand reached up and nervously patted her slightly spiky crop of blond hair. Glancing in one of Jekyl's antique mirrors, she caught sight of her wavering image amid the reflection of swirling revelers. Lip gloss okay? Sure. A tad more mascara? No. Not necessary to impersonate a tarantula.

Carmela Bertrand was beautiful and didn't always realize it. Blue-gray eyes graced with tipped-up dark lashes. A peaches-and-cream complexion that was enhanced by the natural hydration properties of Louisiana's industrial-strength humidity. Thick, blond hair that was, as her friend, Ava, liked to say, artfully skunked and chunked.

Ava. Where was Ava?

Carmela gazed across the top of her chalice-sized goblet of vodka, raspberry liqueur, and cranberry juice, a drink the bartender had called a Purple Haze, and saw that Ava Gruiex, her very best friend in the entire world, was huddled in a corner, gesturing theatrically and talking to a most interesting-looking man. Of course, Ava was a gorgeous and lithesome former beauty queen, femme fatale, and predatory single woman. While she, Carmela, was still trying to puzzle out the etiquette of how to put a discreet move on someone of the male persuasion. Though her divorce from Shamus Meechum, colossal rat and so last year's news, wasn't yet final, was dragging on like a bad third act in a tawdry melodrama, Carmela thought it would be nice to have a boyfriend again. Finally. Before she hit thirty and the old ticktock came into play.

When Ava noticed Carmela looking her way, she let loose a smile and an enthusiastic wave.

In response, Carmela dashed across the dance floor, also known as Jekyl Hardy's living room, trying her best to avoid the writhing mass of partiers, to join her friend. Ava had one bare shoulder nudged possessively up against her latest catch, a good-looking man in his early thirties with soulful brown eyes and sandy-colored hair.

"*Cher,*" said Ava excitedly, pushing back her mass of dark, curly hair and fluttering her lethal-length manicured nails. "Say how do to Archie Baudier."

"How do," said Carmela, amused by Ava's never-fail tactics to intrigue a man.

Archie nodded in return and gave a shy

smile. He seemed suddenly intimidated to be in the company of two such lovely, albeit slightly pushy women.

"Archie is Jekyl's neighbor," explained Ava. "He lives in the apartment directly next door."

"Then you're one of the select few who are envied by pretty much everyone in the Quarter," Carmela told him. "I hear there's a five-year waiting list to get into this building." Jekyl and Archie's apartment building, known officially as Napoleon Gardens, was one of the premier residences in the French Quarter. Built of red brick and originally designed as a warehouse, it dated back to the mid–eighteen hundreds. At the turn of the century, the twentieth not the twenty-first, a wealthy plantation owner had purchased the three-story building and converted it into apartments.

And what palatial places they were! Jekyl Hardy's apartment was only the second one she'd ever visited in this building, but it was a belle époque tour de force. Mahogany floors exuded a rich, dark patina. Tinkling crystal chandeliers dangled from fourteen-foot-high ceilings. Tall, stately windows sported hand-carved plaster cornices. The pitted marble fireplace that dominated the living room was still in working order. A quaint interior courtyard boasted a gigantic live oak tree festooned with Spanish moss and parterre-style plots overrun with tangles of pink ruffle azaleas and Louisiana peppermint camellias. Lacy wrought-iron balconies lent a final touch of elegance.

Of course, interior decoration added to the charm. And Jekyl Hardy, an antique dealer and licensed appraiser by trade, had spared no expense. Dark blue shellacked walls were the perfect backdrop for antique smoked mirrors in gilded frames. Both the living and dining rooms boasted high-backed leather couches as well as over-stuffed chairs with slipcovers in rich brocades and dark damask fabrics. Fringed lamps cast dim shadows. Artwork included oil paintings as well as large brass sculptures of horses, dogs, and Roman statues personally collected by Jekyl.

Speak of the devil . . .

"Jekyl!" called Carmela, breaking into a grin upon seeing her dear friend.

Jekyl Hardy, lean and trim, with long, dark hair pulled back in a ponytail, could have been the model for Anne Rice's vampire Lestat. He consistently dressed in black and worked to project a mysterious air.

Carmela tilted her head slightly as Jekyl joined them and offered air kisses to both her cheeks.

"Are you having a *fabulous* time?" Jekyl asked of Carmela and Ava. "And have you tried my Vampire Bat Wings?" His dark eyes danced with mischief. "Don't tell anyone, but they're really chicken wings soused in chili sauce, honey, and vinegar. I got the recipe from that wonderful lady over on Royal Street — you know, the one with the purple hair who cooks up those scrumptious pralines?"

"I haven't tried the Vampire Bat Wings, but they sound completely yummy," drawled Ava. She owned the Juju Voodoo Shop directly across the courtyard from Carmela's garden apartment and was in love with all manner of oddball things. Of course, the magic charms and amulets Ava sold to tourists were really quite benign. Her love charms consisted of aromatic herbs tied up in little red-and-gold silk pouches. And shrunken heads were mostly carved wood with a few tufts of goat hair.

"You, my dear, need another drink," said Jekyl, eyeing Carmela's almost empty glass.

"Me, too," said Ava, holding out her goblet to Archie.

"Then we shall make our way into yon kitchen and return with fresh provisions for the ladies," said Jekyl. "But first, Archie and

14

I have a few pressing matters to discuss regarding the floats for the Pluvius krewe."

"Problems?" asked Carmela. Her soon-to-be ex, Shamus, was a member of the Pluvius krewe, so she knew firsthand how crazy and disorganized that group could be.

"Mostly tedious issues with their rather imperious krewe captain," Jekyl told her. "He lobbied hard to hire Jimmy Toups but, fortunately, was outvoted."

"Jimmy Toups," said Carmela. "Your big rival." Jimmy Toups was a somewhat arrogant designer and sometime sculptor who designed floats for the Rigadoon and Marquis krewes.

"Not so big," sniped Jekyl.

Carmela turned toward Archie. "How fun that you're helping Jekyl with the Pluvius floats. He told me he'd hired an assistant, and a qualified one at that. Congrats."

"Thanks," said Archie.

"The time was right," cut in Jekyl. Besides making his living in art and antiques, Jekyl was one of the premier Mardi Gras float designers. He often worked on floats for several of the big krewes at the same time and had recently received an offer to write a book about the long and storied history of Mardi Gras.

Archie Baudier favored Carmela with a

friendly grin that morphed into a slight grimace. "Float building is turning out to be great fun. Unfortunately, I had no idea how much *work* was involved." Archie spread his fingers and ticked off each point. "Concept, design blueprints, internal architecture, actual float construction, decoration, sound effects, motion, and lighting."

"Whew," said Ava. "I thought y'all just constructed a big papier-mâché head or something, then people climbed on and tossed strands of beads."

"I wish it was that easy," said Archie. "Fact is, we're running behind big time, and Fat Tuesday's just one week away." Fat Tuesday was the climax of Mardi Gras, that one bawdy day of revelry that local media as well as national networks loved to broadcast to all the world.

"So you're under the gun," said Carmela. Of course, they were. Mardi Gras was a hectic time for everyone. Tough to work and fit in all those parties, too!

"We're *dying!*" said Jekyl.

"Designing floats is just a completely different design paradigm than creating Web sites," Archie added. "Floats are multidimensional, and the scale is enormous."

"That's what you do for real?" asked Ava. She was all but batting her eyes at him.

16

"Design Web sites?"

But Jekyl had already pulled Archie from Ava's grasp, and they were headed toward the kitchen.

"Jekyl always knows the most interesting people," said Ava, as her eyes roved the crowd that milled about them. She nudged Carmela with an elbow. "Take that group over there. So doggone artsy-looking."

"A real French Quarter crowd," agreed Carmela. Indeed, she recognized a number of antique dealers, café and bar owners, as well as folks who were just plain neighbors. You didn't always know their names but certainly nodded to them when you passed in the street. Carmela recognized a man who was a professional mime who hung out in Jackson Square, a well-known photographer who specialized in extremely flattering society portraits, and two outsider artists who were being so heavily collected these days that they were in danger of losing their outsider status.

"Honey," said Ava, grabbing Carmela's arm and shouting into her ear as the decibel level continued to rise, "I can't tell you how excited I am to finally be in a Mardi Gras krewe. And a brand-spanking-new one at that."

"It's about time," said Carmela. "It's *our*

17

time." Last summer, a group of female business owners from the French Quarter had put their heads together and come up with the idea of forming what was euphemistically known as a neighborhood krewe. Calling themselves the Demilune krewe, they planned to roll a single float on Fat Tuesday in the company of two fairly well-established Bywater neighborhood krewes. Of course, there was no competing with the super krewes like Proteus, Bacchus, Endymion, or Rex, who put on lavish, multifloat parades, but it was a fun thing to attempt. And maybe the start of something bigger, too. Who knew? It wasn't so long ago that women hadn't participated in Mardi Gras parades at all.

Ava waved a hand to fan herself. "Whew, getting warm in here. So many bodies all pressed together. Normally, I like that type of situation, but tonight I feel like I'm gettin' the vapors."

"Maybe it's the leather pants," said Carmela, glancing at Ava's skintight black leather pants.

"No, my pants are fine," said Ava. "It's my head that feels like it's going to explode like a can of beans sittin' on a hot burner."

"Plus it's getting late," said Carmela. She glanced at her watch, a Cartier tank watch

18

handed down from her father, and saw that it was a little after ten. "Oh, yeah, I've got to get going." She had two dogs to walk and always liked to lay out her clothes for the following morning. Mornings tended to be a slightly hectic, groggy time for Carmela.

"But the party's just getting started," pleaded Ava. "And we didn't get our second round of drinks yet."

"Ten more minutes then," said Carmela as the two of them elbowed their way through the crowd. Jekyl's parties always went on until the wee hours of the morning. And they always seemed to generate a certain weird cachet. Even now, the room seemed dim and exotic as burning candles strobed like crazy, casting wild shadows on dark walls. The smell of incense mingled with the aroma of floral bouquets, perfume, aftershave, and Caribbean spices. Someone had shoved an old Doors album into the CD player and the tune "Light My Fire" pulsed through the room. All in all, the atmosphere was a little spooky but intoxicating, too.

Pushing their way into the tiny kitchen, Carmela and Ava found two caterers sharing a joint and an overworked bartender frantically washing glasses. But no Jekyl Hardy or Archie Baudier.

"Maybe they went outside?" proposed Ava. "For a smoke?"

"Jekyl doesn't smoke," said Carmela.

Ava shrugged and rolled her eyes at the caterers. "You know . . ."

Yes, she did.

"Then they're probably hanging out on the back balcony," said Carmela. It overlooked the garden below and offered an unobstructed sight line to the gently curving Mississippi River with its never-ending parade of slow-moving, twinkling barges.

The outside hallway was just as jammed as the inside of Jekyl's apartment. More guests had arrived and remained congregated there, drinking, smoking, talking loudly. The music was still blaring, too, the Doors snarling out their song: "Come on baby, light my fire / Try to set the night on fiiiiire."

"How many people did Jekyl invite, anyway?" asked Ava as they hunched and bumped their way through the throng of laughing, joking, drinking-to-beat-the-band guests.

"It's not a question of how many you invite," said Carmela. "It's who the invitees invite." At Mardi Gras time, it wasn't uncommon for friends of friends as well as friends of those friends to tag along to parties.

"Excuse me, excuse me," said Ava as they pushed and inched through the crowd.

"The fire marshal would have a conniption if he saw this jam of people," said Carmela.

"Being Mardi Gras," said Ava, "the fire marshal would probably grab a drink and join in."

"*Laissez les bon temps rouler,*" said Carmela. Let the good times roll. It was still very much the mantra of the Big Easy.

"Hey," said Ava. "There he is." As they reached the end of the hallway, she peered through a wrought-iron door backed with glass panels. That door led out to a balcony, or what was referred to as a *gallery* in New Orleans.

"Jekyl," called Carmela, rapping on the glass. "We're gonna take off in a couple of minutes."

"Speak for yourself," said Ava, glancing back at the crowd. "I might just stay and —"

"That's not Jekyl," Carmela said in a low, cautious voice.

Ava's head spun around. "Then who . . . ?"

"I think it's your friend, Archie. He's bent

completely over the railing and doesn't look like he's in very good shape."

Ava nodded. "Too much Purple Haze. That stuff can mess with your mind."

Carmela clutched Ava's arm as the figure on the balcony straightened up slightly, then bobbed and wove drunkenly. "Dear lord, I think he's really ill."

They watched, startled, as Archie suddenly dropped to his knees.

"Ouch," said Carmela.

"Maybe we oughta give him a little space," suggested Ava, somewhat embarrassed now.

Carmela squinted into the darkness. "Ava . . ."

Ava was starting to move back toward the party. "Yes, *cher?*"

"I think something's really wrong."

"Huh?" Ava's head snapped back.

Making up her mind, Carmela pushed open the wrought-iron door and felt the welcome caress of cool night air.

"Archie?" she called. "Mr. Baudier? Do you need help?"

Her question was met with a low moan.

"What's wrong with him?" asked Ava. She was a few steps behind Carmela, looking hesitant, trying to decide what to do.

Archie's hands clutched his throat, and he was making a strange gurgling sound. Sud-

22

denly, he began yanking and batting at something.

"Collar's too tight," said Ava. "Poor guy probably needs a few breaths of fresh air."

Carmela closed the gap between herself and Archie Baudier. Kneeling down beside him, she was startled to see that his face was bright red, even as his eyes lolled sickeningly in his head. And something seemed to be wrapped tightly around Archie's neck.

What on earth?

Instinctively, Carmela's hand reached out to see what was choking Archie, then recoiled as she hit something sharp. "Ouch!" One fingertip was suddenly ripped open.

"Cher?" said Ava, sounding jittery now.

"There's something wrapped around his neck," said Carmela, barely able to contain her horror. "Some sort of wire or metal."

"Oh my Lord!" exclaimed Ava. She was instantly on her knees beside Carmela and pulling at the collar of Archie Baudier's shirt.

What they saw was positively inhuman. A thick coil of barbed wire was wound so tightly around Archie's neck that it was practically imbedded in his flesh. A garrote!

"He's been strangled!" said Carmela. "Quick, try to find some kind of cutting tool, and have someone phone nine-one-one! He needs help now! Go!"

Ava sprinted off as Carmela eased a gasping Archie down onto his side and struggled again with the wire around his neck. In the few seconds' time she'd been trying to help him, Archie's face had turned from beet red to a hideous purple, and his eyes were beginning to bulge! Pitiful moans came from the back of his throat, and his eyelids fluttered weakly.

Reaching around in back, Carmela found that the stiff wire had been tightened and bent into a kind of knot. She tried frantically to loosen it with her fingers, but nothing she did seemed to work.

More horrible sounds poured forth from Archie Baudier. Dry, choking sobs. And Carmela feared he was running out of precious air.

Now Archie's entire body seemed racked with violent tremors. His head twisted from side to side; his shoulders arched then released.

These were convulsions, Carmela told herself as she viewed them from an almost dreamlike state. His oxygen-starved brain was rebelling, his body dying off, cell by cell.

Carmela fumbled again with the barbed

wire, trying to untwist the metal that held Archie in its wicked embrace. The barbs dug deep into her thumb and index fingers, but still she fought to free him. She was frighteningly cognizant that even as Archie's convulsions began to abate, any semblance of respiration was slowly ceasing.

Ava suddenly dropped beside her in a flutter. "Ambulance is on the way," she announced breathlessly. "And Jekyl's coming with those cutters." Carmela glanced up. A gaggle of people had followed Ava out. Their expressions carried a blend of curiosity and horror at what they were witnessing.

Carmela stared down at Archie's eggplant-colored face with its hideously protruding tongue and froth of bloody bubbles. "It's too late," she told her friend. "He's dead."

CHAPTER 2

All hell broke loose then. Jekyl arrived in a blind panic and tried to cut the barbed wire using garden shears. In the process, he managed to nick and gouge Archie's neck horribly.

"Stop!" begged Ava. "You're just making it worse!"

"She's right," said Carmela. "The poor man's gone."

Jekyl refused to accept the reality of the situation. "But I was just *talking* to him!"

"So were we," said a tearful Ava.

"We were having a drink!" argued Jekyl. The shears dropped with a clatter, and he gazed at Carmela, pain and frustration apparent in his eyes. "Can't we do *something* for him?" he begged. "Artificial respiration? CPR?"

"We can leave him alone," said Carmela. "So the police can do their job." It was slowly dawning on her that Archie Baudier didn't wrap that nasty coil of barbed wire around his neck by himself. Someone had savagely attacked him, gotten the better of him, and strangled him. She glanced up at the shuffling, suddenly sober crowd that hung back from them. Someone . . . here? Someone who was still at this party?

A wail of police sirens suddenly pierced the still of the night.

Jekyl struggled to his feet. "I'll . . . I'll get something to cover him with." Stoop-shouldered, he turned and pushed his way through the silenced revelers.

"Maybe we should all go back inside," suggested Ava. The crowd seemed to hesitate en masse for a few seconds, then they slowly eased away from the body.

Carmela, left alone with Archie Baudier, looked up at the glimmer of stars overhead in the dark, inky sky and wondered if, even now, his poor soul was traveling heavenward. *Upward on heavenly wings,* she thought to herself, remembering a snippet from a song. Or maybe it was a Bible verse.

She gazed down at Archie, thought for a few moments, then dug inside the Coach bag that had slid off her shoulder during the melee.

The word *murder* was running through her mind, etched in glowing capital letters. Like chase lights on a movie marquee. *Murder.* Archie had been murdered.

Carmela found her little Maglite, then snapped it on and began her cursory inspection.

Yes, it was barbed wire that was wound around his neck, all right. But an extra-thick kind of barbed wire. Carmela wondered idly where you'd find something like that. A building supply place? A military surplus store?

She ran the beam of her flashlight down the body. *The body.* Not Archie Baudier anymore. Strange how death instantly depersonalized someone.

Carmela didn't see anything out of the ordinary. Except . . .

She aimed the beam directly at Archie's shoes. Penny loafers. A nice dark brown, good-quality leather. Strangely, they seemed to carry a few flecks of gold paint.

Carmela ran the flashlight back up the body. Besides the fact that he was dead, nothing else looked out of place.

Just as she was about to flick the Maglite off, Carmela noticed the glint of something nearby.

What? A ring? No. Some sort of coin. Must have fallen from his pocket.

Carmela reached down and picked it up

28

just as four uniformed police officers and a pair of EMTs swarmed the balcony.

"Everybody back off," ordered one of the officers. He glanced at her sharply. "That means you, too, lady."

Carmela spread her hands in a gesture of friendliness. "Hey, I was only trying to help." She struggled to her feet, feeling more than a little shaky.

"Let the professionals take over," he told her in a gruff voice.

"Sure," she said, eyeing his name tag. Willy Partridge. "Officer Partridge?"

"You're the one who found him?" asked one of the EMTs. He was a round-faced man who worked briskly and efficiently but seemed to have a kind manner.

"Yes," said Carmela. "He was choking, trying to get that piece of . . ."

"I said out!" yelled Officer Partridge. "What part of my order did you not understand?"

Carmela narrowed her eyes as she backed away. This wasn't going well. Partridge was yelling and threatening, and here she was, an actual witness. Well, a sort-of witness anyway.

"Shouldn't you bring in a crime-scene unit?" Carmela asked.

"Are you going to get out of the way?"

thundered Partridge. "Or do you want to be cuffed and booked?"

This time Carmela put her hands all the way in the air in a gesture of surrender. "Enough already, I'm leaving."

Carmela joined up with Ava and Jekyl in the hallway. Another twenty or so party guests were huddled there, too, talking in low whispers. Carmela wondered where the rest of the people had made off to.

Ava looked shaken but had pulled it together. Jekyl was clutching a white sheet, the sheet he'd gone to get so he could cover Archie's body.

"What's happening?" he asked Carmela in a shaky voice.

"The police and EMTs are at the scene," said Carmela, even though that was fairly self-evident.

"I heard yelling," said Ava.

"Yeah . . . well . . ." said Carmela. "Things are a little crazy."

Another officer was pushing his way through the crowd. "Mr. Hardy?" he called. "Jekyl Hardy?"

Jekyl raised his hand like he was back in school. "That's me."

"We want everyone back inside your apartment," he told Jekyl.

Jekyl nodded miserably. "Sure. Okay."

"People," said the officer, raising his voice. "Clear this hallway. Get back in Mr. Hardy's apartment, okay?"

Nobody moved.

Officer Partridge joined his partner. He pulled out his nightstick, smacked it hard against the wall. "Now! Move!"

A sudden flurry of fur brushed across Carmela's ankles. And then a woman screamed, "Somebody grab that cat!"

The crowd shuffled and parted, revealing a furry black cat cowering against a claret-colored wall, looking absolutely terrified.

"That's Isis," said Jekyl. "Archie's cat. She must have gotten out of his apartment somehow."

"Oh no," said Carmela. "Should we try to catch her?"

"People!" boomed Partridge. "You're still not moving!"

"She's awfully high-strung," said Jekyl.

"Let me," said Ava. She skittered down the hallway and scooped the cat up in her arms.

"Watch out," warned Jekyl as everyone started backing down the hallway toward his apartment. "Sometimes she scratches like crazy."

But Isis seemed calm and comfortable in Ava's gentle embrace.

"I could take her home," Ava offered.

"Would you?" said a grateful Jekyl.

A rush of air swept the hallway, then a clanking metal gurney suddenly appeared.

"Make way, make way!" shouted the round-faced EMT, as they rushed it through.

One hand hooked possessively on the metal strut of the gurney, Officer Partridge kept pace as it rattled past stunned onlookers. A white sheet was drawn over Archie Baudier's dead body.

Carmela turned and dashed after the terrible entourage. "Shouldn't you be questioning these people?" she asked Officer Partridge.

Jaw firmly set, dark eyes blazing, Partridge brushed Carmela off like she was an insignificant, buzzing gnat. "Lady, will you *please* get lost!"

Gazing after the flutter of sheets, Carmela's brain registered the click-clack of wheels. They could rush all they wanted, but it wasn't going to make an iota of difference for poor Archie Baudier.

Feeling helpless, Carmela's fist closed tightly around the coin she'd picked up. She was oblivious to the feel of metal pressing into flesh, unaware of the punishment she was giving her poor, already torn and bleeding hand.

Carmela knew it was too late for Archie Baudier. She also knew this was the worst possible way to handle a crime scene.

CHAPTER 3

"I just can't believe it," said Gabby. "The poor man was murdered right there in Jekyl's apartment?"

"On the balcony anyway," Carmela told her assistant. They were gathered at the big square table in the back of Carmela's scrapbook shop. It was a chipped and slightly dented wooden table that previous tenants had left behind, and they'd laughingly dubbed it Craft Central. Gabby was hanging on Carmela's every word. So were Baby Fontaine and Tandy Bliss, two of Carmela's scrapbooking regulars.

Gabby shook her head, still not believing the news. She was a sweet, rather demure girl who was married to Stuart Mercer-Morris, the Toyota King of New Orleans. While a lot of women opted for glitter T-shirts and jeans with hardware, Gabby always seemed more at home in a twinset. She was wearing one now, in fact. Paprika-colored cashmere topping carefully pressed khakis.

Tandy gazed across the top of her red half-glasses and put a hand to her tight mop of hennaed curls. "Sounds like a mob hit. You think this Archie guy was involved in something illegal? Drugs or something? Organized crime?" She said it casually as she passed around Coconut-Cranberry Bars.

Carmela shrugged. "Search me. All I know is he was a Web site designer who was helping Jekyl design and build floats."

"Doesn't sound too shady to me," said Baby. She was fifty-something and still gorgeous. A blond pixie who wore designer duds and lived in a grand mansion in the Garden District.

"You never know," said Tandy, who seemed to thrive on imagining the worst. "Things have changed down here. Lots of new people moving in to try to take advantage. People from not here." *From not here* was New Orleans slang for saying someone wasn't born and bred there.

"I don't think Archie's new people," said Carmela. "In fact, I think he's from here."

"You say the last name is Baudier?" asked Baby. "I'll have to ask Mrs. Xavier over at the Claiborne Club. She knows absolutely everyone."

"No kidding," said Tandy, rolling her eyes. "She's got lists of pedigrees that stretch back almost two hundred years. Come to think of it, Mrs. Xavier might be pushing two hundred herself."

"That would make her a vampire," said Gabby.

"Honey," replied Tandy, raising thin, penciled brows, "down here that's not far from the truth."

Bam. Bam. Bam.

The sudden, loud pounding caused Gabby to jump in her seat. "Good heavens, what's that?" she exclaimed, clapping a hand to her heart. She was obviously still shaken by Carmela's tale detailing Archie Baudier's gruesome murder.

But Carmela was already up and moving swiftly toward the back door, a heavy metal contraption that required more than a little finesse to open.

"It's probably Ava," said Carmela, jiggling the dead bolt. "She said she'd be dropping by."

It was Ava. This time dressed in buckskin leather jeans and a brown, spangled T-shirt; and bearing a box that held an extraordinarily large king cake! "Greetings, dear hearts!" she announced.

"Why it's Miss Ava with a king cake!"

exclaimed Baby. "More sugar to help elevate our glucose levels. How absolutely perfect."

"And delicious," added Tandy. King cake was a coffee cake–type sweet decorated with purple and green sprinkles. And tradition dictated that whoever found the little plastic king cake baby that had been baked inside was obliged to buy the next king cake.

"I'll put on some coffee," volunteered Gabby. "Chicory okay with everyone?"

"The stronger the better," said Ava, setting her cake down in the middle of the table. She undid the ties to her black cape and let it slip from her shoulders. Then her dark eyes roamed quizzically around the table. "I see Carmela told y'all."

Tandy gave a sharp bob of her head. "A sad situation. But there's always crazy things that happen during Mardi Gras."

Ava slid into an empty chair. "Yeah, but I gotta tell you, this was way nuttier than usual. Did Carmela tell you how Archie was killed? The actual, grizzly circumstances?"

Heads nodded a little more slowly now. The notion of someone being strangled with a barbed wire ligature was particularly distasteful.

"I mean, how weird is that?" asked Ava, flipping the lid on the large bakery box. "A murder like that sounds almost . . . What would you call it? Ritualistic?" As if to punctuate her sentence, she picked up a knife and sliced off a generous slab of king cake.

"I really wish you wouldn't say that," called Gabby from the back room.

"Yeah, but it's true," said Ava, continuing to slice.

"How's the kitty doing?" asked Carmela.

Ava flashed a happy grin. "Isis is a sweetheart," she told Carmela. "Settled down right away, just curled up on my bed."

"Who's Isis?" asked Gabby.

"Archie's cat," said Ava. "Ooh, Carmela, how's your hand?"

"Okay," said Carmela. "The cut wasn't very deep."

"Carmela cut her hand?" asked Baby. "What happened, dear?"

"Caught it on the, uh, barbed wire," said Carmela.

Gabby winced.

"I still think it sounds like a mob hit," said Tandy, as she accepted a piece of king cake from Ava. Tandy liked her theory and was sticking to it.

"Somehow," said Carmela, "I don't envision a Web site designer being connected to the mob."

"Did Carmela tell you I was supposed to

go out with Archie?" asked Ava. "That he'd actually asked me on a date for Saturday night?"

"No," said Baby, reaching over to give Ava a reassuring pat. "Oh, you'd made a connection with him. That's so sad."

"Now I have to find another date for the weekend," said Ava, looking glum.

"I'm sure you'll manage," murmured Carmela. Like pulling a rabbit out of a hat, Ava always managed to find a date.

Ava looked thoughtful as she munched her cake. "Do you think Archie's murder could have had anything to do with the Pluvius krewe?"

"What makes you say that, honey?" asked Tandy.

"Because Archie was helping Jekyl with their particular floats," said Ava.

"That could be an interesting wrinkle," said Baby. Now the group turned their collective eyes on Carmela.

"What?" she said, upon realizing she was suddenly center stage. *"What?"*

"I guess we're just wondering if you talked to Shamus about this," said Tandy. Shamus was Carmela's soon-to-be ex-husband.

Carmela almost did a double take. "Talk to Shamus? I try *never* to deal with Shamus anymore. Or his wacky sister. The less contact I have with those two, the better."

Ava gave an inquisitive tilt of her head. "But Shamus is a member of the Pluvius krewe."

"That doesn't mean he knows what's actually going on," explained Carmela. She gave a sad smile and shook her head. "Shamus is a vice president at Crescent City Bank, but the man can't balance his own checkbook. You have to understand, Shamus's brain doesn't transmit neurons like regular people's gray matter; it fires dumdums. He may be handsome, charming, and glib, but the truth is, I once saw Shamus use his toes to figure a fifteen percent tip."

"Which means he's cheap, too," said Tandy.

"Carmela's probably right," said Baby, adjusting the navy-and-white Chanel scarf draped languidly around her neck. "Shamus never was the brightest bulb in the box."

Gabby set steaming mugs of chicory coffee down on the table for everyone. "I always thought Shamus was kind of sweet," she offered. "Remember the time he sent all those roses?"

"The place looked like a funeral parlor," laughed Tandy.

"It was lovely," protested Gabby. "A little heavy on the fragrance maybe, but awfully

40

romantic."

"Shamus only sent roses that time because he was begging for forgiveness," said Ava. "Trying to avoid the big *D.*"

"Discord?" asked Gabby, wrinkling her nose, trying to recall the exact circumstances.

"Divorce," said Ava. "Although that's exactly what's ended up on his plate. *If* he can manage to get off his lazy butt, get his lawyer to contact Carmela's lawyer, and do a certain amount of negotiation."

"That's a big *if,*" allowed Carmela. Things hadn't exactly been moving along at a breakneck pace.

"I still don't think Shamus really wants a divorce," said Gabby, helping herself to a piece of king cake.

"What is it with that boy?" asked Tandy. "Why can't he let go?"

Gabby gazed across the table at Carmela. "Because he's still smitten."

"Oh please," said Carmela.

"Why else would he be trying to sidestep this divorce?" asked Baby.

"Maybe because he doesn't want to fork over any alimony?" said Tandy.

Ava snapped her fingers. "Excellent point. When it comes to money, Shamus is tighter than Scrooge McDuck."

"Please," said Carmela, looking slightly subdued, "can we just change the subject?"

"No problem," said Baby, patting Carmela's hand.

"In that case," said Tandy, hoisting her craft bag onto the table, "are we going to start our Paperclay projects or what?"

"Yes," said Gabby, hovering behind them. "Absolutely we are. I'll gather all the materials."

"What's Paperclay?" asked Ava. "And what wonderful crafts are you guys going to create this time?"

"Paperclay is this wonderful plasticine material that can be sculpted and molded," explained Carmela. "In fact, we're going to use it today for a jewelry project." Carmela prided herself on coming up with different projects that all dovetailed with scrapbooking, stamping, and crafting. In the past they'd created memory boxes, altered books, and even constructed miniature paper theaters.

"I'm going to do leaf earrings," said Tandy. She reached into her craft bag and pulled out a rubber stamp of an aspen leaf. "Perfect for long, dangly earrings, yes?"

"That should work great," Carmela told her. "Or you can use a coin of some sort to make an impression in the Paperclay." She thought for a moment, then dug into the pocket of her slacks. "Like this."

"What's that?" asked Ava, curious.

"Nothing really," said Carmela. "Well, actually, I picked it up on Jekyl's balcony last night." She gave it an absent glance. "I assume it's one of the doubloons that got tossed during the Sardonyx parade the other night." With Mardi Gras in full swing and leading up to the grand culmination on Fat Tuesday, there was a parade rolling almost every night.

Ava peered at the large bronze doubloon in Carmela's hand. "That was tossed from a float?"

Carmela nodded. "Probably."

Ava reached a hand out. "Let me see, *cher.*"

Carmela handed her the coin.

"Looks kind of fancy," said Ava, studying it. "Do you think it could be a real coin of some sort?"

"I suppose . . ." said Carmela. That possibility had never occurred to her.

Tandy glanced at the coin in Ava's hand. "Looks foreign to me. And the metal seems authentic."

"Do you suppose Archie was a coin collector?" asked Ava.

"Don't know," said Carmela. "That's

something we'll have to ask Jekyl."

The Paperclay project was going great guns. And Tandy's aspen leaf stamp was working perfectly. Per Carmela's instructions, she rolled her Paperclay out so it was quite thin. Then Carmela showed her how to rub silver paint onto the Paperclay.

"Gorgeous," said Baby, who had an Italian mask stamp she wanted to use for a pendant. "Now what?"

"Just stamp the clay," said Carmela.

Tandy positioned her leaf stamp above the clay, then pressed down.

"And again," urged Carmela.

Now Tandy had her second earring.

"Okay, what's next?" asked Tandy, always eager to keep moving forward.

"I like to imbed the wire now," said Carmela, giving her two little gold jump rings. "Just thread those through, and then they're easily attached to ear wires later."

Tandy complied. "But they still look awfully rough," she said, eyeing her project.

"We're just getting to the finishing part," said Carmela. "You need to trim the edges and smooth everything out. Work the Paperclay almost as though it's a piece of metal, smoothing and refining it. Once you get your earrings perfect, I suggest using a

44

silver leafing pen on the edges to finish them off."

"Gorgeous," breathed Baby as she watched Tandy labor diligently with her earrings. "I love 'em."

"How long are these going to have to dry?" asked Tandy. "What I'm really asking, of course, is will they be ready in time for Baby's Mardi Gras party this Sunday night?"

"They need twenty-four hours for sure," said Carmela. "And forty-eight is better. But, yes, they'll be ready. The Paperclay should be nice and dry."

They all worked on their own projects, then. Baby made her Italian mask pendant, Gabby used a Japanese geisha stamp to create a pin, and Carmela worked on a pair of long, rectangular earrings. Carmela's design was a little trickier. She was going to stamp a music staff with notes into her Paperclay, then stamp an image of a pear over that. She planned to use gold paint for her background and then apply copper and rose-gold pigments to highlight the pear.

Of course, it was also a busy day at Memory Mine, so Carmela and Gabby had to take turns jumping up to wait on customers.

One woman came in needing note cards

and metallic ink pads. Carmela helped her coordinate her project in shades of purple and pink.

Another woman wanted to design place cards for her Mardi Gras party but didn't want to use a typical Mardi Gras mask image. Carmela suggested some rubber stamps that carried a turn-of-the-century party motif slightly reminiscent of a classic Mardi Gras ball, as well as some rubber stamp images of palm trees and court jesters. Using light green card stock and overstamping the images in purple, mauve, dark green, and gold inks, they were able to come up with a delightful montage.

"This is really fun," said Baby, when there was a lull in the action. "I think I might have a second career as a jewelry designer."

Carmela studied Baby's pendant. It was gorgeous and a little oversized, like designer jewelry often was. "I think you might be right," said Carmela.

"I'm ready to start a second project," said Tandy. "Hey, Carmela, do you still have that coin? I think a coin impression would make for dandy earrings."

"Very high-fashion," agreed Baby. "Like Bulgari jewelry."

Carmela fished the coin from her pocket. As she passed it over to Tandy, she began to wonder exactly why that coin had been lying next to Archie's body last night.

"Tandy," said Carmela, "can you read the imprint on that coin?"

Tandy slid her red glasses onto her pert nose and squinted. "It looks like the head of a Roman or Greek goddess on one side and . . . uh, on the other side, a vase and the words *Pont Max*. Does that sound like anything?"

"Could be a Roman coin," suggested Gabby.

Could have something to do with Archie's murder, thought Carmela.

CHAPTER 4

Just as Tandy and Baby were packing up to leave, Jekyl Hardy walked in. He usually carried himself with a spring in his step, but today he looked drawn, sober, and awfully down. A complete one eighty from last night when his party was at its zenith.

"So sorry to hear about your friend," Baby told him as she squeezed his hand.

"Thank you," he said in a hoarse whisper. Though Jekyl always dressed in black, somehow his black slacks and jacket looked more than a little funereal today.

"I'm sorry, too, honey," said Tandy. "I guess that fellow, Archie, was a pretty good friend, huh?"

"Good enough," said Jekyl. "We'd lived next door to each other for almost three years. And, of course, he was helping me with the floats for the Pluvius krewe."

"If there's anything we can do . . ." added Baby.

Jekyl gave a somber wave as Tandy and Baby headed out the door, craft bags slung over their shoulders. Then he turned to face Carmela. The look on his face told her all she needed to know.

"You don't look good," she told him, worry coloring her words.

"I'm not good," admitted Jekyl. "The police have been crawling all over me like I'm some sort of international terrorist, and now I'm more nervous than ever about finishing the Pluvius floats on time."

"Things are that backed up?" she asked.

He bobbed his head. "Let me put it this way: it's going to be a race to the wire."

"Maybe I could come over and help," she offered.

Jekyl brightened. "Sunday? That's when I'm planning to engineer my big push. If the volunteers cooperate, that is. If they can stay sober long enough."

"You don't have any other staff?"

"You're looking at him," said Jekyl. "No budget, no staff."

"That's not right," said Carmela. She knew quite a few members of the Pluvius krewe. Most were rather wealthy men from prominent New Orleans families. "Can you get them to do a last-minute budget appropriation?"

"Already tried that," said Jekyl. "They were outraged. Especially Brett Fowler, the krewe captain."

Carmela knew Fowler. In fact, the last time she'd seen him was during last year's Mardi Gras when he was wearing a rubber donkey head and trying to jump from table to table at Grenadine's Restaurant. He'd come away from that little escapade with one fractured ankle.

"Hey, Jekyl," said Gabby, as she brushed past him with a customer in tow, hot on the trail of gold tassels and a butterfly stamp. "If there's anything I can do . . ."

He nodded, then turned sober eyes on Carmela. "We need to talk."

"Okay," said Carmela. She led her friend back to her little office, cleared a stack of foil paper off a side chair, and got him seated. But before Jekyl had a chance to open his mouth, Carmela pulled out the doubloon and held it up between her thumb and index fingers.

"Does this mean anything to you?" she asked.

Jekyl stared at the coin, which seemed to glow slightly in the dim light. "Huh?"

"I picked up this coin on the balcony last night, just before the cavalry came charging in. I didn't think anything of it at the time.

50

In fact, I thought it was probably some silly doubloon that had been tossed from a float. Now I'm thinking it might be something of real value."

Gingerly, Jekyl accepted the coin. "It probably is a real coin," he told her as he eyed it. "In fact, I know it is. Archie was an avid coin collector. He was always going on about antique Roman coins and French ducats and such."

"Well that clears that up," said Carmela. The niggling feeling of dread she'd been harboring began to dissipate. Archie'd had the coin in his pocket and in the struggle, it had probably rolled out. Simple as that.

Jekyl, however, seemed more distraught than ever. He gazed sorrowfully at Carmela, then lowered his head into his hands. "I have a terrible feeling someone at my party was involved in Archie's death," he murmured. "Which means I'm responsible."

"No, Jekyl," said Carmela. "You're not the least bit responsible. Some monster killed Archie, not you."

"But that's how I feel," responded Jekyl. "I was brought up Catholic. I fervently believe in heaven and hell, and I've definitely been taught how to loll around in a big juicy pile of *guilt*."

"Were you able to give the police a guest

list?" asked Carmela. She didn't really want to get into the upbringing thing. That was usually a land mine for everyone concerned.

Jekyl nodded wearily. "I gave them a *best guess* list. Or at least I tried to put one together. I don't know how complete it was. Friends brought friends who in turn brought friends." He gave a sad grimace. "As usual, things got a little crazy."

"So you didn't know everyone who was there last night," said Carmela.

"Lord, no!" exclaimed Jekyl, putting his hands to his face.

"Jekyl," said Carmela, dropping her voice. "You didn't have anything illegal going on, did you?"

Jekyl peered at her from between spread fingers. "What do you mean by illegal?"

Oh, great, thought Carmela. "Drugs?"

Now Jekyl's eyes slid away from hers. "Not really. I mean, nothing spectacularly out of the ordinary."

Which means, thought Carmela, *they were probably smoking grass at the very least.* Okay . . . so what Jekyl did to his prefrontal lobe really wasn't her business.

Jekyl's shoulders rose, held for a second, then drooped as he exhaled loudly. "I don't know what to do," he told her in a thin, papery voice. "I just have . . . no clue."

Carmela reached for his hand. They clasped fingers and gazed at each other.

"Are you talking about the float building?" she asked. "Or how to assuage your perceived but certainly unwarranted feelings of guilt?"

"I'm talking about finding Archie's killer," said Jekyl.

Carmela straightened in her chair. "That's up to the police," she told him in a soft voice.

"They're not doing a very good job of it so far," said Jekyl.

Carmela wasn't about to voice her opinion right now, but secretly she agreed with him. If last night was any indication of how the actual murder investigation was going to proceed, she didn't hold out a lot of hope.

"At the risk of sounding like everyone else," said Carmela. "How can I help?"

Jekyl lifted an eyebrow. "You mean that?"

"Of course," said Carmela. "With all my heart."

Jekyl seemed to weigh his words then. "Carmela," he began, "if you could just sort of poke around . . ."

"What?" This wasn't what she had in mind.

"You live in the French Quarter, after all," continued Jekyl. "Your shop is here. You know people."

"I certainly don't know *those* kind of people," protested Carmela. "People who . . . who commit murder!"

"But you're a good amateur sleuth," said Jekyl, barely stopping for breath. "You've solved crimes before."

"I've stumbled on solutions," said Carmela, trying to explain herself. "But it was simply blind luck. Dumb luck," she added.

"No," said Jekyl, looking serious bordering on pensive. "I think you're a very skilled investigator. You pulled Shamus's fat out of the fryer a couple of times."

"I was more married then," she explained hastily. "I had to help him; it's the law." She tried to make a joke, but it seemed to fall on deaf ears.

"Please," said Jekyl. "I really do need your help. Your smarts."

"Look," said Carmela. "I've got the store to run. This is my busy time. Everyone is storming in here looking for purple and green paper, bags for favors, you name it." She stared at Jekyl's face, noted the dark smudges under his eyes, the look of defeat on his face. And, in her heart, she relented a little.

"Well . . . maybe," she said. "Just a little sleuthing, okay? But no promises. I'm amateur-ville after all."

"Come to my place after work," said Jekyl, "and we'll talk. Better yet, I'll swing back around five and pick you up."

"Yes," said Carmela. "I suppose we could do that." The little niggling feeling in the pit of her stomach was suddenly back in full force and not feeling a bit comfortable. "We'll put our heads together," she told him, hesitation evident in her voice. "Start with a little kumbaya, then try to move on to some creative thinking. But I'm not making any promises."

"You're going to help him," said Gabby, once Jekyl had left. "I just know you are."

"What makes you think I'm going to get involved?" asked Carmela. She was a little taken aback by Gabby's perception. Gabby was usually laid-back and wanted to remain aloof of things that smacked of danger or intrigue.

"Because you always do," said Gabby, fixing her with a curious look. "You're Carmela Bertrand, champion of underdogs."

"Is that what I am, really?"

Gabby nodded.

"Oh dear."

Gabby patted Carmela's arm. "It's okay. I'm beginning to realize it's something that's probably imbedded in your DNA."

"You mean to say I'm powerless?" said Carmela. "I'm driven to help? Or some might say meddle?"

"Maybe," said Gabby. "Probably. But, hey, I applaud you for your chutzpah. All your friends do. You have this crazy knack for sorting through evidence and clues and coming up with some very insightful ideas." Gabby hesitated. "Of course, you sometimes get pulled right into the thick of things, too."

"By *thick of things,* you mean danger," murmured Carmela.

Gabby grimaced. "Well . . . yes. There is that element."

"You're not going to quit, are you?" asked Carmela with a gentle smile. A few times in the past, Gabby had been so nervous about Carmela's involvement in murder investigations, she'd talked about quitting.

"No," said Gabby. "I love my job here. Next to Stuart and my home, scrapbooking is my absolute favorite thing in the whole world. But I'm for sure going to light a saint candle just in case." Saint candles were colorful glass candles with vigil lights inside and thin paper wrapping on the outside that carried images of patron saints. Ava's store sold tons of them, and Gabby was one of her biggest customers.

"Which saint will it be this time?" asked Carmela, touched at Gabby's somewhat backhanded endorsement.

Gabby thought for a minute. "Maybe Saint John the Apostle."

"Remind me again what he's the patron saint of," said Carmela as the phone on the counter started to ring.

"Papermakers," said Gabby, grabbing for the phone. "But I'm pretty sure it's a fairly loose definition and that scrapbookers are included, too." She held the receiver to her ear, listened, made a wry face, then held out the phone to Carmela. "Shamus," she hissed.

Carmela reluctantly accepted the phone. Her soon-to-be ex. Just what she needed.

Carmela drew a deep breath, then said, "What?"

"That's what I'd like to know." Shamus's deep voice dripped with melodrama. "What have you gotten yourself involved in *this* time?"

"What are you talking about?" asked Carmela, all innocence. She knew darned well what Shamus was talking about. He'd just found out about the murder at Jekyl Hardy's apartment last night.

"You were involved in a murder!" Shamus's voice rose a fast few octaves, taking on a decidedly shrill quality. Not all that attractive, Carmela noted.

"I was not involved in a murder," Carmela countered. "I simply happened to be one of several witnesses." She thought for a few moments, then picked her words carefully. "It was a terrible tragedy, one I'm hoping the police are diligently following up on." She almost winced. Her words sounded like she was reading from a prepared statement.

"Your buddy Jekyl got some pretty negative press in this morning's paper, and I'm hoping it doesn't cause any problems with our floats," said Shamus.

This sudden turn in the conversation struck Carmela as particularly odd. Here they were, proceeding as usual, Shamus huffing and puffing like the proverbial big bad wolf. And suddenly he brought up floats. "That's what you're worried about?" asked Carmela. "Your Mardi Gras floats?"

"Well . . . yeah," said Shamus. "Sure." From the tone of Carmela's voice, Shamus seemed to realize he was beginning to tread in some pretty deep doo-doo, so he tried to backpedal. Tried to sound upbeat. "Hey, babe, it's Mardi Gras. We gotta roll our floats. The Pluvius krewe always rolls the best and biggest floats."

"I'm sure Jekyl has things well in hand,"

said Carmela. She could almost picture the self-serving, wheedling expression on Shamus's face. The face she used to sprinkle with kisses.

"I was wondering if you could sort of, you know, ride herd on Jekyl," suggested Shamus, still in hale-and-hearty mode. "Make sure he stays on top of things. See that he doesn't get too distracted."

"Well, I'd be pleased as punch to do that," responded Carmela. "As soon as Jekyl gets all the blood mopped up, finishes with his police interrogation, and arranges poor Archie Baudier's funeral. In fact, I'll be sure to caution Jekyl to stop frittering away his time and get his butt in gear."

"You don't have to put it that way," said Shamus, a hurt sound creeping into his voice. "You make me sound like some kind of ogre."

Carmela didn't bother to respond.

CHAPTER 5

Carmela was by herself, sorting through packets of metal eyelets and snaps, when Jekyl stopped by to pick her up. It was a little after five, already dark outside. Through the front window she could see white twinkle lights glowing from the potted palms that stood in front of Glisande's Courtyard Restaurant across the street. Magic time in the French Quarter.

"You ready?" asked Jekyl.

Carmela nodded. "In a sec. I want to make sure I have a stash of corrugated book covers and batik paper. We got a frantic last-minute call from a customer who wants to put together a set of memory books."

Perusing her floor-to-ceiling racks of paper, card stock, and miscellany, Carmela finally spotted the covers and paper.

"Yup," she murmured to herself, "we've got 'em."

Jekyl lounged at the front counter, studying a display of colored ink pens.

"Are these good pens?" he asked. "Will they write on plastic or glass?"

"They're amazing," said Carmela. "They'll probably write on a NASA heat shield if you want to. Here." She grabbed one of the pens. "Take one with you. In fact, take two." She stuffed the pens into a small brown paper sack with raffia handles, then quickly slapped on one of her crack-and-peel Memory Mine stickers. "For advertising," she told Jekyl as they stepped out the front door. "Every little bit helps. Business *still* isn't back to what it was before Hurricane Katrina."

"Nothing really is," agreed Jekyl.

They strolled down Governor Nicholls Street, enjoying that pause in the day when purple dusk oozed through the narrow streets, horses clopped by pulling colorful open carriages, and antique wrought-iron lamps glowed soft yellow. The nighttime French Quarter was coming to life. Lights shone from shop windows, and a cozy feeling seemed to emanate from the restaurants, oyster bars, and gumbo cafés that were housed in old brick buildings.

"There's something I want to ask you," said Carmela, as they strolled along.

"Okay," said Jekyl. His eyes were downcast, and he seemed pensive.

"Last night, you and Archie went into the kitchen to get refills for Ava and me."

"Right," said Jekyl. "The Purple Haze."

"But you never came back. And Archie ended up all alone on the balcony."

Jekyl remained silent.

"How did that come about?" she asked. "Had you been out there with him? I mean, you said you had some problems to discuss. Problems that had to do with the Pluvius krewe."

Jekyl stopped in front of the window of the Peacock Alley Antique Shop. He stared in at a montage of eighteenth-century blue-and-white vases, a silver bust of Napoleon, a brass desk set complete with quill pen, and a pink-and-green floral china teapot.

"Yes, I was out there with him," replied Jekyl. "But only for a few moments."

"Do the police know that?" asked Carmela.

"No," said Jekyl. "And I'd rather not tell them."

"But all those people in the hallway . . ." said Carmela. "They must have seen you. They must have mentioned it to the police."

Jekyl shrugged. "Maybe, maybe not. The important thing is, I had nothing to do with Archie's death." He turned to stare at

Carmela. "You believe that, don't you?"

Carmela never wavered. "Yes, I do. But someone sure wanted him dead. Can you think of anyone like that? Someone Archie might have been on the outs with? Someone he was having problems with? A client, relative, old girlfriend?"

"No," said Jekyl.

"Can you think of *any* reason someone would want him dead?" Carmela asked, pressing Jekyl a little harder.

Jekyl shook his head. "Again, not really. Although we weren't *that* close. I didn't *really* know what was going on in his personal life."

"What about Jimmy Toups?" asked Carmela.

"He might want *me* dead, but I don't think he even knew Archie."

"So . . . what were you two talking about out there on the balcony?"

"Floats," said Jekyl. "More specifically, the timing, which has really become a huge bone of contention. And we chatted briefly about the design of one particular float."

"Something wrong with the design?" asked Carmela.

"The krewe captain loathes it. Says it's too moribund."

"Is it?" asked Carmela.

"A little," admitted Jekyl. "But you put fifty strings of colored lights on a float and load it up with twenty raucous guys who are tossing strings of beads, and suddenly you've got chemistry." Jekyl focused on the window display again. "You're a good investigator," he told her. "Asking all the hard questions."

"I'm just glad you had answers," replied Carmela.

Creeping down the long, dark, third-floor hallway toward Jekyl's apartment, they knew right away that something was going on. Voices floated toward them. Voices that seemed to be raised in anger and frustration.

"Somebody's in Archie's apartment," said Jekyl, picking up the pace.

The minute they passed the door of Jekyl's apartment, Carmela spotted the black-and-yellow crime-scene tape at Archie's place. "Police are back," she commented.

Jekyl shook his head, more disheartened than angry. "I thought they were finished."

They hesitated in front of the open apartment door. Like an oversized spiderweb, strands of yellow-and-black tape criss-crossed the doorway.

"Hello!" sang out Carmela. She was curious to see if the same cops were back or if this was a new team. Hopefully a better team.

A young officer appeared in the doorway. His close-cropped dark blond hair and deep blue eyes gave him the look of an alert German Shepherd. "Go away," he told them. "There's an investigation in progress."

"He lives here," said Carmela.

The young officer narrowed his eyes at Jekyl. "You mean here? In this apartment?"

"Next door," said Carmela, raising a thumb and indicating Jekyl's apartment down the hall.

But something was seriously bugging Jekyl. He reached up, grabbed a strand of tape, and ripped it down from the doorway. "You realize," he told the officer, outrage beginning to rise in his voice, "that you've strung gummy tape on one hundred and fifty-year-old mahogany."

"Jekyl . . ." began Carmela. She knew he was upset, but this wasn't the time to throw a hissy fit.

"My friend, Archie, the one whose apartment you're in, refinished all that wood by hand," continued Jekyl.

The young cop shrugged. "Tell it to the detective. He's the man in charge."

"Who is the detective?" asked Carmela.

Her words were barely out of her mouth, when Lieutenant Edgar Babcock, a detective Carmela had more than a nodding acquaintance with, loomed in front of them. Dressed in a tweed jacket, sharply pressed tan slacks, and what appeared to be Gucci loafers, Babcock looked awfully dapper for a homicide detective. He was also, Carmela decided, extremely good-looking. Tall and rangy, with ginger-colored hair, Edgar Babcock was square-jawed, brown-eyed, and extremely sexy. At one time she was pretty sure he'd had major hots for Ava. Now he was staring at her as though she were a museum curiosity.

"Interesting meeting you here," said Babcock. His tone was neutral and controlled, but his eyes flicked from Carmela to Jekyl, then back again to Carmela. A sharp yet wary detective's assessment.

Carmela leaned forward and peered into Archie's apartment. Although she'd certainly never been in there before, the place looked a shambles, as though it had been completely torn apart. Tables and chairs were upset, books had tumbled from shelves. "Did you do that?" she asked Babcock. "In your quest for truth?"

"Nope," he said. "Did you?"

"Strange question," said Carmela.

"I understand you were here last night," said Babcock, edging closer to her.

"Yes, I was," said Carmela, backing away slightly. "Jekyl had a little get-together."

"Not so little," said Babcock as he turned his focus on Jekyl. "And my colleagues tell me you had an argument with the deceased."

Jekyl looked pained. "Oh please. We may have exchanged a few words, but they were in no way argumentative."

"Then what *did* you talk about?" asked Babcock.

"We were hammering out a few creative differences," said Jekyl. "But they certainly weren't issues that would precipitate a major knock-down, drag-out fight. For goodness sakes, we were building floats together. We were *friends*. I'd never do anything to harm Archie."

"Someone sure did," said Babcock.

"I'd feel a lot more confident in your investigative skills," said Carmela, "if you'd please stop focusing on Jekyl."

"Some of the witnesses said they heard an argument," continued Babcock.

"It wasn't me," snapped Jekyl.

"Maybe it was the murderer," said Carmela. She put a hand on her hip and stared pointedly at Babcock.

"Could have been," said Babcock. His eyebrows seemed to raise a millimeter. She was pretty sure he was just placating her.

"Mr. Hardy," said Babcock finally, "I'd like to speak with Carmela alone."

Jekyl spun on his heel. "Fine," he said, throwing one hand up in a petulant wave. "I'll be in my apartment."

"What's up?" asked Carmela, once Jekyl had moved off.

"Don't get involved in this," said Babcock without preamble.

Carmela shrugged. "I'm not involved."

The corners of his mouth twitched. "Of course, you are. You're always involved. Right now your eyes are working like twin lasers, trying to peer around me and figure out what went on in there."

Carmela focused on the midpoint of Edgar Babcock's earnest-looking forehead. "Not really. I'm just . . . curious." There. That seemed like a neutral enough word.

"Don't be." Lieutenant Edgar Babcock leaned forward a little. "Listen to me, Mrs. Meechum . . . Carmela. Whoever murdered Archie Baudier is a nasty, violent person. Someone you don't want to get mixed up with. Possibly someone who's had martial arts training. Jujitsu or even kung fu."

"Then you should cross Jekyl Hardy off

68

your suspect list," said Carmela. "He's about as athletic as a noodle. Not even hatha yoga or Pilates for him."

"If you say so," said Babcock, still staring intently at her.

"What happened in there?" asked Carmela. "That it's all torn up?"

"Just off the top of my head," said Babcock, "I'd say someone was searching rather desperately for something. Of course, the deceased could have just been a very bad housekeeper."

"May I come in?" asked Carmela. "Take a quick look around?"

"Absolutely not!" protested Babcock, moving to block the doorway. "Have you not been listening to me? I don't want you involved in this case."

"Now you sound like Shamus," she said, frowning.

That disarmed him for a moment. "How is Shamus?" asked Babcock. "You two divorced yet?"

"I don't see how that question is pertinent to your investigation," said Carmela.

Babcock chose to ignore her remark. "Hear me out, please. Whoever did this is very disturbed. For your own good, I suggest you stay as far away from this investigation as possible."

"You realize," said Carmela, "I was the one who found Archie on the balcony."

"Yes, that was in the report," agreed Babcock.

"Then you read the witness interviews, too?" asked Carmela. "What few there probably were?"

Babcock nodded.

"So you've undoubtedly developed a list of suspects?"

Babcock gave nothing away. He did move a little closer to her, however. So close she could smell the scent of his aftershave. Something slightly peppery with a hint of sandalwood. Made it hard to breathe for a moment.

"Listen carefully," said Edgar Babcock. "The barbed wire garrote that was used against Archie Baudier is a highly lethal form of strangulation. It causes severe pain, unconsciousness, and then brain death. Mind you, this nasty little scenario takes place in as little as thirty seconds. Strangulation is a form of power and control that also has a devastating psychological effect on victims. Once overpowered, it's next to impossible to fight back, and they realize rather quickly that they're going to die. Are you hearing me?"

"Yes," said Carmela.

"Only eleven pounds of pressure placed on both carotid arteries causes unconsciousness." Babcock reached out a hand and closed his fingers gently around Carmela's throat. "For comparison purposes, it takes only eight pounds of pressure to pull the trigger on a gun." He removed his hand and gazed at her, looking very serious. "Now have I convinced you to back off?" he asked.

"Of course," said Carmela, swallowing hard. But in her heart she knew she really wouldn't. She couldn't. After all, she'd promised to help Jekyl.

And there was one other thing: she'd gotten a tiny whiff of the potential danger. Besides unnerving her, that essence of danger had also ignited something deep within her.

CHAPTER 6

Carmela gazed about Mumbo Gumbo and smiled. It was a cozy little restaurant located in the old Westminster Gallery space, and it never failed to make her feel relaxed and welcome. Crumbling brick crept halfway up the interior walls, then the ensuing smooth walls were painted a cream and gold harlequin pattern. A large bar the color of a ripe eggplant dominated a side wall. Above the bar, glass shelves displayed hundreds of bottles. Heavy wooden tables with black leather club chairs were snugged next to antique oak barrels that held glass and brass lamps. Potted palms and slowly spinning ceiling fans added to the slightly exotic atmosphere. The music was zydeco interspersed with haunting Cajun ballads.

And the menu . . .

Well, the menu was what Carmela and Jekyl were sorting through right now. A multipage accordion piece that Carmela had designed for Quigg Brevard, the proprietor. Quigg also owned Bon Tiempe, a slightly fancier restaurant located in an old mansion in the Bywater. She'd done some design work for that restaurant, too. In fact, after she'd separated from Shamus, the *first* time she'd separated from Shamus, Carmela had accepted a date with Quigg to attend a dinner party. They'd had a good time together, but that had been well over a year ago, and now she wasn't sure *what* their relationship was. Besides simply being cordial.

"I can't believe the gumbo variations they serve here," exclaimed Jekyl as he studied the menu.

"Quigg's got a thing for gumbo," agreed Carmela. Indeed, the menu listed chicken andouille gumbo, seafood okra gumbo, crab and oyster gumbo, and even lobster gumbo. Of course, there were also dishes like crawfish pie, red beans and rice, and alligator piquant.

"I'm going with the seafood okra gumbo," said Jekyl. "And maybe a glass of wine. Do they have a good wine list?"

"Quigg's your basic obsessive-compulsive oenophile," said Carmela. "So, yes, they have lots of great wine."

Jekyl signaled to their waiter then, and

they ordered. Carmela opted for the gulf shrimp fettuccini, and they decided to split a bottle of Chardonnay.

"So what was that detective . . . ?" began Jekyl.

"Babcock," filled in Carmela.

"What was Detective Babcock being so secretive about? From the way he looked at you, or dare I say leered, he gave the distinct impression he wanted to hook up."

"Not really," said Carmela. "He's just another male who's interested in running my life."

"I wouldn't presume to do that," said Jekyl.

"No, you wouldn't," responded Carmela.

"But Shamus sure did," said Jekyl.

"Still tries to," said Carmela.

"And now this guy Babcock?"

Carmela nodded. "His confidential conversation was basically him administering a rather stern warning."

"About what?" asked Jekyl.

"He suggested I stay away from the murder investigation."

"Are you going to be the good little schoolgirl and obey him?" asked Jekyl. He ventured a wicked grin, suddenly looking like his old devil-may-care self.

Carmela paused while the waiter lit the

white pillar candle that sat on the table between them. "Of course not," she said once he'd moved on. "I promised to help you, and I mean to keep my promise."

"You're an angel," said Jekyl. "An absolute angel."

No, thought Carmela, *I'm no angel. But I might be a bit of a thrill seeker.* Now that Shamus was pretty much out of the picture and unable to ride herd on her, Carmela could feel her inner wild child beginning to emerge.

Have to watch that, she cautioned herself. *Be a little careful.*

"Carmela."

Carmela glanced up. Quigg Brevard was smiling down at her. A broad-shouldered man with olive skin, piercing dark eyes, and a handsome although slightly slick appearance.

"I brought you an upgrade," he told her in a throaty growl.

"Pardon?" Carmela wasn't quite following him.

Quigg held out a glistening bottle of wine with all the care and respect one might show in handling their firstborn. "A better wine. The Chardonnay you chose is good, but this wine is exceptional. A full one hundred points awarded by the *Wine Spectator.*"

Quigg turned his smile on Jekyl. "Hello."

Carmela made quick introductions. "Quigg Brevard, this is my friend Jekyl Hardy."

"The man who makes the floats," said Quigg.

"Trying to," responded Jekyl. "Although this year there seems to be a black cloud hanging over my head."

"Jekyl's friend was murdered last night," explained Carmela. "Over in Napoleon Gardens."

"Say now," said Quigg, looking serious. "I heard about that. Sorry. Sounded like a dreadful way to go." He tapped the bottle of wine. "Sure you wouldn't like something stronger?"

Jekyl shook his head. "I'm sure your selection is lovely."

"I'll check on your dinners personally," Quigg told them, then raised a hand to summon their waiter. "Duncan?" He passed the bottle to Duncan, who had suddenly snapped to with smiles and accommodating nods. "Kindly open this with utmost care. And do not spill a precious drop, as the wholesale price far exceeds your weekly salary."

"You don't really feel like there's a black

76

cloud hanging over your head, do you?" asked Carmela as she scraped at her last bits of fettuccini. It had been absolutely delicious. Creamy, cheesy, and probably stratospheric as far as calorie count. *Gotta cut back,* she told herself. Just like she was really gonna hit those books next year in study hall.

Jekyl stared at her. "How did you feel when Shamus walked out on you?"

"Cursed," said Carmela. "Like a witch with green paint all over her face slithered out of a swamp and turned Shamus into his own evil twin."

Jekyl nodded. "I feel terrible about Archie, and even, as I mentioned before, *responsible.* And I'm also nervous about my dealings with the Pluvius krewe. For the first time in ten years of float building, I've got an unhappy client on my hands. That's something I've never had to deal with before."

"I know what you mean," said Carmela. "That stuff can just rot away at your confidence." Last month, she'd spent an entire afternoon pulling album selections, sheets of paper, and rubber stamps for a woman who wanted to make a vacation scrapbook. But nothing she showed the woman was quite right. And every creative suggestion

77

was met with a firm rejection. Finally, the woman had flounced out without buying a thing, leaving Carmela feeling like she was pretty much devoid of creative ideas.

"I'm just lucky the Pluvius krewe isn't going to roll until Fat Tuesday," said Jekyl. "Gives me time to straighten things out."

Carmela nodded. Since Hurricane Katrina, parade routes and dates had been changed around quite a bit.

"How was the wine?" Quigg Brevard was back.

Quigg was large and in charge, Carmela decided.

"Outstanding," Jekyl told him. "A wonderful selection."

"Dinner's on me tonight," said Quigg.

"Oh no," protested Carmela.

"I'd really feel better about paying," said Jekyl. "Especially in light of that wine."

"Absolutely not," said Quigg. "Consider it my treat."

"Well, thank you," said Jekyl. "Thanks very much."

Quigg focused on Carmela. "Think of it as an inducement to do a slight favor for me." He wiggled his eyebrows at her. "A menu revision. We're adding so many new dishes."

"Of course," Carmela told him. "Anytime.

Glad to help."

Quigg rocked back on his heels. "Good. Great." He hovered above Carmela, making her feel nervous.

"How's your house coming along?" she asked him, trying to make small talk, feeling a little ill at ease. Quigg's house on Lake Pontchartrain had been destroyed by Hurricane Katrina. After much wrangling with his insurance company, he was finally building a new one.

"It's good," he told her. "Big. Four bedrooms and five baths. Three-car garage."

"A McMansion," said Jekyl.

"A lot more room than a single guy like me really needs," said Quigg.

Carmela remained silent. She never knew when Quigg was coming on to her or when he was toying with her. Hmm. Did that mean she was clueless when it came to men? Too bad there wasn't a Psychology of the Male Mind 101 course you could take. Come to think of it, there was: Ava.

"Aren't you worried about building so close to the lake?" asked Jekyl.

"Not really," said Quigg. "Lake Pontchartrain isn't the toxic dump everybody thinks it is. In fact, the catfish have come back like gangbusters."

"You don't serve that fish here, do you?"

asked Jekyl, suddenly looking wary.

"Sure do," said Quigg. "Coated with bread crumbs and baked to perfection."

Much to Carmela's consternation, Quigg insisted on sending over dessert as well. A humongous piece of bread pudding soaked in rum sauce. While the bread pudding Carmela made was pretty straightforward, calling for regular bread, Mumbo Gumbo's recipe used thick slices of brioche. So the end result was a rich, poufy, buttery bread pudding. Practically sinful.

Thanks to the wine, good food, and casual atmosphere, Jekyl seemed to be feeling a lot more relaxed.

"I'm really going to have to pick up the pace," he told Carmela as they were finishing up. "And try to keep the Pluvius krewe on task. It could be I gave Archie a little too much free rein in creating a theme and pitching it to the Pluvius krewe. After all, when an overall concept is selected, it becomes, for all practical purposes, a krewe's marketing effort. The one big theme they hang their hat on."

"I hear you," said Carmela. Over the years, Mardi Gras floats had carried themes that showcased Greek mythology, the oceans, insects, famous works of art, nursery rhymes, and music. A couple recent themes had been Through the Eyes of a Child and Habitat for Insanity.

"Of course," continued Jekyl in a sarcastic tone, "the captain of the krewe, Brett Fowler, was hot to hire his brother-in-law, who owns a sign shop in Natchitoches."

"That was his sole qualification?" asked Carmela. "Owning a sign shop?" She dabbed surreptitiously at her lips with a linen napkin. For some reason the sticky rum sauce seemed to be spreading by osmosis onto the handle of her fork, her hands, her face.

"That was it," said Jekyl. "Thank goodness the other Pluvius members were sold on Archie's presentation and the theme he came up with."

"What theme was that?" asked Carmela, as she tried in vain to wipe rum sauce from her fingers.

"Ruins and Doubloons."

"Doubloons," said Carmela slowly. "What is it with Archie and doubloons?"

Jekyl threw two twenties down on the table for the waiter, then stood up. "C'mon, I'll show you."

CHAPTER 7

They crept back up the stairs to Jekyl's apartment. For some reason, the stairwell and hallway seemed darker than usual. Maybe a light was out?

"Do you think the police have gone?" asked Carmela. She was having trouble focusing in the dim light.

"I think so," said Jekyl as they eased down the hallway.

A soft creak sounded just off to Carmela's right. A door being snicked open. "What?" she said, startled.

"Jekyl, is that you?" came a whispered voice.

A one-inch crack revealed a single bright eye peering out.

"It's me, Miss Norma," said Jekyl.

The door closed, and Carmela could hear a chain lock sliding along its metal track.

"My landlady," whispered Jekyl.

Carmela nodded.

When the door opened again, a waft of perfume emerged, and a woman looked out expectantly. She was in her late sixties, early seventies, and heavily made up: false eyelashes with a little too much powder that had caked in the crevices around her mouth, lipstick shade a little too coral.

Miss Norma coughed a rattly smoker's cough, then said, "A girl can't be too careful. After what happened last night, I'm absolutely terrified."

"The police were here earlier," said Carmela. "And I have a feeling they'll be back again. So I don't think you have too much to worry about."

"This is my friend Carmela," said Jekyl.

Miss Norma extended a plump arm, and a dozen gold bangles jangled like crazy. "Hiya, Carmela. Nice to meet you."

"Hi, Miss Norma," said Carmela. That was the funny thing about New Orleans. Women, older women, even if they'd been married, were often referred to as Miss. Miss Norma. Miss Idetta. Miss Grace. Carmela even knew a pair of sisters who were known as Old Miss and Young Miss.

"Did the police question you?" asked Jekyl.

Miss Norma gathered her silk, multicolored muumuu closer to her ample bosom and rolled her eyes expressively. "Did they ever."

"Did you happen to see anything?" asked Carmela.

Miss Norma blinked. "You mean last night?"

Carmela and Jekyl both nodded.

"Not a thing. But I had the volume on my TV cranked up. I was watching a rerun of *Sex and the City*." She smiled fleetingly at Carmela. "You ever watch that show?"

"Sometimes," said Carmela.

Miss Norma waved a hand. "Those girls are such potty mouths. Gives me a chuckle." Her head swiveled toward Jekyl. "Did you see what they did to the wall?"

"A cop hit it with his nightstick," said Carmela.

"Tore a gash in the wallpaper," said Miss Norma. "Gonna have to be patched." She glanced over her shoulder, suddenly looking impatient. "Oh, commercials are over. Gotta go."

"Night," said Carmela, as Miss Norma closed her door.

"Sweet old girl," said Jekyl.

"What is she besides the landlady?" asked Carmela. "Or should I say, what *was* she?"

"Showgirl," said Jekyl. "Miss Norma claims to have been a Rockette at one time, but I wouldn't be surprised if she didn't work most of her life in one of the burlesque houses over on Bourbon Street."

Jekyl stuck his key into his lock and pushed open his door. "C'mon in."

"You know what, Jekyl?" said Carmela, suddenly feeling the effects of an eight-hour day, a large meal, and two glasses of wine. "It's kind of late, and I should get home. Walk the dogs."

"But I want to show you something," said Jekyl, in a suddenly mysterious tone. He grasped Carmela's hand, led her through his apartment and into his bedroom.

"Jekyl?" said Carmela. What was this about, anyway?

He pulled open a pair of ornate double doors and ushered her into his walk-in closet.

Carmela looked around at the rows of elegant clothes, multiple shoe racks, and his large section of costumes, one of which included a red-sequined devil suit. "Jekyl, what are we doing in here?"

He put an index finger to his mouth. "Sssh."

Kneeling down, facing the back wall, he pushed gently on a piece of wood paneling.

What the . . . ? thought Carmela.

There was a little ping, and then a trapdoor sprang open, revealing a gaping, dark hole.

"Whoa," said Carmela, with an intake of breath. He had her attention now. The dark hole was about four feet high, maybe two and a half feet wide. It looked like a hobbit door leading to Middle Earth. Or, better yet, something straight out of *Alice in Wonderland.* Carmela expected a white rabbit to poke his furry head out and declare that he was inexcusably late.

Except she knew that this secret doorway led directly into Archie Baudier's apartment.

Carmela couldn't help herself. She got down on her hands and knees and peered through. "This is weird."

"Isn't it?" replied Jekyl. "About a hundred years ago this all used to be one huge apartment."

"How did you find out about this? *When* did you find out?"

"Couple years ago."

"You know what this reminds me of?" asked Carmela, her brain clicking into overdrive. "*Rosemary's Baby.* Remember how the Woodhouse apartment had a secret passageway into Minnie and Roman Castevet's place?"

"Nothing that sinister," said Jekyl.

"Oh yeah?" said Carmela, studying the opening. "This could be how the murderer escaped. Or, worse yet, how the murderer gained access to your apartment, to your party. We know for sure that somebody was in Archie's apartment last night, because it's all torn up."

Jekyl was quiet now, mulling over her words.

"I don't think they crawled through here," he said finally. "Nobody really knows about this."

Carmela looked grim. "Well, you certainly can't keep this a secret."

Jekyl peered at her and wrinkled his nose. "Aw crap. You're saying I have to tell Lieutenant Babcock?"

"Yes," said Carmela. "I'm afraid so. I *know* so. This passageway could be extremely relevant. I'm sure the police are going to want to come in here and do their CSI thing."

"Right here in my closet," said Jekyl. He was obviously unhappy.

"Yes, right here in your closet," Carmela said adamantly. "You have to allow this. Don't you want the police to catch Archie's killer?"

"Of course," allowed Jekyl. But he was still waffling.

"Then make the call," said Carmela.

"Okay," said Jekyl. "I will. But there are a couple things I need to take care of first. And you're going to help."

Carmela watched as Jekyl, on his hands and knees, wiggled through the tiny tunnel. Then it was her turn. Gulp.

Once they were both on the other side, Archie's side, Carmela was even more nervous. Following Jekyl, she slipped out of Archie's somewhat smaller closet and gazed about his bedroom. Again, it was smaller than Jekyl's place. A four-poster bed dominated the room, and a small desk was shoved up against the wall.

That's where Jekyl was. Pulling open drawers, pawing through stacks of files.

"What are you looking for?" asked Carmela.

"These," said Jekyl. He held up two small leather-bound books. "His appointment book and his address book."

"You're going to take them?" asked Carmela.

"For safekeeping," said Jekyl. "Here." He thrust them into her hands. "You keep them."

"The police should have these," Carmela pointed out.

"The police already photographed the

contents," Jekyl told her, "when they came through this morning. The *first* time they were here."

Carmela flipped through Archie's address book. Only a few names and addresses were printed in neat, square lettering. Most of the pages were blank.

A pang of sympathy swept through Carmela. Had Archie been somewhat shy? Or a loner? "What can you tell me about Archie?" asked Carmela. "Did he have any family?"

"Not exactly," said Jekyl, as he headed for the living room. "As far as I know, both his parents are dead, and his brother is in prison."

"In prison where?" asked Carmela, following him. Her footsteps whispered on plush carpets as she gazed about Archie's living room. Everything was still topsy-turvy, but she could tell it was tasteful topsy-turvy. A leather couch, two chintz chairs, nice bookcases. Through an archway, she spotted a small white-tile kitchen.

"I think his brother's in Angola," said Jekyl.

"Oh no!" responded Carmela. The Louisiana State Penitentiary at Angola was one of the country's tough-ass prisons. Pretty much filled with lifers. "Do you know why his brother is in there?"

"I think maybe . . . drugs?" said Jekyl.

"Must have been serious drugs," said Carmela.

"Nothing to see out here," murmured Jekyl. He grabbed Carmela's hand and pulled her back into the bedroom. Then they squeezed back through the secret passageway and pulled the door shut behind them.

"That was an adventure and a half," declared Carmela.

"We're not done yet," said Jekyl.

"What?"

He bent down and, in a practiced motion, rolled up a small Oriental carpet. He leaned it against his shoe rack.

Carmela stared at the wooden floorboards, which were really fairly wide planks. Now what?

But Jekyl already had a pocket knife out and had inserted the blade between two of the boards.

"Holy shit!" said Carmela, as one of the boards lifted up.

"Secret compartment," said Jekyl, laboring with the second board. "We kind of shared it. It's where Archie kept his coins."

"Right," said Carmela, staring into the narrow hole. "You did mention that he collected coins." This little adventure was getting stranger by the minute.

Jekyl lifted out a strongbox, grunted softly, then laid it at Carmela's feet. "What if . . . ?" began Carmela, trying to collect her thoughts. "What if Archie was killed because of these?"

"You mean that his killer knew about this collection and was trying to get his hands on them?"

"Yeah," said Carmela. "Maybe."

Jekyl flipped a latch and threw back the lid on the strongbox. Rolls of coins in plastic tubes glinted in the light. Other coins were stored individually in small plastic bags, the same kind of small ziplock bags Carmela used to corral beads and small charms. A few coins were set into foam inserts and nestled in small plastic boxes.

"All told, what do you think they're worth?" asked Carmela.

"Maybe five to ten grand," said Jekyl.

"Not a huge amount of money in the scheme of things," said Carmela. "Although people have certainly been killed over far less."

"Agreed," said Jekyl. He had once been beaten and robbed over near the French Market for a Movado watch and fifty-odd dollars.

Silence hung in the air between them.

"Coins," said Carmela. "Greek and Roman coins."

"And the odd pirate's doubloon," added Jekyl. "Archie did have a passion for treasure hunting."

"Not much treasure hunting around here," said Carmela.

"Actually, Archie was convinced he was close to finding Lafitte's treasure."

Time suddenly stood still for Carmela. "You're not serious. *Jean Lafitte's* treasure?" Jean Lafitte was probably the most famous pirate of the Western world. He was the swashbuckling pirate credited with coming to the aid of Andrew Jackson during the Battle of New Orleans to help roundly defeat the British.

"Oh yeah," said Jekyl. "Archie was crazy wild over Lafitte."

"Tell me the whole story," said Carmela. "Start from the beginning."

"Not much to tell," said Jekyl. "Archie loved coins and doubloons and, as you can see, amassed a small collection of them."

"What about the treasure-hunting part?" urged Carmela.

"Archie did a lot of research on Jean Lafitte as well as the legends that abound concerning vast amounts of undiscovered treasure. He was always at the Vieux Carré

Historical Society studying maps and reading old accounts. In fact, with the local landscape so radically altered by Hurricane Katrina, Archie thought the treasure might be even easier to find."

"Or more difficult," said Carmela.

"That could be, too," agreed Jekyl.

Carmela thought for a moment. "Not that I'm buying into this treasure theory, but what exactly did Archie think the treasure might be worth?"

"He thought that at current numismatic and historic value, the treasure could be worth anywhere between two and five million dollars."

"Yowza," said Carmela.

Jekyl reached into the strongbox, felt around, and pulled out a set of keys.

"What are those for?" asked Carmela.

Jekyl looked grim as he jingled the keys on his index finger.

"Archie has a crypt over in St. Louis Cemetery No. 1. He always said if something happened to him . . ."

"Dear Lord," said Carmela. "He was awfully young to be thinking about his own burial."

"And now it's come to pass," said Jekyl in a somber tone. He looked up, locked eyes with Carmela.

"This sounds a little strange," said Carmela, "but if Archie was talking this treasure thing up around town . . ."

"And somebody took him seriously," said Jekyl. "Then that someone might tear his place apart looking for leads."

"Or kill Archie because he wouldn't reveal anything," said Carmela.

Silence hung between them once more.

"Now what?" asked Jekyl.

"First things first," said Carmela. "You need to barricade that passageway. If somebody got to Archie, they could get to you the same way. For whatever reason."

"Nobody knows," said Jekyl.

"Honestly," said Carmela, "I think someone *does* know."

"And you're worried I could be the next victim?"

"I have no idea," said Carmela. Her head was spinning with ideas and theories. "But why take a chance?"

Jekyl bobbed his head. "I suppose you're right. No sense taking chances."

"And you promise me you'll phone Lieutenant Babcock? Right away?"

"I promise."

But the evasive look on Jekyl's face made Carmela nervous.

CHAPTER 8

"Is it too late to come over?" asked Ava.

Carmela dropped the phone to her chest and thought for a moment. No, not really. It was barely eight thirty, and Ava had left a note saying she'd already walked the dogs. "Come on over," she told Ava. "I've got tons of crazy stuff to tell you."

"Excellent," said Ava.

Two minutes later, the brass knocker on Carmela's front door sounded.

"It's open!" called Carmela, as Boo and Poobah raced wildly for the door.

"Darlings!" cried Ava, dropping to her knees to accept a barrage of canine kisses. "How are the best puppy dogs in the whole world? Even though I haven't seen you in sixty whole minutes!"

Turns out the puppies were just fine. Boo — a girly-girl Shar-Pei with a fat muzzle; loads of wrinkles; and a tight, curly tail — jockeyed for position as the alpha dog.

Poobah, a mongrel with a slightly torn ear, that Shamus had found wandering the streets, wasn't far behind. He wormed his way into the snuggle pile and nuzzled Ava affectionately.

"How's the cat?" asked Carmela. She fished for the name. "Isis. She doing okay, Stepmom?"

Ava rose to her feet as Boo and Poobah continued their assault. "In ancient times," said Ava, "cats were regarded as gods. You'll be happy to know they still are."

"I take it you're catering to her every whim?"

"Of course," said Ava. "She's an absolute darling. Even though she only eats that *expensive* cat food in the silver package."

"Isn't it funny how animals can actually sense when your Visa card is maxed out?" said Carmela.

Ava nodded. "And I'm not sure how I feel about a kitty who has prettier hair than me."

Carmela gazed at Boo, with her lush, reddish-fawn fur. "Get used to it."

"So, did you eat already, *cher?*" asked Ava. There was a plaintive tone in her voice, and her eyes roved toward Carmela's kitchen. Carmela was a darned fine cook, and Ava knew she always had a stash of pecan biscuits or peanut pralines in her cupboard as well as red beans and rice or jambalaya in her freezer.

"Oh yeah," said Carmela. "Jekyl and I went to Mumbo Gumbo."

Ava's eyes lit up. "And how's that fine-looking restaurateur? Was he present and accounted for?"

"Quigg was there," said Carmela. "He was even nice enough to comp our dinner."

"A truly generous man," said Ava. "You could probably be quite happy with him."

Carmela groaned. "You thought I'd be happy with Shamus."

"That was a major miscalculation on my part," said Ava. "But I really think you could be *satisfied* with Quigg. He could give you great companionship."

"I already have two dogs," said Carmela. "So I'm covered in that department."

"Then think of the food aspect," said Ava. "You'd dine like a queen every day of your life."

"Is Quigg offering you a commission or something?"

"No," laughed Ava.

"The food is tempting, but I'd probably get fat in the bargain," said Carmela. "Changing the subject only slightly, did you eat?"

Ava patted her midsection, where there

was a two-inch gap between her tight, low-slung jeans and her tight red T-shirt. "I gotta watch my weight. Can you believe it? I finally get my head together, and now my body's fallin' apart!"

"You're not falling apart; you're as toned and as taut as you ever were. You do not need to watch your weight."

Ava gave a slow wink. "Then how about you watch it for me?"

"Sure," said Carmela.

"In that case," said Ava, "do you by chance have any of your famous crab cakes stashed in your refrigerator?"

"No, but I've got some leftover crawfish jambalaya that I could heat up. It's nice and spicy, just the way you like it."

"Be still, my heart," declared Ava. "And would you have a couple of stray pecan biscuits?"

"Frozen, but easily popped into the microwave," said Carmela. "How many would you like? One or two?"

"Three," said Ava, "since we've decided that watchin' my weight doesn't actually entail doing anything about it."

Carmela set to work in her small kitchen, while Ava wandered idly about Carmela's apartment. It was a cozy apartment that, over the last couple years, had received the belle époque treatment. A refinished walnut dining room table with cane chairs defined the dining room. The living room consisted of an antique leather couch, glass cocktail table, antique fringed lamps, and prints in elegant gold frames hung on the walls. Just last month, Carmela had added an Aubusson carpet. Of course, Boo and Poobah had staked that out as their favorite nap spot.

"You got some new books," said Ava, checking the wrought-iron shelf to the left of the small fireplace. Carmela collected vintage children's books, and she'd just recently found a 1938 first edition of *Bumblebuzz* by Rosalie Fry in a Magazine Street junk shop.

"I hit the jackpot," said Carmela. "Somebody brought in a box of old books that probably got soaked clear through during the hurricane. I'm still working on drying them out and cleaning off the grime using methyl cellulose, but I think if I'm careful and persistent, most of the books will be fine."

Indeed, in the weeks and months following Hurricane Katrina, Carmela had labored intently to help her customers with their soggy and mud-spattered photos. She'd cleaned the damaged photos in a special emulsion, then dried and pressed them. She hadn't been able to recover every damaged photo that had been brought to her, but she'd enjoyed an almost 80 percent success rate.

Carmela stuck a wooden spoon into the saucepan and gave her jambalaya a quick stir. Then she grabbed an already-open bottle of Vouvray from the refrigerator and pulled the cork out.

"You want to hear something funny?" said Carmela as she poured generous-sized servings into generous-sized wineglasses. "I watched this Martha Stewart episode recently where Martha suggested freezing your leftover wine in ice cube trays so you could use 'em later to pop in sauces."

"Extra wine?" said Ava, with a puzzled expression. "What extra wine would that be?"

They settled in at Carmela's dining room table, the dogs milling about their feet, begging for crumbs and scraps.

Carmela told Ava all about the secret passageway and the coins that Archie had stashed in the floor of Jekyl's closet.

"Secret passageway," said Ava. "Now I've heard everything."

"Not by a long shot, you haven't," said Carmela. "Jekyl had a few more wacky revelations. He told me that Archie was hot on the trail of the Jean Lafitte treasure."

Ava did a double take. "Treasure? Are you serious? I thought Jean Lafitte sailed off into a Caribbean sunset with chests full of money. And that buried treasure, *locally* buried treasure, was just a tall tale."

"Apparently Archie didn't consider it all that tall," said Carmela, "because he was doing hard research on it. He'd even drawn some conclusions as to where he thought the treasure might actually be buried."

"Where did he think it was buried?" asked Ava.

"No idea," said Carmela. "Jekyl said Archie only mentioned it to him. I don't think Archie had an actual map or anything."

"Nothing in that strongbox, huh?"

"Not that I could see."

"Too bad," said Ava. "Find that treasure, and you could really tell Shamus to kiss off. Tell him to take the minuscule alimony payment he proposed and shove it where the sun don't shine."

"Better yet," said Carmela. "I could buy the Crescent City Bank right out from under him. But keep him on as a handyman or something."

"Make him clean the toilets," giggled Ava.

■ ■ ■ ■

Curled up on the couch, Ava sipped a second glass of wine while Carmela talked a little more about Archie's murder, the warning she'd received from Edgar Babcock, and her theory on why Archie might have been killed.

Ava listened thoughtfully, then said, "Sounds like Babcock was really trying to scare you." She took a final sip of wine. "Last time I ran into him was at the Creole Christmas Festival here in the Quarter. He looked pretty good." She glanced sideways at Carmela. "He still look good?"

"Oh yeah," said Carmela. "If he ever dropped the attitude, he'd be your basic adorable little Ken doll."

"Sounds like you're interested in him," said Ava.

"Right now, I'm only interested in those of the male persuasion who don't try to intimidate me or tell me what to do."

"That's not him," said Ava. "Babcock's just filled with opinions."

"You're right," said Carmela. "But a girl can look, can't she?"

"It's awful what he told you about strangulation," said Ava. She touched a hand to the slight hollow at the front of her throat. "Good thing I didn't go out on the balcony with poor Archie."

"A ligature snapped around the throat from behind," murmured Carmela. "Terrifying. You'd really have no way of fighting back."

Ava sat up straight. "Remember in that movie, *The Godfather,* when that fat guy, Luca Brasi, got strangled in the bar?"

"Yes," said Carmela, wondering where Ava was going with this.

"Creepy," said Ava. "Oh, and I think they stuck a knife through his hand, too. Pinned him to the bar with his eyes all bugged out." She set her empty glass down. "I'm rambling. Time to switch to RC Cola."

"I'll get you one," offered Carmela.

"Hey," said Ava. "I brought my Demilune costume along. Can you give me a little help?"

"Sure," said Carmela, as Ava reached for her Gucci tote bag and dumped it upside down. Her costume spilled out, along with keys, wallet, three lipsticks, a box of false eyelashes, and a glossy gossip magazine.

"Oh, I gotta show you this really cool dress I'm in love with." Ava grabbed her magazine and thumbed through it quickly. Gossip magazines were one of her guilty pleasures. "I love this section where they show all the celebrities dressed to the nines and walking the red carpet. Here it is! Chanel couture. I'd sell a kidney to get a dress like that." She passed her magazine over to Carmela in exchange for the cola.

"Oh yeah," agreed Carmela. "To die for. Well, at least to limp around for." Carmela suddenly looked around. "Where's Boo?" It was quiet in her apartment. Too quiet.

"She was just here," said Ava.

There was the faint sound of lapping coming from the bathroom.

"Having a quick drink," laughed Ava.

"Eeyew," said Carmela.

Ava was close to finishing her Demilune krewe costume. Designed to match the twenty-foot float with its elaborate gold moon and silver star motif, Ava was determined to sew tiny moons and stars onto the bodice. Carmela wasn't sure that, in a screaming French Quarter throng of fifty thousand people crazed for grabbing strands of beads, the little doodads would even be noticed, but Ava was insistent. She had to match.

"Is this right, *cher?* Is this how you do a running stitch?"

Carmela studied Ava's efforts. A little

104

ragged, but she had to admit the tiny charms did look cute. "Almost perfect."

"I can't *wait* to wear this thing," said Ava as the phone suddenly rang. She reached out an arm and snagged the phone off the hook. "Carmela's House of Earthly Delights. We accept Visa, MasterCard, and good old greenbacks."

There was a slight hesitation, then a male caller said, "Ava?"

Ava made a face. "Shamus?"

"Yes, it's Shamus." Now he sounded cranky.

"In that case, I meant Carmela's House of Pancakes." Ava erupted with shrill laughter.

"You're twisted, you know that?" snapped Shamus. "You're a terrible influence on Carmela. Always have been."

"Thanks for your vote of confidence, you sack of shit," said Ava. "You think *you're* the paradigm of virtue? You're out prancing around with a new, barely legal floozy every night. Your floozy du jour." Ava was rolling now, enjoying her verbal joust with Shamus. "And tell me this, Mr. Shamus Allan Meechum. Why is it you don't want to give Carmela a reasonable divorce settlement, when she's put up with all your various and sundry crap?"

Carmela mouthed *Good one* at Ava, then took the phone. "What's up?" she asked him.

"That's a fine way to greet your husband," grumped Shamus.

"Soon-to-be ex-husband," corrected Carmela.

Shamus let loose a deep sigh.

Uh-oh, thought Carmela. A deep sigh was always Shamus's preamble to bad news.

"Babe," said Shamus, "we're workin' on all that legal stuff. But my lawyers are still hung up on a few logistical points."

"And what exactly would those points be, Shamus?"

"Well, uh, actually, a number of things. Nothing big, mind you, but still details that need to be hammered out."

"Hammered out?" said Carmela. "Listen, Shamus, I deserve a decent settlement. Compensation for all the heartache you put me through. The walking out on me, the cheating, the walking out again, the humiliation. You hear me, Shamus? Reasonable alimony for the next three years. And child support for Boo and Poobah. After that, I don't care what happens. I'll be on my own. I think that's more than fair."

"It's just a darn shame we didn't sign a prenuptial agreement," lamented Shamus.

"Then we wouldn't be having these problems."

"Because you didn't *want* a prenuptial," said Carmela. "Your loony sister, Glory, pushed for one and, in an unprecedented show of independence against your family fortune, you chose to ignore her suggestion."

"You know what, Carmela?" said Shamus. "You've got a mind like a computer hard drive. Every sticky little thing is lodged in there just waiting to be retrieved."

"Then retrieve this, Shamus: please don't call again until we have an agreement."

"I have to see Boo and Poobah. I have parental rights, you know."

"Not when things are at a stalemate."

"Visitation at least," whined Shamus.

"I'll have to get back to you on that," said Carmela. And she hung up before he could reply.

CHAPTER 9

Today was rubber stamping day at Memory Mine. Carmela had declared it so, and Tandy, Baby, and Byrle had readily agreed. But to change things up a bit, Carmela wasn't having them do traditional stamping on paper. No, today the creative challenge was to stamp designs on ready-made black velvet bags.

"They're evening bags, really," said Tandy, gazing at the eight-by-eight-inch square bag that lay flat on the table and fingering the long woven cord handle. "Especially if you use fancier stamps along with metallic inks."

"Who wanted the butterfly stamp?" asked Gabby. She had enthusiastically dug through their trove of rubber stamps and pulled out the ones she thought would lend themselves to more elegant designs.

"Me," said Baby, raising her hand. "I want to create a border of vines and then put a couple butterflies smack-dab in the middle."

"Lovely," said Carmela. "And if you over-stamp your vine design with a number of color-coordinated inks, you'll create a much more dimensional look."

"Dimensional," said Tandy. "You use that word a lot."

"That's because it makes the difference between a so-so project and a killer project," said Carmela. "The more layers you can build up, whether we're talking about colored inks, different papers, or decals and stickers, the more pizzazz your project's going to have."

"So I could add even more dimensionality by sewing on tiny pearls," said Baby.

"Exactly," said Carmela. "Or you could even try some of those colorful glass Czech beads we just got in."

"Now I have to ask," said Byrle. "Would this work for a velvet pillow, too?"

"Sure," said Carmela. "Really, you can rubber stamp on almost anything. I've stamped designs on white terry cloth towels and given them away as shower gifts." Last October she'd even rubber stamped a T-shirt for Ava. She had taken an assortment of Halloween-themed rubber stamps — bats, jack-o'-lanterns, and historic-looking grave-stones — and stamped them in purple, gold, and rose-gold ink onto a black T-shirt.

Carmela had been thrilled when her creation turned out to be one of Ava's favorites.

Gabby laid out another assortment of stamps. "This is a grouping of angel and rose designs," she explained. "From the Rose Cottage Romance Collection."

Baby reached a hand out tentatively. "Ooh! May I?"

"Please do," said Gabby, pushing the stamp set toward her and grabbing another boxed set of rubber stamps. "And these little gems have wonderful Parisian poster and landmark designs."

When all the questions ceased, when her customers were working away contentedly and Gabby was up at the front counter helping customers, Carmela slipped into her small office at the back of the shop. She was eager to take another look at Archie's phone directory and check out his appointment book. Maybe, buried in there somewhere, was a tiny clue that would shed some light onto why he'd been murdered.

Unfortunately, Carmela didn't find much to go on. The directory was mostly blank pages, and Carmela wondered if Archie hadn't stored his phone numbers either on his computer or in his cell phone. She'd have to look into that. Or ask Babcock to.

So, okay, that left Archie's appointment calendar. A small, thin, black book that also didn't look like it had been used much.

Carmela thumbed through the month of January. A few notations had been scrawled in. But most of them pertained to business meetings. Sure, there he'd noted a meeting with Jekyl and the Pluvius krewe. Getting the ball rolling on the floats, probably.

Turning to this week, the current week, Carmela found only one notation. Archie had scheduled a meeting for tomorrow morning at ten o'clock with a person by the name of Robert Tallant.

Carmela closed the book and leaned back in her chair. Where had she heard that name before? Why did it sound so familiar?

Grabbing the phone book, she thumbed through the *T*s. There was a Robert Tallant listed. His address was 1815 Calhoun Street. If Carmela's memory served her correctly, that was over near Tulane University. Near Audubon Park.

An address didn't tell her much, though.

Idly, Carmela turned to the business listings, ran her finger down the column of *T*s. There was Talent Scouts Modeling Agency, Tall and Big Men's Clothing, and, lo and behold, Tallant, Robert — Rare Coins and Curios.

A rare coin dealer. Hmm.

Carmela's left hand crawled up to the back of her neck as she let her mind wander. She ran her fingers through her hair, rubbing her scalp briskly, then spiking her hair slightly. She hoped the scalp massage would activate her brain cells. Send them into hyperdrive.

Maybe, she decided, Archie was simply planning to buy more coins from Robert Tallant. On the other hand, maybe he was going to sell coins. Maybe he'd gotten himself into some sort of trouble and needed to make some fast money.

Trouble, she thought. *Yeah, he'd gotten himself in trouble, all right.*

Swiveling in her chair, Carmela's fingers sought out her keyboard. There was something else she wanted to check out. A few taps, and she was on the Internet, doing a Google search on *barbed wire.*

She was stunned when more than a thousand hits came back.

Barbed wire was that popular?

Turns out it was.

There were barbed wire collectors, barbed wire museums, barbed wire historians, and barbed wire manufacturers.

Interestingly enough, barbed wire was also referred to as devil's wire. Carmela gave a

112

shudder. An appropriately nasty name.

"Carmela?"

In her Web surfing trance, Gabby's voice sounded faraway. And then Carmela's chair snapped forward, both her feet hit the floor, and she was hustling toward the front of the store where a gaggle of customers had seemingly appeared from nowhere to blot out the sun.

"A little help, Carmela?" Gabby asked again, but Carmela was right there.

"Absolutely," said Carmela, putting on a bright, hopefully helpful-looking smile. "Who's next?"

"I am," said a lady with slightly rose-tinted glasses and a waft of gray hair. "I'm looking for a calligraphy pen."

"Got those," said Carmela, plucking one from a display.

"And," said the woman, pulling an old ledger from her tote bag, "I need your advice. I found this old ledger and was wondering if I could use it to create a family history album. I've got tons of old pictures, but I'm not sure how to incorporate them."

Carmela took the ledger in her hands. It was a handsome brown fabric-covered book with a 1920s Deco design on the front and tan leather binding and corners. "This is gorgeous," she told the woman. "And, yes, I think it will make a lovely album."

"But how do I put it all together?" asked the woman.

"Do you have old papers besides your photos?" asked Carmela. "What scrappers call ephemera?"

The woman nodded. "Quite a lot. I have some old birth certificates, wedding announcements, newspaper clippings, and even some old bus tokens and gas rationing stamps from World War II."

"What you do," said Carmela, "is create a sort of time line. Here . . ." She reached for some Roman numeral rubber stamps. "Use these to establish a time frame for your earliest photos, then use them to highlight every decade. For example, if you're starting in the 1920s, stamp 1920 at the top of the page, arrange your photos and memorabilia, and then maybe add a few highlights."

"Such as?" asked the woman.

"Maybe make a piece of tag art, using one of our vintage rubber stamps. Add an old button or two, and maybe a piece of sheet music from that era."

"I get it," nodded the woman. "I *like* it."

"Maybe use brown leather corners to mount your photographs in keeping with the book's cover. And then, when you get it all put together," said Carmela, turning toward her display of ribbon, "finish it off by wrapping some ribbon around your ledger to give it the feel of an old, historic album. Here." Carmela pulled off a yard and a half of fawn-colored velvet ribbon with antiqued edges. "Tie it all up with this."

"Perfect," declared the woman.

"Carmela," called Gabby, still looking a little frantic, "we've got some customers who are asking about our new classes. You *do* have those finalized, don't you?"

I do now, thought Carmela.

"We'll be starting two new classes," she told the group as they crowded around her, "in three weeks' time. The first will be a class called Scrapping Sew Easy. This is a class that focuses on how to incorporate fibers, fiber art, hand sewing, and machine stitching onto scrapbook pages and cards."

"Hand sewing?" asked one of the women. "That works?"

"Sure," said Carmela. "Of course, you can also create amazing looks using your sewing machine to stitch fabric onto paper."

There was a murmur of approval as Carmela continued. "My second class is called Asian Accents. In that class we'll learn how to create Asian-themed scrapbook pages using rice paper, wax seals, calligraphy, origami, Chinese symbols, Japanese washi papers, blue and white beads, and bits of cinnabar."

"Wow," said one of the women, "where do we sign up?"

"Right here," said Gabby from behind the front desk. "Classes are limited to the first fourteen people, so you *do* need to make a reservation."

Carmela and Gabby remained frantically busy for the next hour, pulling sheets of paper for customers, demonstrating uses for some new metal tags, showing off new crackle paper. So of course Edgar Babcock chose that time to show up. He pushed his way through the crowd at the front of the store and only stopped when he was within six inches of Carmela.

Pushy, she thought, gazing into his bright brown eyes. *Cute, but pushy.*

Babcock aimed for her right ear. "Tell me about the illegal absinthe."

Carmela stared at him quizzically. "What?" she whispered back. "And please keep your voice down. I don't want you upsetting my customers." She pulled him back toward her office. "I don't know anything about illegal absinthe."

Babcock narrowed his eyes. "You're telling me that you and your crazy friend . . ."

"Wait a minute," said Carmela. "Hold everything. Are you referring to Ava? Calling her crazy?"

"Well, yeah," said Babcock. "She always struck me as being a little wild."

"Well, she's not," said Carmela. "Far from it. In fact, she's one of the most levelheaded people I know." Carmela dared not glance at the sky for fear a bolt of lightning would shoot down and strike her. Cook her like a baked potato in a blast furnace. "And for your information," she continued, "we do not drink absinthe. Wine, yes. Now and then a Sazerac or a mint julep. But definitely not absinthe." Carmela had to force herself to take a breath. A cleansing breath. "Why are you asking about this anyway?"

"Because traces of thujone just happened to show up in Archie Baudier's toxicology report," said Babcock. "I find that a little strange." Thujone was the toxic substance that made old-fashioned absinthe so dangerous.

Carmela stared back at him. "It's not like absinthe hasn't reared its head here before." Absinthe had a long and storied history in New Orleans. In fact, a historic building still standing in the French Quarter and dubbed the Old Absinthe House dated back to the early eighteen hundreds. The plaque on the outside of the building listed the names of Oscar Wilde, Sarah Bernhardt, and Walt Whitman as former customers who'd bellied up to the bar for the now-outlawed drink.

"Tell me about it." Babcock sighed. "There are even two legal versions of absinthe now."

The look on Babcock's face told Carmela that this could have been the thing Jekyl hedged on when she asked about drugs.

"You must have found a better clue than that," prodded Carmela.

Babcock narrowed his eyes. "There were also flecks of gold paint found on Archie's shoes. You know anything about gold paint?" He glanced around Carmela's store, his eyes taking in the ink pads as well as the jars, tubes, bottles, and cans of paint. "I guess you do. I'd say you have about twenty different kinds here."

"Maybe thirty," said Carmela. "Does that mean I'm on your suspect list now?"

His frown morphed into a reluctant smile. "Probably not." He hesitated. "Do you know you get this tiny little line right between your eyebrows when you're mad?" He lifted a finger to her forehead, not quite touching her, but Carmela could feel the warmth of his nearness.

118

"Maybe I missed my Botox shot last month." She laughed.

"You're too young for that," he told her.

Carmela brightened. "You think so?" Then, realizing he was flirting with her and that she was flirting back, she quickly tried to change the subject. "What can you tell me about your suspects so far?"

"I can't tell you anything," said Babcock pleasantly.

"I don't mean a name," said Carmela. Watching him carefully, she noticed a slight flinch. "Wait a minute, you do have a name, don't you? You have *something?*"

Babcock remained curiously silent.

"No," she said, sounding a little self-satisfied. "You don't. Okay then, have you developed any sort of profile?"

Babcock looked around. "You've got to keep this under your hat."

"Please," said Carmela. "Who would I tell?"

Babcock glanced around again. "Just about everybody."

"Well, I won't," said Carmela. "I promise."

He drew a deep breath. "Male. Probably with a history of violence. Possibly someone fascinated with knots and cords."

"Really," breathed Carmela. When an actual homicide detective worded it that way, the profile sounded awfully plausible.

"Take my word for it," added Babcock, "this guy's a real squirrel."

"You're sure it's a he?"

"I'm sure."

"But it has to be someone Archie knew," said Carmela. "Someone who was able to infiltrate the party and get close to him."

Babcock looked unhappy. "Probably. Why are you so all-fired interested in this? Because you happened to be there? Because Jekyl asked for your help?"

Carmela shrugged. "Could be." She hesitated. "Listen, speaking of Jekyl . . ."

"Yes?" said Babcock.

"I was at his place last night . . ."

"Yes," said Babcock again.

"And he kind of let it slip . . . that is, he showed me something . . ."

"What are you trying to tell me?"

Carmela decided to just blurt it out. "There's a secret passageway."

"What!" Edgar Babcock's expression changed from curiosity into anger.

"It leads from Jekyl's apartment into Archie's place."

"How is it you *know* this stuff?" hissed Babcock.

"Because I was there," said Carmela. "Jekyl gave me the grand tour. And . . . I

120

guess he just trusts me." What was left unspoken was that Jekyl didn't trust the police.

"But if it makes you feel any better," continued Carmela, "I was the one who urged Jekyl to call you. I'm just sorry he didn't. No. Actually, I'm darned upset that he didn't call."

"Oh, he called all right," said Babcock. "His number showed up on my cell phone. I've just been chasing all over the city this morning so I haven't gotten around to responding to that particular message. Frankly, I assumed he was calling to gripe, not deliver a key piece of information."

"So he really did call," said Carmela. "Well . . . good."

Babcock grimaced. "So I suppose I've got to head over there now. And I'll have to call in my crime-scene guys again. Not what I need right now."

Carmela's busy morning wasn't over. Five minutes after Edgar Babcock stepped out the door, Federal Express arrived with a huge box.

"Wow," said Gabby. "Is that for us?"

Carmela checked the label. "For my Demilune krewe."

"What on earth is in that *ginormous* box?"

121

asked Tandy, who had drifted toward the front of the shop.

"Beads," said Carmela, as she grabbed an X-Acto knife and slit open the top. "Throws."

Inside were literally thousands of strands of beads, held together in packs of fifty by paper bands.

"They're gorgeous," said Tandy.

Carmela broke open one of the packs and held a few strands up to the light. The beads were shimmering purple pearls with a single gold crescent moon, hung like a medallion.

"I see purple and gold," said Gabby. "But no green."

Carmela dug deep within the box, pulled out gobs of green beads with the same gold crescent moon.

"Excellent," said Tandy, as they spilled onto the counter. "The colors of Mardi Gras, which haven't varied since 1872 when the Russian Grand Duke Alexis Romanoff came for Mardi Gras, and our fair city adopted his royal colors."

"Purple for justice, green for faith, and gold for power," said Gabby.

"Don't you just love Mardi Gras?" said Tandy. "Don't you just love all the different throws?"

"When I first moved here," said Gabby, "I

couldn't quite believe that the krewes actually tossed out beads, cups, mirrors, stuffed animals, Moon Pies, doubloons, combs, and even ladies' panties!"

"Maybe that's why they call us the Big Easy," mused Tandy, a mischievous grin on her face.

Gabby decided to let that remark slide by. "Ladies," she said, calling to Baby and Byrle, who were still in back. "I'm ordering lunch from the Pirate's Alley Deli. Does anybody want to put in their order for a po'boy?"

Hands immediately flew up.

CHAPTER 10

The po'boys were a huge hit. The favored sandwich that became a New Orleans signature consisted of a long French roll stuffed with a huge variety of fillings. Po'boys could be ordered bursting with meats and cheeses, filled with fried shrimp or oysters, and even stuffed with roast beef and gravy. Pickles and lettuce were usually piled on, so was plenty of mayonnaise.

Carmela cleared away the remains of the sandwich wrappers as well as empty coffee mugs. Baby and Byrle had taken off a short while ago; Tandy was still firmly ensconced. Carmela had promised her a special lesson.

"You can really stamp on candles?" asked Tandy as she pulled three large white pillar candles from her tote bag.

"Works like a charm," said Carmela.

Tandy set her candles in front of her, then picked through the rubber stamps Carmela had set out. "So I just use my ink pad?" she asked.

"Nope," said Carmela. "You have to use paint. That will make your design permanent and give better color saturation."

"Interesting," said Tandy. "Why don't you just go ahead and do one. That way you can show me what technique to use." She pushed a rubber stamp toward her. "Here, maybe use this sun stamp."

Carmela nodded as she squirted a gob of dark blue acrylic paint into a shallow tin pan. Then, using a small roller, she ran it through the paint, then applied the blue paint to the rubber sun stamp.

"Ah," said Tandy.

"Once your rubber stamp has enough paint on it," said Carmela, "you place one edge of the stamp on the candle, then roll the stamp gently across until you've completely transferred the motif. Then you simply repeat your motif all around the candle." She worked quietly for a few minutes. "In this case, I stamped five sun images."

"It looks good already," remarked Tandy.

"And once the paint is dry," said Carmela, pushing the candle toward Tandy, "you can overstamp an image. In this case, I'd recommend a smaller, complementary stamp."

She rummaged among the rubber stamps. "Say this image of a star. Maybe use gold acrylic paint and stamp the stars right on top of the suns. Then, when your second images are dry, you can tie a cord or ribbon around your candle and even add a charm if you want."

"Love it," said Tandy. She held up her candle for Gabby to see. "See how great this looks already!"

"Very pretty," said Gabby. She turned her focus on Carmela. "Were you going to do something with this extra sandwich?" She held up a brown paper bag. "It's starting to leak."

"I'm going to run it over to Ava," said Carmela. Her eyes roved quickly about the shop. "In fact, can you spare me right now?"

"Go ahead," said Gabby. "Just please come back."

Carmela was out the back door, down the alley, and pushing through the front door of the Juju Voodoo Shop in a matter of minutes.

Overhead, a mobile of bare, white bones clacked together to announce her arrival. Shelves filled with plastic skulls, charms, candles, amulets, and decks of tarot cards filled the little store. Incense, an intoxicat-

126

ing blend of sandalwood and cardamom, hung in the air.

Ava's head suddenly bobbed up from behind the counter and a grin split her gorgeous face. "Carmela! What brings you over here?"

Carmela dangled the paper bag in front of her. "Lunch."

"Bless you," said Ava. She slipped out from behind the counter, looking slinky and lithe in a black jersey wrap dress. "Mmm," she exclaimed, grabbing the leaky bag and peering into it. "A po'boy. Always one of my faves. Thanks loads."

"I have an ulterior motive," said Carmela.

"Okay," said Ava.

"A major question to ask," said Carmela.

Ava set the bag on the counter, safely out of the way of her display of soft-sculpture voodoo dolls. "Shoot."

"Do you know any absinthe dealers? The kind that sell the illegal stuff?"

Ava's eyebrows shot up. "That *is* a major question. Are you thinking of, how shall I phrase this? Indulging?"

"Not really," said Carmela. "But here's the thing. Detective Babcock dropped by Memory Mine just before lunch. He was all freaky about the fact that traces of heavy duty absinthe turned up in Archie's toxicology report."

"The green fairy," mused Ava, using the intriguing phrase that was part of the vernacular surrounding absinthe. "Interesting. And always a little dangerous."

"A little taboo," agreed Carmela.

"So Archie was drinking the illegal version the night of Jekyl's party, not just the Purple Haze?"

"Looks like," said Carmela.

"This guy was edgier than I thought he was," said Ava.

"So what I'm wondering," said Carmela, "is if you know anybody who might have a connection to selling that kind of absinthe? If we can get a handle on Archie's provider, maybe we can take a small step forward in this investigation. Not that we've made all that much progress as yet."

"You think Archie was murdered over absinthe?"

"I have no idea," said Carmela. "But if he was buying illegal absinthe, he might have been mixed up with some seriously dangerous people."

Ava looked thoughtful. "Come to think of it, I know a guy who *might* know a guy."

"Can you call him? Maybe press him a little on this?"

One of Ava's brows arced a little higher.

"You mean flirt?"

"Give it all you've got," urged Carmela.

Ava glanced around. One customer was studying the ingredients list on her love charms, another was checking out her new rack of amulets. "Okay, but I'm gonna have to go in my office, *cher.* Close the door and keep this little matter confidential."

"Sure."

"Hey," said Ava, grabbing a leather cord and handing it to Carmela. "Check out my new evil eye charms. Just got 'em in. The blue ones are from Turkey, and the red ones are from Romania. Pretty cool, huh?"

"Delightful," said Carmela, staring at the strange red ceramic bauble with the wonky, staring eye.

"And they work, too," said Ava. "Hey, Miguel," she yelled to a young man who was balancing atop a stepladder, hanging bright red Chinese Fu Manchu masks from the ceiling. "Watch the counter, will you? And don't you dare put your mitts on my sandwich!"

While Ava was in her office, whispering into her phone, Carmela poked around Ava's shop. It was a quaint shop, literally filled to the rafters with crazy and slightly spooky merchandise. Once tourists found their way into Juju Voodoo, they were usually enchanted beyond belief, figuring they'd discovered the *real* New Orleans. In actuality, most of Ava's stuff was imported from the Far East.

Five minutes later, Ava came hurrying out of her office, high heels clicking like castanets. "Okay, I've got something for you," she told Carmela. "But I really had to twist my guy's arm. Kinda promised I'd go out with him."

"But you got a name," said Carmela, excitement pinging in her chest. "Or a phone number."

"Both," said Ava. "A cell phone number that belongs to a guy named Miguez. He's supposed to be some sort of crazy Cajun."

"What's the prefix for the number?"

Ava showed her a scrap of paper. "Do you know where this is?"

"No," said Carmela, studying it. "Do you?"

Ava shook her head. "Nope. Still think I should make the call?"

"There's a chance it could lead to something," said Carmela. "So yes, why not? What have we got to lose?"

Ava looked a little hesitant. "So I should call and . . . what?"

"Try to set up a meeting," said Carmela. "For tonight, if possible. Then we'll just take things one step at a time, see where they lead."

"Okay," agreed Ava, "I'll take care of it."

As she was hurrying back to her scrapbook shop, Carmela made an impulse decision. She would detour down Dumaine Street and make a quick stop at the Vieux Carré Historical Society. Jekyl had mentioned that it was where Archie had spent a lot of his time doing research. So maybe, just maybe, if she paid them a visit, she could learn a little more.

Housed in an old brick building with tall, shuttered windows and coach lamps hung to either side of its well-worn wooden door, the Vieux Carré Historical Society seemed as charming as its name. Inside, the pegged wooden floor looked like the building's original, and brick walls were hung with antique etchings and prints that depicted a rough-and-tumble French Quarter filled with bars, warehouses, and apartments. It was no wonder that, by 1810, New Orleans had been the fifth largest city in the United States.

Carmela went to the front desk, a circular affair straight out of the forties, and introduced herself. She was immediately directed to Margot Destrehan, the society's curator.

Margot was open, friendly, and looked the part of a museum curator. Although she was still in her mid-thirties, scholarly wire-rimmed glasses perched on the tip of her nose, and she wore a long, black skirt and a simple, black cowl-necked sweater that was accented by a large sterling silver free-form pin. Carmela couldn't decide if the design was supposed to be a star or a flamingo.

"Oh, you're Mrs. Meechum!" exclaimed Margot.

Not for long, thought Carmela.

"Your sister-in-law, Glory Meechum, sits on our board of directors," said Margot with great enthusiasm. "In fact, she's been responsible for a good percentage of our funding."

"Wonderful that's she been so generous," remarked Carmela in a neutral tone. Glory, who she always thought of as *she of the tight fist and great stone face,* had never been particularly generous to her.

"Are you thinking of getting involved with the Meechum Family Foundation?" asked Margot.

Dodging that question deftly, Carmela said, "Actually, I'm sort of looking into the murder of a friend. I'm sure you know him. Archie Baudier?"

Margot's smile collapsed, and her brown

132

eyes immediately welled up with tears. "A shock," she whispered as she hastily dug in the folds of her skirt for a Kleenex tissue.

"I take it you knew Archie quite well?" said Carmela.

Margot nodded as she dabbed at her eyes, then blew her nose. "Oh my, yes. Archie was one of our Honor Circle members."

"Honor Circle," said Carmela. "What exactly does that mean?"

"Archie took part in any number of symposiums and panel discussions here," explained Margot, giving a final honk. "And he did a good deal of just plain volunteer work. You know, cataloguing books and things. He was a lovely man. We miss him already. So charming and interesting . . . and imbued with a true love of history. There's not so many people like that anymore."

Carmela decided to take a chance. "Did you know that one of Archie's hobbies was trying to locate Jean Lafitte's treasure?"

"Oh, absolutely," said Margot with a wistful smile. "Treasure and ancient coins were Archie's absolute passion. I don't think a week went by that he didn't pop in here to do a little bit of research or pore over some of our old maps."

"You have a lot of old maps?" asked Carmela.

"Come take a look," invited Margot. She pushed open a swinging door and led Carmela into a much larger, brighter back room. Floor-to-ceiling bookcases, jam-packed with books, lined the walls. A row of filing cabinets sat bunkered in the middle of the room. In front of those were three antique library tables surrounded with comfortable-looking leather-covered chairs, the kind of chairs with nubby brass nails that held the leather in place. The ceiling had a partial skylight, which afforded plenty of natural light.

Margot led the way in. "Besides books, photographs, maps, and historic documents that pertain to the French Quarter, we also have a good deal of material on the Louisiana Purchase, the Battle of New Orleans, the Baratarians, and, of course, Jean Lafitte himself."

"This is a wonderful little historical society," marveled Carmela. In all her time in the French Quarter, she'd never once poked her head in here. Now she felt a pang of regret. This place was a little gem.

"We're very proud of our collection," said Margot.

"Tell me," said Carmela. "The Lafitte

treasure . . . do you believe in it? Do you think it exists?"

Margot fixed her with a sad smile. "No. I'd *like* to believe in it — much the same way I'd like to believe in unicorns and leprechauns. But there doesn't seem to be much documented evidence that any such treasure ever really existed."

Carmela shifted from one foot to the other. "What about undocumented evidence?"

"Now you're talking legends and lore," said Margot. "Folk stories and apocryphal tales. Crazy newspaper stories from eighty, ninety years ago." She peered at Carmela, as if checking to see if she was still interested. "That we have a little on."

Carmela *was* interested. "May I see it?" asked Carmela.

Margot shrugged. "Sure, why not? I have to warn you, though, it's a mess downstairs."

Margot led Carmela through a narrow back hallway and down an even narrower flight of stairs. "This is our basement archive," said Margot. "And I use that term loosely."

Carmela gazed about the dark, musty space and tried not to sneeze. Rusty file cabinets leaned against damp walls, dusty books comprised uneven piles. Cardboard boxes, many of which seemed to be deconstructing in the moldering dampness, were stacked everywhere.

"Most of this stuff has been deacquisitioned," said Margot, leading the way through the jumble. "Problem is, I can't seem to let myself throw it away." She looked a little embarrassed by the mess and clutter. "Anyway, if you're looking for legends and lore, this is pretty much the mother lode, most of it being old newspaper accounts." Margot pushed her glasses up on her nose, frowned, stopped in front of a battered file cabinet. She slid open the top drawer, studied the peeling labels on the files, then pulled out a file crammed full of slightly yellowing paper. "This might be of interest to you. Letters, maps, and a packet of clippings from defunct newspapers. If you ask me, I think most of those old swashbuckling stories about Lafitte were written with the sole intention of selling newspapers."

Carmela accepted the file, considered the heft of it. "May I take this home?"

Margot was suddenly hesitant. "I really shouldn't let anything out of the building. If our executive director, Mr. McCuen, ever found out . . ."

"I'd be very discreet," promised Carmela.

"And I know for a fact that Glory is thrilled with all the great work you do."

Margot suddenly looked a lot less hesitant. "If you could get the file back in a day or two?"

"A day or two," said Carmela. "Of course." She knew she could scan anything she wanted rather quickly once she got back to Memory Mine. Then she'd have her own master set.

Carmela tucked the file folder into her shoulder bag as they climbed the stairs. Margot walked her to the door and held it open.

"If there's anything I can do," said Margot, "please don't hesitate to call. Truly."

"Thanks so much," said Carmela, clutching the file and hurrying away before Margot Destrehan changed her mind.

CHAPTER 11

"Cher," said Ava, as she sprawled languidly at Carmela's dining room table. "I swear you are one of the best cooks in all of New Orleans."

"Hardly," said Carmela. Tonight she'd served Ava her famous Crab Cakes Carmela: tender lump crab generously seasoned with herbs and drizzled with a cream sauce. Side salads were a mixture of endive, beets, and goat cheese.

"I'm serious," said Ava. "Emeril's got the name and all the fancy cookbooks, and K-Paul's got the serious reputation, but you, my dear, have the magic touch."

"Thank you, darlin'," said Carmela, as she tried her darndest to keep Boo and Poobah from snatching food directly from the table. They'd definitely turned into a couple of wild kitchen dogs, much more focused on people food than their own humble dog food. Only last week, Poobah had somehow crawled on top of the counter and helped himself to a piece of steak that had been sitting there defrosting. He'd mangled it so badly it had looked like steak tartare.

Ava reached for the bottle of pinot noir that sat between them. "We still have plenty of time, right?"

Carmela glanced at the clock in her kitchen, a black and white Kit-Cat clock complete with moving eyes and tail. "It's only eight. We're meeting this guy, Miguez, at ten?"

"That's it," said Ava, picking up the wine bottle and topping off her glass. "Hey, you mind if I undo the snap on my jeans?"

"Unsnap away," said Carmela.

"Whew," said Ava. "I should know better than to wear my skinny jeans when you're cooking."

"The only time I can get into my skinny jeans," said Carmela, "is after a good bout of stomach flu."

"It's food poisoning that generally helps me," said Ava, tipping the bottle to top off Carmela's wineglass, too.

"You sure you've got the directions?" asked Carmela. Now that the meeting was on with the mysterious Miguez tonight, she was feeling jittery and on edge.

"No problem," Ava assured her. "I've got

everything covered."

"Got something to show you," said Carmela. She stood, picked up their empty plates, and carried them into the kitchen. When she came back, she was carrying the Jean Lafitte file that Margot Destrehan had given her. "Take a look at this." Carmela plopped the fat file down onto the table.

Always curious, Ava stuck a lethal-looking fingernail between a couple of pages and pulled out a folded newspaper page. "This is about Jean Lafitte," she said, her voice tinged with curiosity.

"Archie's historical love and favorite fascination," said Carmela. "According to Margot Destrehan, the curator at the Vieux Carré Historical Society."

Ava gazed at her. "That pretty much confirms what Jekyl said, too."

"As bizarre and anachronistic as it all sounds," said Carmela, "I think Archie might have been hunting for Lafitte's treasure."

"If you ask me," said Ava as she turned over more pages and scanned them quickly, "Archie is beginning to sound a tad wacky. *Cher,* how'd you get this stuff, anyhow?"

"Margot Destrehan was kind enough to let me unofficially spirit it out," said Carmela. "As long as I promised to return everything in a couple of days."

"Listen to this," said Ava, reading from one of the old articles. " 'Deep in the southwest corner of Louisiana, in what is today Calcasieu and Cameron parishes, is an area once known as the Neutral Strip. Comprised of wilderness and marshland, this mysterious tract of land was notorious for being a safe harbor for pirates, buccaneers, and lawless social outcasts.' " She put down the sheet of paper and wrinkled her nose. "Phew. This paper smells moldy."

"That's because it is," said Carmela. "What paper is that article from?"

Ava glanced at the top of the crinkled, yellowing page. "*Lake Charles Chronicle.* Dated April 18, 1885." Slightly intrigued now, she shuffled through a few more papers. "Here's something from an even earlier date, 1856."

"What's that one say?" asked Carmela.

Ava's eyes roved down the sheet as she mumbled to herself. Finally, she said, "Ah, this is pretty interesting stuff. It says, and I quote, 'an island in the Contraband Bayou, a tributary of the Calcasieu River, served as a well-known hiding place for the celebrated pirate, Jean Lafitte. A nearby elevation, known to this day as Money Hill, is the reputed spot where Lafitte buried his vast sums of treasure.' "

"But those are old legends," said Carmela, thinking about what Margot Destrehan had said. She'd referred to the Lafitte treasure stories as legends and lore. Stuff you'd *like* to believe in because it was romantic and fanciful and smacked of derring-do.

Ava closed the file. "You're right. They're just old stories. Probably told and retold by old guys who sit on front porches and drink Wild Turkey and brag about their hound dogs. Frankly, I don't see much connection with poor Archie Baudier getting strangled to death with that hunk of barbed wire."

"Unless he was seriously looking for the treasure," said Carmela. "Unless Archie had a bead on where that treasure might be."

"That's a pretty big *unless*," said Ava.

"Yeah it is," agreed Carmela.

"I think," said Ava, looking thoughtful now, "that if there really was a treasure, if Lafitte and his merry men didn't squander their buckets of gold on rum and loose women, some smart, enterprising party would have found it by now."

"Mmm," said Carmela. "Maybe. But I still want to pursue that treasure angle a little more. And I just happen to have found a source who might know a good deal about treasure and doubloons," said Carmela.

"Who's that?" asked Ava, closing the file.

"Robert Tallant," said Carmela.

Ava thought for a minute. "Tallant. Isn't that the name of that coin shop down on Royal Street? The one with the gold coin jewelry in the front window?"

Carmela nodded. "Archie had scheduled an appointment with Robert Tallant for ten o'clock tomorrow morning."

"Let me guess," said Ava. "You're going to keep that appointment for him."

"Tallant is one guy I definitely want to talk to."

"So . . . an information-gathering meeting," said Ava.

"Hopefully," said Carmela.

"Good luck to you then," said Ava. "But I still think your idea of following the absinthe connection is a stronger angle. From what I understand, the high-test version is a hot underground commodity these days. Which probably means a lot of dangerous people have eased themselves into the business."

"Probably good money to be made," said Carmela. "Things that are illegal always possess a certain amount of allure."

"Which in turn creates a demand," said Ava. "Funny, isn't it, how money always seems to go hand in hand with greed and danger?" She glanced at her watch. "Still got a little time."

"We could open another bottle of wine," suggested Carmela.

"*Cher,* I was afraid you'd never ask." Boo rubbed up against Ava and presented her fat muzzle for scratching. Ava, of course, complied. "Maybe a red wine?"

They settled in Carmela's living room with their second bottle of wine, a shiraz from Napa's Rutherford region.

Ava stretched out on the leather chaise and pulled one of her gossip magazines from her oversized purple leather purse. "Got somethin' to show you." She thumbed through a few pages, then tapped one of the glossy pages with her index finger. "You see how thin these women are?"

Carmela glanced at the photos. "Awful. You can see every node in their collarbones."

"You know how they get so skinny?"

"Enlighten me," said Carmela.

"They use some kind of horse asthma drug."

"Weird," said Carmela. "And so not good for you."

"Ah," said Ava. "Here's something better." She held up her magazine. "Photos of those hot new Chanel bubble purses."

"Now those are hot," agreed Carmela.

Ava closed her magazine, extended one leg, and studied her pink painted toenails.

"Can you believe it? Two gorgeous gals like us sitting at home on the weekend? And not a date in sight?"

"It's Thursday night," pointed out Carmela. "Technically not the weekend yet."

"Thursday's the new Friday," said Ava. "Just like tea is the new coffee, and sixty's the new forty."

"You do have a certain way with logic," admitted Carmela.

"Hey," said Ava, reaching for the *Big Easy Weekender* paper that lay on Carmela's coffee table. "Why don't we check the local personal ads. Might be a good way to find ourselves a couple of likely candidates."

"I'm not sure that's a good idea," laughed Carmela.

Ava opened the paper toward the back. "No, come on, this'll be fun." She turned a few pages. "Soon's I get through all these escort service ads. My, there sure are a lot of ladies named Brandy and Tiffany who want to meet discreet gentlemen. Think they're any competition to us?"

"Let's hope not," said Carmela.

Ava finally came to the personal ads. "Okay, I see a serious possibility right off the bat. Listen to this, *cher.* 'Lonely, elderly man seeks female companion for meals out, concerts, movies, conversation, and

Scrabble.' " She set the paper down and grinned widely. "He could be perfect for me."

"Ava," scolded Carmela, "you're gorgeous, sexy, and not even thirty. Don't you think you might be hunting in the wrong age bracket?"

"Then how about this," said Ava. " 'Single white male, financially secure and easygoing, seeks lady, noncontrolling, attractive, and a good driver.' "

"I don't think you'd qualify," said Carmela.

Ava peered over the paper. " 'Cause I'd flunk the noncontrolling part?"

"That's a consideration, yes. And then there's the good driver part."

"Please," said Ava, looking offended. "Anybody can wrap a Honda around a stupid lamppost. I mean, the city puts those darned posts in the absolute worst places."

"You mean on the streets?"

"Yes!"

Five minutes into their second bottle of wine, Jekyl called.

"I've made plans to hold Archie's memorial service this Saturday," he told Carmela. "Right in St. Louis Cemetery No. 1, near his crypt."

"Okay," said Carmela. She mouthed the word, *Jekyl,* to Ava.

"Say hey to Jekyl," called Ava.

"Ava says hey."

"Hey back," said Jekyl. "What I really want to know is, are you still willing to design a memorial program?"

"Of course," said Carmela. "Just give me the details." She gestured at Ava for a pen, grabbed the little newspaper from her and made a scribble mark in the margin. "Okay, shoot."

"I don't have every single detail," said Jekyl, "but I'll give you what I have."

Carmela listened, then jotted a few notes, while Ava got up and strolled into the bathroom.

"I'll e-mail the rest of the details once I finalize the arrangements," promised Jekyl.

"Great," said Carmela. She quickly filled him in on the file she'd picked up earlier, then said, "Jekyl, while I've got you on the phone . . ."

"Yes?" said Jekyl, in a voice that sounded harried and a little hesitant.

"You know Archie had been drinking absinthe? The illegal kind?"

"Who told you that?" asked Jekyl.

"Detective Babcock. It showed up in the medical examiner's toxicology report."

There was dead silence for a few moments, then Jekyl said, "Okay."

"Did you know he was into absinthe?" asked Carmela. "Are you into absinthe?" Her words just sort of rushed out.

"We playing truth or dare?" asked Jekyl.

"No," said Carmela, knowing he was resorting to coyness. "Only truth."

"Truth then," said Jekyl. "I tried some that had been smuggled in from the Czech Republic. Didn't really like it. The price was a bit too high for me."

"We're talking retail?" asked Carmela.

This time Jekyl chuckled. "The price of a hangover." He hesitated. "But I know Archie had developed a taste for it."

"Well, the police are going to be asking more questions," said Carmela. "You might want to have a few answers ready."

Ava came out of the bathroom looking radiant with newly applied lipstick, blusher, and mascara. "Are you talking about the absinthe?" she asked in a loud whisper.

Carmela nodded.

"For gosh sakes, don't tell him we're going off tonight to meet a genuine absinthe *dealer!*"

Carmela tried to cover the phone, but Jekyl's sharp hearing had caught part of Ava's words. "Don't tell me about what?"

he asked. "What are you two cooking up?"

"Nothing," said Carmela. "Nothing at all."

"Time to head out," announced Ava, once Carmela had hung up the phone. "Think we should take the doggies along for protection?"

Carmela gazed at Boo and Poobah, who were sprawled on the floor, looking like stuffed animals that had had the stuffing knocked out of them. Fast asleep, their paws twitched in their doggy dreams, and they both emitted loud snoring noises that came pretty close to mimicking a buzz saw.

"Somehow, these two dogs don't strike me as rough-and-ready guard dog types," said Carmela.

"Good point," said Ava. She peered down at Boo. "She's so dang cute, but does she always drool when she sleeps?"

Carmela nodded. "The joys of living with a Shar-Pei."

Chapter 12

"Left! Turn left!" screamed Ava. They were whipping down Lesseps Street in Carmela's Mercedes, a car that had been a gift from Shamus a couple of years ago. For reasons unknown, Ava seemed to be waiting until the last possible moment to give Carmela precise directions.

Carmela turned, slowed, and popped the clutch into first. "This street's completely blocked."

"Oops," said Ava, making a face. "A slight tactical error. Sorry."

"Do you actually know where we're going?" asked Carmela.

Ava held up her paper with the scrawled directions and rattled it, as if to reassure herself. "Course I do. I've got the finely honed instincts of a professional cartographer."

"That's comforting," said Carmela in a droll tone. "But do you know which street to take right now?"

Ava looked left, then right, then squinted at her map. "I think we should head across the river on St. Claude Street and figure it out from there."

Carmela backed into a driveway, then turned back the way they'd been headed. "So cross the Inner Harbor Canal?"

"Right," said Ava. "I mean correct."

"Then what?"

"I'm workin' on that, *cher*. But it's hard to be exacting under such pressure."

"But you've got the address?"

"Oh sure," said Ava. "Hey, turn here at this little neighborhood bar. Azalea's. You ever been in there? Good comfort food."

"Great stuffed artichokes," said Carmela.

"Now go right, turn right on Reynes."

Carmela braked hard, barely sluiced her way through the turn. "I need a little more warning," she told Ava.

"A few more blocks," said Ava, "then we'll take a left."

They glided down several more blocks. "Dark around here," remarked Carmela. They seemed to be leaving that part of the city that was still inhabited and twinkling with lights.

"Stuff hasn't been rebuilt yet," said Ava as they drove past homes and commercial buildings that were still boarded up.

"And time is taking its toll," added Carmela. Three years later, so many buildings were still deserted. This part of the city was in flux, property owners still hesitant about whether to tear down and rebuild or just abandon their properties entirely, wait until the city declared eminent domain.

"Spooky," said Ava. "Hardly any lights on. Hardly any *people*."

"Now what?" asked Carmela. Being in this part of town made her feel jittery. You never knew what could go wrong. And crime in New Orleans was still at an all-time high.

"Go left!" directed Ava.

What are we in for? wondered Carmela.

"Perfect," declared Ava, as Carmela executed her turn. "Now just pull over to the curb."

"You're not serious," said Carmela, when she saw where they'd ended up. "You know where we are?"

"Gateway Community Hospital," said Ava. She checked her hand-drawn map. "Yeah, this is it, all right."

Carmela was shocked. "This is where we're supposed to meet your Miguez character? The place is completely deserted! It's been closed since Hurricane Katrina!" She peered out the car window at a ten-story brick building that, in the dark, loomed like a gigantic wrecked hulk. It reminded her of the burned-out buildings in Berlin that she'd seen in World War II films. After the Russians had stormed the city and pretty much pounded everything to rubble.

"This can't be right," Carmela muttered again.

"Oh, this is it," Ava assured her. "Miguez said to come here, and he'd phone with the rest of the directions."

Carmela's head snapped right. "He's going to *call* us? We're just supposed to sit here like . . . like sitting ducks?"

"He was very clear that he'd direct us on a need-to-know basis."

"Guess what," said Carmela, her unease ratcheting to a new level. "I need to know right now!"

As if on cue, Ava's cell phone tinkled the first few notes of Bon Jovi's "We Got It Going On." "Bet that's him now," she said brightly. She thumbed her On button, held the little phone to her ear. "This is Ava."

"Good lord," murmured Carmela, still peering out her window at the devastated neighborhood.

"Yup, it's us," Ava said into the phone. She smiled at Carmela, gave an exaggerated nod of her head. "Really? Around back?"

Carmela shook her head no.

"Okay," said Ava. "If you say so." Dropping her phone into her purse, Ava smiled at Carmela. "Looks like he's gonna meet us at the back door."

"I don't like this," said Carmela. "There's something screwy here."

"Guy's probably just being cautious."

Against her better judgment, Carmela stepped out of the car. Her eyes took in the dark building with its shattered windows and boarded-up front door, as well as the battered chain-link fence that stretched around the perimeter. She couldn't think of a more foreboding place.

"Careful where you walk, *cher*," said Ava. "There's a lot of junk lying around."

"No kidding," said Carmela, as she stepped over a soggy cardboard box, then a jumble of boards with sharp nails protruding from them. They walked gingerly in the darkness, following the fence around to the back.

"Dark back here," commented Ava. Now she sounded a little less sure of herself and their plan.

When they arrived at a gaping hole in the chain-link fence, Carmela shook her head. "Man, I *really* don't like this. You sure this Miguez guy is on the up and up? I'd hate to walk into some sort of trap."

Ava pulled her sweater tight around her shoulders. "I think he's okay." Her dark eyes met Carmela's. "What do you want to do, *cher?* Turn around?"

Carmela eyed the hole in the fence. "Not sure." Her upper teeth worried her bottom lip for a few moments. Finally, she made up her mind. "We've come this far . . ."

"My sentiments exactly," agreed Ava.

Ducking through the hole, taking care not to get caught on the pieces of rusty wire that poked out, they walked the twenty paces to the back door of the ruined building. A heavy chain stretched loosely between two door handles.

Ava reached down and jiggled it. "It's not padlocked or anything, just looped. We can go in."

"I guess," said Carmela.

Pulling open the back door, they were immediately enveloped by a gust of stale, damp air. Carmela, always a believer in accumulated karma, could only imagine the enormous misery that had occurred here during the dark days of Hurricane Katrina.

Ava's phone tinkled again from the depths of her purse.

She dug for it quickly. "Hello? Where are you?" Now she didn't sound all that sure of herself. "You were supposed to meet us." Pause. "Downstairs?" She gazed at Carmela, indicated a dark stairwell off to their left. "He wants us to . . . uh . . . come downstairs."

"No way," said Carmela. "It's pitch-black. We're liable to fall and break a leg."

"What?" said Ava into her phone. She turned to Carmela. "Apparently he left a flashlight for us over by the wall."

Carmela looked around warily. "I must be crazy," she muttered. Then her eyes fell upon a small metal tube propped against a dingy cinder block wall. "Okay, I see it."

"We got it," said Ava. "I guess we're coming down."

Clutching each other, the thin beam of light barely cutting through the thick cloud of darkness, Carmela and Ava eased themselves down the stairway. Damp and littered with trash, the steps were a nightmare to negotiate. The walls that closed in on them were scabrous and covered with gray mold. But finally, crazily, they made it.

"Now what?" asked Carmela. Her voice sounded hollow and small in the dank basement corridor.

"Not sure," said Ava. She flashed the light around, revealing corridors that led off in three different directions. "Man, this is scary."

As they stood motionless for a few moments, Carmela's eyes began to grow accustomed to the darkness. "Down there," she said, pointing to where a faint light seemed to glow from behind frosted glass. "There's a light burning."

"Okay," said Ava, "then I guess we head that way."

The long hallway was worse than the stairs. Shards of glass crunched underfoot, and there were faint sounds of scurrying and rustling.

"Tell me those aren't rats I hear," said Ava. Her respiration was fast and audible. Ava was terrified of rats.

"They're not rats."

"You're sure?"

"Just squirrels with skinny tails," said Carmela.

"Eeyew," breathed Ava.

They drew nearer to a large set of double doors. The frosted glass glowed a little brighter. Someone was definitely waiting beyond those doors.

"What's that say?" asked Ava, squinting at flaked and cracked letters peeling away from the door.

Carmela grasped Ava's wrist and aimed

the flashlight. "It's says . . . Morgue."

Ava froze in her tracks. "You're kidding!"

Gathering her courage, Carmela kicked at the door with her foot. It creaked open on rusted hinges. "You won't find any bodies in here," she told her friend. "Not any dead ones, anyway."

"Oh my," whimpered Ava as they shuffled into the room.

And what a room it was. Metal tables stood in two rows, their ungodly plumbing kinking down into pipes that descended into the filth-strewn floor. Trays of instruments sat catawampus on metal stands; Stryker saws dangled overhead.

Hearing a faint scraping sound, sensing a change in the room's atmosphere, Carmela aimed the flashlight toward the back of the room.

"Holy shit!" squealed Ava. Standing in the shadows was a man, six feet tall, with a tangle of dark hair.

"Miguez?" asked Carmela, concentrating on not allowing her voice to crack.

Miguez stepped out of the shadows and gave an inquisitive cock of his head. "At your service." He had a deep, resonant voice that bore the distinct cadence of the Cajun dialect. "You come alone?" he asked. "No one followed?"

"Who would want to?" said Carmela.

He laughed softly, then turned and fiddled with an electrical cord. A slight hum filled the room, then soft light puddled around them.

Now Carmela was able to get a better look at Miguez. He was in his early thirties, clean-shaven, and fairly good-looking in a dark, brooding sort of way. He was dressed in blue jeans and a tight black T-shirt. Probably a concert T-shirt, since it had a faded Aerosmith logo. Gazing at them, Miguez wore a lazy half smile on his face. He certainly didn't *look* all that threatening.

"You know why we're here?" asked Carmela.

Miguez gave a careless shrug. "You tell me."

Carmela felt emboldened. "Why on earth would you ask us to meet you down here?"

Miguez swept a languid arm toward the morgue tables. "You don't like my place?"

"I think you need a better decorator," Carmela shot back.

Miguez let loose another soft laugh. "But this is the perfect place," he told her. "For someone in my business." Now he indicated the bank of oversized stainless steel drawers that stood behind him. "You see . . . excellent storage."

The tiny hairs on the back of Carmela's neck stood up.

"What about electrical power?" asked Ava. "It's dark as sin down here and there hasn't been electricity in this part of town since the hurricane."

"Generator," was his one word answer. "But enough with the questions. Now we do business." Miguez retreated a few steps, slid open one of the drawers.

Instinctively, Carmela and Ava shrank back.

Miguez seemed not to notice. He reached in and extracted a slender bottle of green liquid, balanced it carefully in his hand. "I can let you have one-half liter for one hundred dollars. Or I can give you two bottles for one eighty." He stared at them, challenging now. "The price is firm. No negotiations. This is the real stuff, made with wormwood."

"What if we want more at a later date?" asked Carmela.

"Not possible," said Miguez. And now he eyed them with suspicion. "Things have changed. It appears I'm . . . uh . . . getting out of the business." He held up the single bottle, wiggled it enticingly. *La dame verte,*" he said. "The green fairy. You want to buy? You got cash money?"

"Oh, we're not here to buy," said Ava.

Miguez seemed not to understand. "*Excuse* me?"

"What we really want is a little information," said Carmela. "Then we'll be out of your hair."

Ava gave a nervous grin. "That's right. You can forget we were even here."

Now a sly smile spread across Miguez's face. "You ladies want information? Then you are most definitely here to buy."

"No, really," said Ava. "We just have a couple quick questions." She glanced at Carmela, obviously looking for backup.

Miguez stared at them. "What did I tell you before? One hundred dollars? Excuse *moi,* but the price is now one hundred fifty dollars." He extended his right arm, palm up.

"You're not serious," said Carmela.

Miguez stared at her with crackling dark eyes until she decided he was most definitely serious.

"I don't suppose you, heh-heh, take Visa," said Ava. When an answer wasn't forthcoming, she said, "No? Well okay."

Carmela dug in her purse, pulled out five twenties, placed them in the palm of his hand. Miguez continued to stare at her.

Carmela and Ava had a whispered conversation and then two more twenties appeared.

"Close enough?" asked Carmela.

Miguez folded the bills and nodded. Slipped them into the pocket of his jeans.

"What I want to know," said Carmela, "is if you sold absinthe to Archie Baudier?"

"Yes," he responded slowly. "I sold to him. But not so recently." Miguez continued to stare at Carmela, as if anticipating another question. And Carmela had the distinct feeling that Miguez had absolutely no idea Archie was dead.

"Do you know who supplied Archie most recently?" asked Carmela, deciding to take a different tack.

Miguez hesitated a few long moments. "Possibly. There's a new guy around. A Russian."

For the first time, Carmela detected a look of nervousness on Miguez's face. Or maybe it was fear.

"And he's your new competition," said Carmela. It was a statement not a question.

"Fancies himself a real tough Mafia guy," said Miguez. Once again, he'd tried to pass off a casual answer but looked decidedly unsettled.

"Is he really Russian Mafia?" asked Carmela. "Or just self-appointed?"

"Hey," said Miguez, roughly. "Enough." And now his voice rose. "Like I told you, I'm getting out of the business. The situation is becoming a little too intense."

"All we want to determine —" began Carmela.

But Miguez was decidedly unhappy with their line of questioning. "I said enough! Too pushy!"

"Don't go *bracque*," said Carmela, using a little Cajun. Don't go crazy. "No need *boude*." No need to be angry.

Miguez stared at her, his anger suddenly on hold. "You speak Cajun?" He sounded surprised.

"A little," she admitted.

"You're Cajun?" he asked.

"Some."

Miguez visibly relaxed. "Okay then, I be *obligeant*." I'll be more considerate. "But I think our business here is done."

"Great," said Ava. " 'Cause I'm about ready to blow this pop stand."

Miguez laughed, suddenly turning his attention on Ava. "Pretty *bébé*," he told her. "Is that your real hair?"

Ava was both amused and outraged. "Of course it is." She touched manicured nails to her lustrous locks. "You think this is one of those cheap TV shopping channel clip-ins? No way, honey, this is part and parcel of my DNA."

"Beautiful," said Miguez, his voice smooth and silky now. "You maybe go out with me sometime? We go to a fancy restaurant. Maybe Antoine's or Galatoire's?"

Ava seemed more than a little flattered. "Well . . . maybe."

"Have some oysters Rockefeller and some champagne." Miguez leered at her. "The food of lovers."

Carmela was horrified. "Ava!"

Ava shrugged. Honestly, what was a girl to do?

"One more question," said Carmela.

Miguez's eyes burned bright.

"What else can you tell me about this Russian dealer who's come on the scene?" pressed Carmela. "What's his name? Where does he live? Where does he hang out?"

Miguez's good humor seemed to wither away, and Carmela could tell he was ready for them to leave. Was probably regretting they'd ever come. "I heard he lives in a big mansion in the Garden District. Rented place, but he still try to look like a big shot." He gave a snort. "A Russian immigrant who tells everyone he once lived in Transylvania." Miguez shook his head. "He loves that shit."

"What . . . uh . . . ?" began Carmela. "Oh, you mean vampires?"

"Yeah, yeah," said Miguez. "That's supposed to be one of the reasons he moved here. Loves the New Orleans cemeteries. All the crazy stories and vampire shit." Miguez paused. "And he's supposed to be an ex-mercenary hiding out."

"Oh, that's not good," said Ava.

"What kind of ex-mercenary?" asked Carmela.

"The bad kind," said Miguez, seriously emphasizing his words. "One who worked in Sierra Leone and now is heavy into selling guns to certain interested parties in South America. New Orleans makes a convenient home base."

Carmela thought about that for a minute. As preposterous as it sounded, Miguez's words could be true. Things were still crazy and unsettled in New Orleans. The police were still a little overwhelmed, and there'd definitely been an influx of bad-ass criminals.

"You go now," said Miguez. He placed the half liter bottle of absinthe in Ava's hands. "For your trouble," he told her. Although the look on his face indicated that *he'd* been the one who'd incurred the trouble.

■ ■ ■ ■

"Can you believe it?" asked Ava, as they climbed the stairs. "He gave us a bottle of totally illegal absinthe!" She sounded excited but nervous, too. As though a bunch of narcs or the guys from ATF would swoop down in a fleet of black helicopters and take it away from her.

"For all the trouble Miguez put *us* through," said Carmela, "we should have gotten a bottle of Cristal champagne."

"Still," said Ava, clutching the tapered bottle of shimmering green liquid, "this is intriguing."

Carmela leaned the flashlight back against the wall, and they exited the building. The night air felt cool and refreshing and welcome after their time inside the crumbling hospital.

"Good Lord," said Ava, looking at her watch. "I can't believe how late it is. It's after midnight."

"You know what happens tomorrow night, don't you?" asked Carmela. "Or, rather, tonight. Since we're already into Friday."

"You've got a hot date."

"Not quite," said Carmela. "Think bigger."

"Two hot dates," said Ava.

"You've heard of the Vampyre Danse?"

About ready to duck through the gap in the fence, Ava paused and stared at Carmela. "No kidding, that's tomorrow? I mean tonight?" The Vampyre Danse was one of hundreds of fantastical parties and balls that were held during the Mardi Gras season. Only difference was, instead of formal dresses and tie and tails, the participants were vampire lovers, vampire wannabes, and Goth fans, all suitably attired in full vampire regalia.

"It's something to consider," said Carmela.

"You're thinking this Russian guy could show up there?" said Ava.

"It's the biggest vampire soiree I know of," said Carmela. "And Miguez says this Russian guy is really into vampire legend and lore. So . . . yeah. Maybe."

Ava was already thinking ahead. "Of course, we can't just go waltzing in. We'd need an invitation."

"But if this Russian guy does attend," said Carmela, "we could pick up a valuable lead."

"*If* we can score an invitation," said Ava.

"That's a mighty big if," admitted Carmela. "But I'll call Jekyl first thing tomorrow. See what he can shake out of his net-work."

"You know what the best thing would be?" giggled Ava. "We'd get to dress up in sexy costumes!"

CHAPTER 13

A bell tinkled discreetly as Carmela stepped inside Royal Coin and Curios; soft Oriental carpets whispered underfoot. Much to Carmela's delight, the shop had a distinct old-world feel. Tiffany lamps sat atop antique glass cases, and a handsome grand-father clock ticked reassuringly. As if on guard duty, a fuzzy orange cat squirted across in front of her, leapt to the counter, and curled around a cut-glass vase filled with a bountiful array of purple anemones.

"Hey, kitty," said Carmela, just as Robert Tallant emerged silently from behind a pair of gold brocade curtains. He wore a pink shirt with a cream bow tie that seemed to go well with his carefully practiced smile and somewhat studied manner. His brown hair was parted low, his gray eyes were nar-row, his lips thin. He was in his late forties, maybe early fifties, with a certain coolness surrounding him.

"This is a lovely shop," said Carmela, realizing for the first time that there were quite a few antique daggers as well as a suit of armor on display, too.

"Thank you," said Tallant, crinkling his eyes to imitate a smile.

Carmela extended a hand across the glass case, noting a display of gold coins that would have made any pirate's heart beat faster. "I'm your neighbor, Carmela Bertrand. I own the scrapbook store, Memory Mine, over on Governor Nicholls Street."

Tallant shook her hand. "Of course," he said without a flicker of recognition.

"Your name was in Archie Baudier's appointment book. In fact, you two had a meeting today."

Tallant's faint smile dissipated quickly. "So we did."

"You're aware Archie was killed last Tuesday evening?"

"Yes," said Tallant. "I saw the news report, and then two police officers dropped by yesterday afternoon. A sad affair, it would seem."

"That's kind of why I'm here," said Carmela.

Tallant steepled his fingers while his eyebrows formed twin arcs. "Oh?"

"I'm just following up on anything or

anyone who may have had recent dealings with Archie."

"And you are doing so — why?" asked Tallant.

"As a friend," said Carmela. "A concerned friend."

Now Tallant's gray eyes sparkled. "A fellow shopkeeper playing detective?"

"Something like that," said Carmela.

"Working in concert with the police?" He looked skeptical.

"Absolutely," said Carmela. Sure, she was. Sort of. "The thing is, I was just wondering about the nature of your meeting today. Was Archie buying coins or possibly even selling coins?"

Tallant stared at her, seemingly reluctant to disclose that information. Finally he said, "Mr. Baudier was interested in purchasing a small collection that I'd recently acquired."

Carmela gazed into the display case that stood between them. "How fascinating. Is that particular collection on display? The one Archie was interested in? May I see it?"

Tallant let loose a low sigh. "It's not on display, but, yes, you may see it." He held up an index finger. "Wait please." Then he disappeared behind the curtain.

Carmela stared at a pewter mug and a

crucifix inlaid with rubies, wondering if Tallant was watching her right now on closed-circuit camera. Figured, yeah, he probably was. The shop was filled with valuable items, and he seemed a twitchy sort.

Tallant came bustling out with a small red velvet box. He set it on the counter, reached for a black velvet mat, then placed the box on top of that, centering it carefully.

"They're Dutch coins," he told her as he opened the lid on the hinged box. "Guilders, to be exact." He grasped a small black velvet pouch, tugged it open, and poured a half-dozen coins into Carmela's hand.

"Gorgeous," she exclaimed, surprised at her own strong reaction. The coins were the smoothest, richest, yellowest gold she'd ever laid eyes on. In fact, they seemed to be lit from within.

"Twenty-four-karat gold," whispered Tallant.

Carmela could barely pull her eyes from them. Puddled in the palm of her hand, the coins looked and felt like liquid butter. "And Archie was planning to buy these?"

Tallant nodded. "Probably. They would have made an exquisite addition to his collection."

"They're like some wonderful treasure,"

said Carmela, returning the guilders to his hand.

"Indeed," said Tallant, as he slipped the coins back into their velvet pouch.

"I'm just curious, Mr. Tallant. As a rare coin dealer, have you ever gone treasure hunting yourself?"

Tallant gave a curt laugh. "Me? Hardly. I let the dreamers and fools do that. I'm strictly a businessman. One who tries to purchase interesting collections . . . treasure falling into that category, of course."

"So you actually purchase found treasure?" asked Carmela.

"Absolutely," said Tallant. "I've acquired pieces from Mel Fisher's *Atocha* gold. And, let's see, about a hundred of the twenty thousand Roman coins that were unearthed a few years ago in South Gloucestershire, England. Those were lovely, attributed to Constantine the Great. And then I run across the odd piece of Confederate gold now and then. It's amazing what turns up."

Carmela decided this was as good a time as any to ask the sixty-four-thousand-dollar question.

"Do you know anything about the Jean Lafitte treasure?"

Tallant smiled. "You mean the gold coins supposedly given to Lafitte by Colonel

Andrew Jackson? For throwing in with him and helping win the Battle of New Orleans?"

"Bingo," said Carmela. This conversation might just be easier than she thought.

But Tallant was shaking his head in a dismissive gesture. "Pure myth. According to modern historians, the meeting between Jean Lafitte and Andrew Jackson never took place. There was no great strategizing between the two men. So, obviously, there was never any payoff."

"But modern historians weren't there," said Carmela. "Or maybe Lafitte's treasure wasn't entirely payoff money. Maybe it was gold coins and bullion that Lafitte had amassed over the years. After all, he raided countless Spanish galleons as well as French and English trading ships that plied the Mediterranean as well as the Gulf of Mexico. You might say Jean Lafitte was an equal opportunity pirate."

"And his myth grows with each passing year," said Tallant, sounding even more skeptical.

"Archie Baudier didn't think it was a myth," said Carmela, hoping to elicit some sort of reaction.

Tallant looked like he was about to say something, then didn't.

Carmela continued with her line of conversation. "Apparently, Archie was doing considerable research at the Vieux Carré Historical Society, studying old maps and newspaper accounts."

Tallant simply nodded, as though he was a patient shopkeeper listening to a rambling customer. "There are a lot of old accounts. And theories concerning the treasure's location."

"A few people think Archie might have been on to something," said Carmela. She was grasping at straws now, hoping Tallant had something to add. But nothing seemed to be forthcoming.

Finally, Tallant said, "You know, I wouldn't mind getting my hands on Archie's collection. He wasn't exactly an *amateur* collector, so he had some fairly decent pieces. Do you by any chance know who's in charge of his estate?"

"No," said Carmela, deciding Tallant was pretty much a clod for asking. Especially since Archie hadn't even had a proper burial yet. "No, I don't."

Carmela had barely stepped outside Robert Tallant's coin shop when Edgar Babcock accosted her.

"Are you crazy?" he shrilled. "Have you completely lost your mind?"

Carmela whirled to face him. "What are you talking about?" Was he upset that she'd visited Tallant?

"Gateway Community Hospital," said Babcock, his face beginning to take on the red tinge of freshly boiled crawfish. "Last night. You and Ava went to see that crazy Cajun!"

"You were tailing us?" asked Carmela. Now her surprise quickly turned to anger. What was Edgar Babcock doing, putting a tail on her? What was his problem? Hot spots exploded behind her eyes. "I can't believe you were watching us!"

"I had people there, yes," snapped Babcock.

"Because you think Ava and I had something to do with Archie's *murder?* Are you *kidding* me?" Carmela was livid with anger now.

Babcock looked suddenly confused. "No," he said. "That's not it at all."

"Then what are you talking about?" demanded Carmela.

"We were staking out that Cajun guy — trying to bust him!"

"Miguez?" said Carmela.

"That's one of his aliases, yes," said Babcock. "And for your information, we've been after him for quite some time!"

Carmela forced herself to calm down, tried to quell her rapidly beating heart. "He told us he was getting out of the business."

"Hah!" exclaimed Babcock. "I seriously doubt that. There's been a whole ring of smugglers operating in New Orleans and across the river in Algiers and Gretna. Absinthe, Ecstasy, roofies, ice — they're dealing it all."

"Are you telling me European absinthe is the new club drug?" asked Carmela. She didn't quite believe that.

Babcock stared at her. "It hasn't exactly replaced X, but it's becoming pretty darn popular."

Should she tell him? Sure, why not.

"I, uh, heard there was some Russian guy who was pretty much trying to control the illegal absinthe franchise," said Carmela. "That he's importing and distributing it."

"Is that what Miguez told you?"

"Well, yeah," said Carmela.

"That guy is scum," snorted Babcock. "He'll tell you anything." Edgar Babcock leaned down, and Carmela could smell Dentyne and Hermes aftershave. "Did you give him money?"

"No," lied Carmela. How could she tell Babcock they'd given Miguez a hundred and forty bucks? For what might turn out now to be bogus information!

Babcock continued to keep pace beside her as she headed back toward her shop. "So he actually said there was a Russian involved?" He sounded dubious.

"Yes, that's what he said. Made it all sound highly mysterious. Like the guy was connected to the Russian Mafia or something."

"We're working with ATF on this," said Babcock. "Alcohol, Tobacco, and Firearms. I'll check with them, see if they've heard any rumors about other people involved, particularly your mysterious Russian."

"ATF," said Carmela. "That's federal, right?"

Babcock frowned. "Hell yes, it's federal."

Carmela paled slightly, picturing the tall, elegant bottle of green liqueur sitting on her kitchen counter even as she ambled through the French Quarter with an officer of the law.

"The wormwood absinthe," said Carmela. "You think it's that bad?"

"Doesn't matter what I think," said Babcock. "Point is, the stuff's illegal."

CHAPTER 14

Back at Memory Mine, nervous over the notion of the ATF raiding her apartment at any moment, Carmela was pleasantly surprised to find two of her regulars waiting for her: Tandy and Baby. Surely they'd help take her mind off all the recent craziness.

"Here she is," proclaimed Tandy as Carmela made her way toward them. "And thank goodness."

"What's up?" asked Carmela, trying to appear cool and collected.

"We could use a little help, please," said Tandy. "Seems we're fresh out of ideas for new scrapbook pages."

"I can hardly believe that," said Carmela. Usually, Tandy was a fiend for coming up with new page themes.

"It's true," said Baby. "We're completely flummoxed." She shook her head, and the charms that hung on her Louis Vuitton gold hoop earrings made a tinkling sound, like

179

tiny wind chimes.

"What are you trying to scrap?" asked Carmela, easing herself down at the table.

"I *still* haven't done anything with my Christmas photos," said Tandy, sounding a little embarrassed. "And Baby's got a new grandchild, of course. Dawn had a baby girl last month."

"I know," said Carmela, trying to think. She put her hands flat on the table, buying a little more time, then said, "Okay, I think I've got a couple of ideas."

"About time." Tandy laughed.

Carmela bustled about her shop, pulling out sheets of paper and foil, bits of lace and ribbon, embellishments, and vellum envelopes. Then she sat down with Tandy and Baby, and they all three put their heads together.

An hour and a half later, both women had the makings of a top-notch scrapbook page.

Baby's page for her granddaughter had adopted the theme, Pocketful of Miracles. This line, in bouncing contemporary type, was on a background of pink-and-white checked paper along with two adorable photos, lace bows, and an actual vellum pocket. Inside the pocket were little heart-shaped pieces of paper on which Baby and other family members would write heartfelt wishes for this new child.

Tandy's Christmas page had an O Christmas Tree headline slaloming across red and green paper torn into tree shapes. Three photos were cut into circles like ornaments and ringed with gold vellum. Green foil formed holly leaves and red foil the accompanying berries. A star garland twisted its way across the bottom.

"Fantastic," declared Tandy, while Baby just beamed.

"I love 'em," said Gabby, leaning over their shoulders to admire the two new pages. "Carmela, I don't know how you come up with such wonderful ideas."

Carmela smiled knowingly. She didn't know how she came up with a steady stream of ideas, either. Somehow, they just bubbled up inside her head, like some sort of wellspring. She supposed that's what was known as inspiration.

Luckily, things were relatively quiet for a while, so Carmela grabbed a carton of strawberry yogurt from their small refrigerator and retreated to her office. She wanted to sort through the last dozen or so pages of the file she'd picked up at the Vieux Carré Historical Society. The ones she hadn't gotten to yet. And then, of course, she'd make copies of anything that seemed pertinent.

Scanning an old article written by a fellow named Hubble Whitley, Carmela noted that Lafitte's group had often been referred to as the Baratarians.

"Barataria Bayou," she murmured to herself. She knew a little bit about that area. Shamus's family had a camp house there that they used occasionally for hunting and fishing. It was a small wood frame house with a big front porch that sat on stilts over dark water. The downstairs was pretty much one big kitchen and living room; upstairs was a sleeping loft. During storms, the patter of rain on the corrugated tin roof was like a bayou lullaby.

Okay, she thought. *It seems like Lafitte left his imprint in lots of places.*

Carmela thumbed through a few more pages. One was a sketchy, hastily drawn map that showed Money Hill and its surrounding lakes and bayous. Another map focused on Port Arthur, Texas.

Probably, she decided, a lot of would-be treasure hunters had concentrated their efforts in those particular areas of southwest Louisiana and neighboring Texas.

The final paper in the file was a clipping from the *New Orleans Times-Picayune.* It was a short blurb about a group of local speculators who'd launched a search for Jean Lafitte's treasure in southwestern Louisiana some five years ago.

So, people are still looking.

Carmela was about to put the page aside when a name jumped out at her: Robert Tallant.

What? She studied the article more closely. It didn't give many more details, but it certainly flew in the face of what Tallant had just told her this morning about letting dreamers and fools hunt for treasure.

"What a dirt ball," Carmela muttered to herself, even as she wondered if Tallant could be a viable suspect in Archie's death.

A gentle rap sounded at her door. "Phone call," said Gabby. "It's Jekyl."

"Hey," said Carmela, picking up the phone. "Guess who I met with this morning?"

"That police detective? Babcock?"

"Actually," said Carmela, "I did run into him. But first I had a very interesting meeting with Robert Tallant, the owner of Royal Coin and Curios."

"Tell me what was so interesting," said Jekyl.

"For one thing," said Carmela, "Tallant is a serious collector. His shop is filled with extremely rare coins."

"The kind Archie collected," said Jekyl.

"Exactly," said Carmela. "Tallant also acted somewhat blasé about Archie's death. He assumed a kind of too-bad attitude about the whole thing. Didn't even mention the fact that there was a murder investigation going on. But then, toward the end of our meeting, he asked if I knew how he might go about purchasing Archie's collection."

"The guy is all heart," said Jekyl.

"But the story gets even stranger," said Carmela. "Tallant professed to only be a dealer in rare coins. When I asked him if he'd ever done any actual treasure hunting himself, he was extremely scornful. Yet I found an article . . . hold on a minute." Carmela scrabbled to retrieve the news clipping. "You remember that file I mentioned last night? The one I borrowed from the Vieux Carré Historical Society?"

"Yes?" said Jekyl.

"It was in there. From a five-year-old article that ran in the *Times-Picayune*. Robert Tallant was mentioned as one of the members of a modern-day expedition that went searching for Lafitte's lost treasure."

"So your logic is . . . what?" asked Jekyl. "If Tallant lied about one thing, he'd lie about other things, too?"

"Something like that," said Carmela.

"Then we should maybe tell the police about him," said Jekyl. "Alert your Detective Babcock."

"I think you're right," said Carmela, thinking how Jekyl had certainly done an about-face in being candid with the police. And just maybe, by telling Babcock about Tallant's treasure-hunting foray, she might get herself back in Babcock's good graces again, might be able to glean a little more information from him.

"You can handle that?" asked Jekyl. "You seem to have a real connection with Babcock."

Not really, thought Carmela. She was still smarting from his rant about meeting Miguez last night.

"Since we're on the somewhat touchy subject of suspects," said Jekyl, "I made a few calls concerning the Vampyre Danse tonight. So you could maybe check out that Russian guy."

"Any luck on scoring an invitation?" asked Carmela. She'd sent Jekyl an e-mail earlier, explaining how she and Ava had met with Miguez, but downplaying the danger of their meeting. He'd fired an e-mail back. Along with the final details for Archie's funeral, he'd scolded her for keeping last night's meeting secret. He'd also assured her he'd try to wangle an invitation.

"I had more than luck," Jekyl told her. "The Fates, fickle as the little darlings generally are, smiled down upon us."

"That's a yes?" asked Carmela.

"Thanks to some rather cunning sources," continued Jekyl, "I managed to score three tickets. Now we can all go and enjoy a somewhat ribald party while we hopefully snoop on your mysterious Russian. If he even bothers to show up."

"Ava, too?" asked Carmela.

"Of course, Ava, too," said Jekyl. "Oh, and the Vampyre Danse is being held at a private underground club this year. A place called Club Taboo."

"Where's that?" asked Carmela.

"In the CBD," said Jekyl, referring to the Central Business District, that part of New Orleans that encompassed retail stores, luxury hotels, and, on the edge, large old warehouses. "You'll like Club Taboo. It's in the basement of an old tobacco warehouse. A big dungeony place that holds *beaucoup* revelers. So get your vampire costume ready!"

Costume, thought Carmela. *Gulp.* She wasn't nearly ready to attend a glammed-up party tonight, even if it was a Vampyre Danse.

"Listen," said Jekyl, "I'm frightfully busy, so I don't really have time to drop by with your invitations. But if you could just sort of scoot down the alley to my apartment, I'll leave them stuck halfway under the door."

"Then you'll meet us there tonight?" asked Carmela. "At Club Taboo?"

But Jekyl had already hung up.

Carmela immediately called Ava. "We're in luck; we're going to the Vampyre Danse!"

"Fantastic!" was Ava's comeback. "I can't *believe* it!" But then she got deadly serious. "*Cher,* this is a major cultural event in our lives, and we've barely got time to prepare!"

"I know that," said Carmela, glancing at her watch. "So I'm probably just gonna throw something together from my closet."

"No," came Ava's emphatic cry. "No, no, no, no, no! This is a really big deal, honey. We've got to seriously dress the part and look like vampire club kids. I mean, people come from *all over* to attend the Vampyre Danse. It's comparable to partying at Sky-bar in L.A. or Tao in Las Vegas!"

Was she serious? "I had no idea you felt so strongly about this," said Carmela.

"I'm stoked!" said Ava. "Besides winning

the Miss Teen Sparkle Queen crown a few years back, this is one of the happiest moments of my life! Hey, what say you meet me at Rag and Bone around four o'clock? That's probably our best shot for scoring some over-the-top costumes."

"Maybe," said Carmela. "What's Rag and Bone? Used clothing?"

"It's that Goth boutique over on Esplanade Avenue."

"What!"

"Please don't completely freak out," begged Ava. "Besides Goth paraphernalia, Rag and Bone also has tons of funky stuff: wearable art, designer resale stuff, a shitload of jewelry and scarves." Ava forced herself to calm down and breathe. "The thing is, can you be there?"

"Okay," said Carmela, deciding it wouldn't hurt to look a little vampy, a little vampirey. "My schedule's tight, but sure. Why not?"

"Crazy," squealed Ava. "See ya there!"

CHAPTER 15

Back at craft central, the situation was, thankfully, calm. Tandy and Baby were still busily scrapping. Gabby was waiting on customers, then popping back to check on things when she was free.

"Hey you!" exclaimed Tandy, as Carmela emerged from her office. "We were just talking about Baby's party. You're still coming, right?"

"I wouldn't miss it for the world," said Carmela.

"Atta girl," said Baby, pleased.

Every year, on the Sunday evening right before Fat Tuesday, Baby threw a huge party at her rather splendiferous Garden District home. The music, the food, even the guests, were over-the-top. Carmela never missed one of Baby's parties!

"I love the fact that it's a costume party this year," said Tandy. "Darwin and I have ours all figured out."

Costume, thought Carmela. *That's right. I've got to come up with another costume!*

"And don't you love the theme?" asked Gabby.

"Riverboat Ramble," said Tandy, grinning at Baby. "Very fitting. Very catchy."

"Hopefully," said Baby, "everyone will adopt a sort of Mississippi riverboat theme into their costumes."

"And you're still going to have a sketch artist?" asked Tandy.

"And a jazz band?" asked Gabby.

Baby nodded happily. "And Del is going to have a couple of poker tables set up. All guests will start with a hundred dollars in play chips. Redeemable, of course, for some very interesting prizes at the end of the night."

Carmela listened as she pulled sheets of paper from her floor-to-ceiling racks, picked out a brass stencil of an arched cathedral window, then selected a couple of rubber stamps. "Are you using the same caterers as last year?" she asked Baby.

Baby straightened in her chair, looking serious. "No. I'm trying a brand-new place over on Prytania called Alex and Athena Catering. Ever hear of them?"

Carmela shook her head as she pulled out a sheet of light-green mulberry paper with banana fibers woven through it. "Don't think so," she told Baby.

"I think I have," said Gabby. "Maybe they catered a fund-raiser for the orchestra last fall?"

"They did," said Baby. "In fact, that's how I found out about them. Alex and Athena are actually this wonderful young couple who recently graduated from the Culinary Institute in Napa Valley."

"I bet you worked out a really good menu, huh?" asked Tandy. Skinny and hyperthyroid, Tandy could pack away a monumental amount of food.

"Oh, my gosh," said Baby. "Let's see if I can remember. We're serving shrimp-stuffed merliton baked in tomato sauce, an oyster and shrimp bouillabaisse, blackened catfish, and fresh salmon fillets topped with beurre blanc sauce."

"Good Lord!" exclaimed Gabby. "What a banquet!"

"Tell us about dessert," demanded Tandy, also the resident sugar freak.

"Well," said Baby, "king cake, of course." They all nodded.

"And peach cobbler and mud pie and probably coffee ice cream," said Baby. "Oh, and my aunt Laila gave me her recipe for lace cookies. So I'm going to do a little bak-

191

ing of my own."

"Everything sounds so good," said Carmela, pulling out a chair and sitting down at the table.

Baby suddenly leaned forward, took in the brass stencil, the rubber stamps, and the mulberry paper that Carmela had arranged in front of her. "Oh, honey," she said, suddenly looking sober. "You're working on a memorial program!"

Carmela nodded. "That's right. Archie Baudier's funeral is tomorrow morning."

"Dear me," said Tandy, one hand flying to her skinny chest. "And here we are, going on about Baby's party like a bunch of silly, irreverent ducks."

Baby looked utterly crestfallen. "Talking about riverboats and music and food."

Carmela smoothed out her paper. "No reason you shouldn't," she told them.

Once Carmela and Ava hit Rag and Bone, it took Ava about thirty seconds to pick out her costume and try it on. A strapless black stretch PVC dress with a racy, lace-up back.

"I love it," Ava declared, making a pirouette in front of a wavering full-length mirror. "It's so *me*."

"It's your basic little black dress, all right," said Carmela. "Except it looks like you were

melted down and literally poured into it."
She chuckled. "Liquid Ava."

"I love the way that sounds," purred Ava.
"And, *cher . . .*" Ava pawed through a
nearby rack. "I think *you* should get this
adorable one-shoulder fishnet top."

Carmela gazed in horror at a tiny bit of
black netting that hung limply from a padded hanger. "There's nothing there! It
would be like wearing the emperor's new
clothes!"

"Maybe add a black push-up bra underneath?" suggested Ava. "Just to keep things
legal."

"How about a black bra underneath a
black *dress?*" asked Carmela. "I have an
old black evening gown. Maybe I could fray
the hem a little, give it a vampire spin."

"Way too many layers," scoffed Ava. She
searched the rack again and pulled out a
black satin bustier with three red buckles
slashed across the low-cut front. "Better you
should get this bustier and borrow my black
leather skirt."

Carmela eyed the bustier with nervous ap-
prehension. "You think?"

Ava nodded knowingly.

But Carmela wasn't sure. The bustier was
small, tight, and somewhat lacking in mod-
esty. "Could I throw a black cape over it?"

she asked. Lord knows, she needed *some* sort of cover-up.

"I'll allow a cape," said Ava. "But *only* if it's extremely thin and fluttery."

They searched for accessories then. Carmela opting for a black batwing purse and Ava exclaiming over a coffin-shaped vinyl purse. Then, warming up to the whole Goth thing, Carmela fell in love with a jeweled batwing pendant, while Ava chose a Medusa necklace with a red jewel in the forehead just below a crown of writhing snakes.

"Oh," said Ava. "And I'm gonna need these metallic red false eyelashes. They'll be the perfect finishing touch."

"Very foxy," said Carmela, trying to keep a straight face. "A really excellent look for you."

"And maybe these clip-in hair extensions?" said Ava, holding up two strands of silvery-white hair attached to tiny clips.

"For that vintage Lily Munster look," agreed Carmela.

"Cher," drawled Ava, reaching for a package that held a pair of small glass vials. "This is what *you* need for a change of pace. Green cat-eye contact lenses."

"You don't think colored contacts are a little over-the-top? Maybe a little too Marilyn Manson?"

Ava shook her head. "I say you go for it." She reached for a black feather boa. "And maybe a touch of feathers?"

"I have to be nuts," laughed Carmela. "Taking advice from a woman who thinks black vinyl is the perfect little party dress!"

Her outfit tucked carefully under her arm, Carmela headed down Esplanade. The evening was fast approaching, and she still had lots to do.

For one thing, Carmela wanted to return the file to Margot Destrehan at the Vieux Carré Historical Society. Margot had been kind enough to lend it to her, and she'd made copies of quite a few articles she'd deemed important, particularly that clipping concerning Robert Tallant.

Pushing open the front door to the little historical society, Carmela found herself staring into an empty room.

"Hello?" called Carmela. "Anybody here?"

Probably, she figured, most of the folks had already gone home for the evening. For the weekend, really. On the other hand, the door had been left unlocked . . .

"Margot?" called Carmela. "It's Carmela."

This time she got an answer.

"Back here," came a woman's voice.

Carmela found Margot sitting at one of

the library tables, a half-dozen old books spread out in front of her. Sitting alongside were latex gloves, a glue bottle, snips of leather, heavy-duty scissors, and assorted jars.

"You're still hard at work," said Carmela.

Margot pushed a few strands of hair from her face and smiled at Carmela. "It never seems to end." She picked up a piece of leather and wrapped it around the spine of one of the books, measuring it.

"That looks awfully crafty," Carmela commented. "Like you're designing an album or making an altered book."

"I wish," said Margot. "Fact is, I'd like nothing better than to while away an afternoon at your scrapbook shop, absorbed in some wonderful craft or arranging my photos in some marvelous design. Unfortunately, my creativity seems only to extend to bookbinding."

Carmela gazed at the leather books that were shelved floor-to-ceiling. Most looked old bordering on antique. Many seemed frayed and moth-eaten. Probably, these old books were forever needing to be patched or rebound. She knew how fragile book bindings could be and how easily the combination of paper and glue could give out.

"We try to keep up," explained Margot,

"but the bindings on these poor old tomes just keep cracking."

Carmela studied the book Margot was working on. The binding was terribly frayed, but Margot was doggedly replacing the leather and touching up the corners.

"It looks like you're doing a lovely job, though."

"Probably be better if we hired professional bookbinders to work on these," said Margot. "But that's not in our budget."

"Maybe I could speak to Glory," said Carmela, then regretted her words instantly. Glory hated her. She would probably cut off funding altogether if Carmela even *mentioned* that she was somehow connected with the Vieux Carré Historical Society.

"You're very kind," said Margot. "But there's no need. We'll just keep muddling along. We always do."

"I brought your file back," said Carmela. She pulled it from her shoulder bag and set it on the table.

"Oh, aren't you a dear. It's so nice when folks do what they say they're going to do." She peered at Carmela. "Was it at all helpful?"

Carmela shrugged. "Interesting, anyway."

Margot nodded. "That's what I thought. Good reading, but not much substance."

"Are you coming to the memorial service tomorrow?" asked Carmela.

Margot sighed gently, and her shoulders seemed to droop. "Yes. But it's going to be a difficult one. Archie was so young."

"All funerals are difficult," said Carmela.

From the historical society it was only a hop, skip, and a jump to Jekyl Hardy's apartment.

Climbing the sagging wooden staircase, Carmela was acutely aware of how dark it was. Spooky almost. Of course, Napoleon Gardens was an old building, constructed long before electric lights were even a consideration.

Rounding the final turn, walking the final creaking half flight up to Jekyl's third-floor apartment, Carmela didn't find the lighting situation any better. It was as if someone had replaced all the hundred-watt bulbs with twenty-watt bulbs. Or turned off half the lights in the hallway.

Which suddenly reminded her of an old joke. How many Louisiana politicians does it take to change a lightbulb? Four. One to change it and the other three to deny it. Ha!

Her chuckle was short-lived as she crept down the hallway. The dark aubergine walls seemed to close in on her, and she was acutely aware of how quiet and deserted the place was.

At this time of day? Shouldn't everyone be coming home about now? Turning on the TV to watch the evening news?

She listened, heard nothing.

Weird.

Continuing down the hallway, Carmela finally arrived at Jekyl's door.

Yes, there it is.

Stuck halfway under the door was a bright red envelope.

Carmela leaned down to grab it. And just as she did, heard a door snick open somewhere down the hall.

She straightened up, looked around fast, saw nothing. Only the dark walls cloaked in shadows.

Gingerly now, she reached down and grabbed the envelope, stuffing it in her bag. The feeling of someone watching her was overwhelming.

Could it have been the door to Miss Norma's apartment that had snicked open?

Did it mean that Miss Norma was watching her? If so, the woman was either nervous, nosy, or . . . watching for something?

CHAPTER 16

The evening was moonlit and magical. A gilded moon bobbed atop billowing clouds like a galleon riding the sea. Cool breezes, sweeping north from the Gulf, whooshed into the Big Easy and fluttered the hems of legions of costumed vampires as they glided silently through the night, drawn like a magnet to this one place.

A half block from Club Taboo, Ava was all atwitter. "You think Ann Rice will be there?"

"I think she's since moved on," replied Carmela, tugging at her bustier. Her costume was short, tight, and way too revealing for her sensibilities.

"Still," chirped Ava, as they joined the ranks of black-caped vampires congregating at the front door, "you never know."

"Invitation please." A red-robed doorman, head shaved, multiple pieces of hardware piercing his ears and eyebrows, scanned their invitations, then nodded. "Downstairs," he told them. "Watch your step."

Then they were descending a circular stone staircase.

"This is so cool," said Ava as they caught the first pulse of techno music.

"Great," said Carmela, who'd managed to catch her heel a half-dozen times. "If only I . . ." As they rounded the final turn, she stopped in midsentence.

Now a thunderous wave of techno music rolled across them as they entered Club Taboo. The place was dark and huge. Stone walls with a rough-hewn wood beamed ceiling. Giant pillar candles flickered everywhere, reminding Carmela of film footage she'd seen of Roman catacombs. An enormous stained glass window hung above a long, wooden bar, its backlit shards of red, purple, and yellow glass forming an elegant crest pattern. Because this was the Vampyre Danse, coffins were arranged everywhere, some with red vigil lights inside, others occupied by fashion models in skintight vampire costumes. A fog machine cranked out a diaphanous layer of swirling mist.

And everywhere, writhing to the music, bellying up to the bar, hanging out at small, intimate cocktail tables, were revelers in vampire costumes.

"Whoa!" said Ava, looking around excitedly. "This is my kind of customer. If I could get these people into my shop, I bet I could really crank up sales."

"Maybe you should put one of those ads on the bathroom stall doors," suggested Carmela.

"Get 'em coming and going," cackled Ava. "Not a bad idea."

"Look over there," said Carmela, gesturing to a wooden booth, the kind you might see at a county fair. Only this booth was wound with black crepe paper bunting entwined with thorns. "A biting booth."

"Now that's a little weird," said Ava.

Carmela gazed around, utterly amazed at the spectacle of so many wannabe vampires in one place. Even though New Orleans was known for its vampire groupies and vampire underground, this was still an amazing sight. "Some of these costumes are absolutely incredible," she remarked to Ava.

"Custom-made," agreed Ava.

Indeed, there were women in tight, slinky Morticia Adams–type dresses, men in tuxedos with velvet capes, even a few younger vampires with skimpy leotard costumes and lots of body paint.

And almost everyone had fangs. Short fangs, plastic fangs, ivory-looking fangs, snaggled animalistic fangs.

"I can't believe it," said Ava, shaking her head in dismay. "We forgot to buy fangs. We *knew* it was the Vampyre Danse, and we still forgot the darn fangs."

"Hard to drink with those things in your mouth," Carmela pointed out.

Ava grinned as she raised one eyebrow and let it quiver for an instant. "Depends on what you're drinking."

Carmela grabbed Ava by the elbow. "Speaking of which, let's head over to the bar. We'll get ourselves a nice cocktail and wander around some. Scope out this place. Try to find Jekyl."

What else could two bewitching vampire ladies order except Bloody Marys?

"Mmm," said Ava, taking a sip. "Now this is what I call a drink." The lip of her oversized goblet was rimmed with lethal black pepper, and her drink was garnished with a curled pink shrimp. Carmela's Bloody Mary was equally peppered and sported a giant spear of dill pickle.

They wandered out of the bar area, circled around the dance floor, eased themselves into a second room that was slightly quieter. Dark booths rimmed the walls, and in the center was a scattering of low tables and club chairs. The place would have been cozy except for the fact it was lit with an eerie blue light.

"This isn't a bit flattering to my complexion," remarked Ava.

"Nobody looks good," giggled Carmela. "In fact, they all look like Smurfs!"

"If hell had a bad lounge act," said Ava, "this would be the place."

"Not the green room, but the blue room," said Carmela.

"And the devil would —" began Ava.

"Speaking of —" said Carmela, interrupting. She'd just noticed a familiar-looking red-sequined devil suit bobbing and weaving its way through the crowd. "Jekyl!" she called. "Over here!"

"Halloooo!" exclaimed Jekyl, suddenly popping up in front of them. "Having a fun time, kiddies? Making lots of new friends?"

"Trying to," said Ava, throwing a dazzling smile at a goateed man in a crimson-lined black cape.

"Did you locate your mysterious Russian yet?" he asked.

"Not yet," said Ava, nibbling at her shrimp. "But we're just getting started."

Jekyl inclined his head toward Carmela. "I see you got the invitations okay."

"Is your building always that dark?" asked Carmela. "I felt like I was creepy-crawling a haunted house."

"That's called character," said Jekyl. "And I think there have been some recent problems with the wiring." He stared at her quizzically. "Why? Something happen?"

"I had the strangest feeling I was being watched," said Carmela.

"Maybe you were," said Jekyl. "I do have neighbors, after all. And after what happened . . ."

"But it didn't exactly feel like your friendly neighborhood watch group," said Carmela. "Let me ask you something. Is your friend, Miss Norma, always home?"

"I don't know," said Jekyl. "I guess so. She's the landlady. Isn't that what landladies do? Stay home and keep an eye on things?"

"But she doesn't own the building," said Carmela.

"No, no," said Jekyl. "It's been in the Caruthers family for years. Two elderly brothers who are both pushing ninety. Who knows what's going to happen to the place once they're gone. Some idiot developer will probably turn it into overpriced condos. Yech."

"So Miss Norma works for the Caruthers family?"

"The Caruthers brothers," giggled Ava.

Jekyl nodded. "She collects rent and sort of rides herd on the commercial cleaning people and the gardeners who maintain the flowers and pond in the courtyard. Why are you asking?"

"No reason," said Carmela, wondering if Miss Norma knew about the secret passageway. "Just curious."

"Sure," said Jekyl. "Okay." He raised a hand and gave an enthusiastic wave to a woman in a low-cut purple velvet dress. "Hey there, Miranda! You wanton woman!"

"And Miss Norma . . . she's not well off?" asked Carmela.

"Lord no," said Jekyl, beginning to edge away. "In fact, she always seems to be on the fine edge of disaster."

Ava clung possessively to the arm of her goateed man as she made introductions. "This is Eduardo, *cher.*"

Carmela smiled politely. "Hello, Eduardo, I'm Carmela."

Inclining her head slightly, Ava said, "He says there's a VIP room. The Red Room."

Carmela was suddenly interested. "Can he get us in?"

Ava snuggled closer to Eduardo. "Can you get us in?"

"No problem," he told her, looking happier by the minute at being in the company of such an attractive woman. "I'm a card-carrying member. Lifetime."

"Lifetime," said Ava. "That could be a long time for a vampire." She giggled. The enormous Bloody Mary was starting to get to her.

"It's just a hobby," Eduardo told them. "Like building models or collecting stamps."

"Not quite," murmured Carmela.

Thanks to Eduardo's membership card, the black leather padded door with the brass studs eased open for them, admitting them into the Red Room.

Set into an alcove at the far end of the room was a giant stone Buddha. Red vigil lights flickered at its bare feet. Deep, red leather circular booths lined one wall, and a long, ornate bar ran along the other wall. The music pulsed, low and seductive. Definitely a more refined vibe and ambience than the front part of Club Taboo.

"Cool," said Ava. "Now, this is more my style."

As Ava and Eduardo drifted off, Carmela's eye roved about the room. She studied the people drinking and whispering together in the booths, decided they all looked like your garden-variety New Orleans types. That left the bar, where a dozen people perched on cushy barstools. Seven men, five women.

Carmela studied the men. Only one really

stood out to her. A bearded, bearish looking man in a vampire costume that seemed to fit a little too snugly.

He seemed more animated, more effusive, more . . . Russian?

Now the big question was, should she just walk up to him and start talking?

Well, why not? she decided as she tossed her cape back over her shoulders.

Carmela moved slowly down the row of barstools, aware that she looked good in her costume. Cute, youngish, hopefully sexy.

Okay, she told herself, trying to ratchet up her courage, *if you've got it flaunt it.* It wasn't her typical mantra, but this wasn't your typical club.

Trying to recall a few words of Russian she'd heard over the years, Carmela eased up to the man at the end of the bar.

"Privet!" Hello!

He spun toward her, a smile lighting his broad, lined face. "You speak Russian?"

She shook her head. *"Net."* No.

He looked askance at her. "Sounds like you do."

"Sorry, but I just ran out of words," Carmela told him.

"You have a name?" he asked her, curious. He was no older than mid-forties but looked like he'd logged some serious miles.

"Carmela."

He touched a large hand to his chest. "Vasiliy. Sit down, have a drink. Vodka," he grunted to the bartender. "Two."

"I think I might know a friend of yours," said Carmela, easing onto the stool next to him.

Vasiliy squinted at her. "Yeah?"

"Miguez."

Vasiliy shook a cigarette from a battered pack and stuck it in his mouth. "No friend of mine." He flicked a gold lighter, inhaled deeply.

"Me neither," said Carmela. "But I think the two of you have something in common." The bartender set drinks in front of them. Hers remained untouched.

"What you want?" asked Vasiliy. Suddenly he wasn't quite so open and friendly.

"Here's the thing of it," said Carmela, deciding to lay her cards directly on the table. "I'm doing a little investigating . . . into the recent murder of a friend."

He stared at her, his mass of bushy eyebrows bunching together. "You want to know if I killed your friend — the pretty boy who liked to drink absinthe and collect the coins."

His statement, laid out so straightforward, rocked Carmela to the core. "You knew

Archie?" she blurted out. This was what she'd come for, of course, but she hadn't expected the mysterious Russian to suddenly turn candid!

Vasiliy nodded. "A little."

"He was a customer?"

"Once or twice."

"And how did you know about his coins?" asked Carmela.

Vasiliy shrugged. "He told me. Asked if I could get my hands on antique Russian coins."

"You're kidding," said Carmela. "What kind?"

Vasiliy chuckled. "Your friend was looking for hammered silver coins from the reign of Ivan the Terrible. He also asked about pure gold Alexander II coins from 1905 that were minted in Bulgaria." Vasiliy paused and sipped at his drink now. "See? Very specific. But I told him coin dealing was not my thing." He lowered his voice, looked around the room. "I only deal in guns."

"And illegal absinthe," said Carmela.

"Guns are my real business," growled Vasiliy. "Absinthe is just a small sideline. My entrée to meeting lots of interesting people." He eased forward in his chair, seemingly interested in her again. "And, of course, beautiful women."

"What are you really doing here?" asked Carmela.

"Prastite?" Pardon?

"I mean in New Orleans."

"I like this place," he told her, winking. "Your local government is all screwed up. Just like Russia. *Worse* than Russia."

"And you're trying to set up a nice little home base," said Carmela.

"Much better conditions than when I was in Red Army," he replied easily. "Thanks to well-stocked Soviet arsenals, now I can afford luxurious living."

"You *are* dealing in arms," said Carmela.

"Just small stuff," said Vasiliy, fluttering a hand. "Kalishnikovs and RPG's." He shrugged. "Everybody want rocked-propelled grenades today. Very popular." He pronounced it *pup*ular.

"I understand you spent time in Sierra Leone," pressed Carmela. "You must have gotten your hands a little . . . dirty." She'd almost said *bloody* but held back at the last moment. "You must be one tough guy."

"Me?" laughed Vasiliy as he inhaled a huge draft of vodka. "I'm really just a pussycat."

But, somehow, Carmela didn't think so.

"You found him," said Ava. She was sitting on the edge of one of the booths, scrunched in next to Eduardo and five other people. Carmela had come over to join them. "Anything?"

"Not much," said Carmela, leaning down so she could whisper in Ava's ear. "This guy, Vasiliy, admits to knowing Archie, and says Archie asked him to locate some Russian coins."

"Do you believe him?" asked Ava.

Carmela thought for a minute. "Not sure."

"How much did he say about the absinthe?"

"Vasiliy claims absinthe is just a small sideline."

"And the guns?" asked Ava.

Carmela rolled her eyes. "I think that's not such a small sideline."

"Bad news," murmured Ava.

"Oh jeez," said Carmela. She watched as a sturdy-looking man in a dark suit approached Vasiliy and whispered in his ear. Vasiliy listened intently, nodded, then made a small hand gesture in the direction of her and Ava. "Maybe time to mosey on out of here."

"Let me just say good-bye to Eduardo," said Ava, picking up on Carmela's nervousness. "Give him my phone number."

"Did he follow us, *cher?*" Ava asked as she

212

hurried alongside Carmela.

Carmela managed a quick glance back at the black padded door they'd just exited through. "Not yet."

"Think he will?" asked Ava.

"Maybe the Russian was just trying to scare us?" proposed Carmela.

"He succeeded," said Ava. "Maybe we should get our asses out of here."

They elbowed their way through the writhing crowd in the Blue Room. The Vampyre Danse was well under way, and the caped and fanged guests seemed to be having the time of their lives. A champagne fountain had been wheeled into the room, and people were filling their glass flutes to the brim.

Carmela and Ava skirted the dance floor again, heading for the front bar.

As Carmela darted around a woman in a black fishnet dress, the kind of crazy dress Ava had wanted her to don, she ran smack-dab into a tall vampire with a white-powdered face. He had a woman on his arm, also white-powdered with black feathers for hair. "Oh, excuse me . . . I . . . ." She stared at the vampire.

Robert Tallant?

"Tallant," she said, her voice this side of a growl.

Tallant stared at her with kohl-rimmed eyes and an imperious air.

"The coin dealer?" asked Ava, peeping over Carmela's shoulder.

"Darn straight," said Carmela, staring at Tallant now, a confrontational look on her face.

"*Excuse* us," said Tallant's date in an arrogant, nattering tone of voice.

"And you told me treasure hunting was better left to dreamers and fools," said Carmela forcefully. "That you were only a businessman who purchased interesting collections."

"What?" he said, staring at her.

"So I guess your purely business attitude isn't quite so pure."

"What are you *blathering* about?" snapped Tallant.

"I ran across an article in the *Times-Picayune* that mentioned your treasure-hunting foray of a few years ago," Carmela told him.

Tallant glared at her. "I do as I please."

"Robert," snapped the woman at his side, "who *is* this person?"

"Nobody," barked Tallant.

"Now wait a minute, pal," began Ava. "That's no way to —"

The woman put a hand on Ava's arm.

"Will you please *move!*"

"Just what exactly is your problem?" asked Ava. She pushed closer to the woman, towering over her by a head. Angry but slightly cowed, the woman shrank back.

"Never mind, Rain," Tallant told the woman. "Just ignore them." He grasped Rain's shoulder firmly and turned her back in the direction they'd come.

"I was thinking of buying that coin necklace in your window," Ava called after him. "Fat chance now!" She turned to Carmela. "Who was that ghastly woman with him? Did you know her?"

"I have a feeling it was Rain Munroe," said Carmela.

"What's a Rain Munroe?" asked Ava. "Besides somebody who puts a damper on things?"

"She's a socialite of sorts," said Carmela. "Shamus has mentioned her a number of times, and I've seen her name in the paper. She sits on the board of directors of the museum and maybe the orchestra."

"So she's a vampire-socialite," laughed Ava. "Or is that term redundant?"

"C'mon," said Carmela. "Forget about them."

They threaded their way back up the circular staircase and popped outside into

215

cool darkness.

"Nice not to have that music blastin' in my ears," remarked Ava, shaking her head.

"I'm not sure that's really our scene," said Carmela.

"I know," said Ava. "I love the spooky stuff, but some of that shit was *way* off the hook."

Thirty feet from her car, Carmela had the feeling (again!) that somebody was shadowing her. Feet scuffed against gravel, a shadow flitted behind a black Jaguar that was parked nearby. She dug into her batwing purse, grabbed her car keys, and pressed the Open button. The headlights of her little Mercedes flashed on, illuminating the way, and they scrambled in. Another push of a button assured doors were locked hastily.

As Carmela revved her engine, she wondered if Vasiliy or his flunky had followed them. Or had it been Tallant or perhaps Miguez? Or maybe even her ex-husband, Shamus? Or was it someone else?

Tromping down on the gas pedal, leaving a scatter of gravel behind, Carmela wondered just how many enemies she'd managed to make in three short days!

CHAPTER 17

The gaping mouth of a skull melted into carved stone. Beneath it was the epitaph, "This life of mortal breath leads only to a portal we call Death."

St. Louis Cemetery No. 1, the oldest cemetery in New Orleans, was appropriately gray and grim on this rainy, cool Saturday in February. Appropriate weather, it would seem, for Archie Baudier's memorial service.

Bare trees were etched black against an overcast sky, ancient tombstones, like so many broken teeth, canted and tottered in different directions. Large tombs and sarcophagi were chipped from countless decades of neglect. Like all the cities of the dead in New Orleans, the residents here were buried in aboveground tombs. This being a practice that began when early settlers buried their dearly departed, only to find their caskets slowly floating to the surface due to the fact that the city was located well below sea level.

Looking demure in a fitted black suit, black leather boots, and a black velvet headband, Ava wound her way through the crowd, passing out the programs Carmela had designed.

Carmela had stayed by Jekyl's side, consulting the notes on his clipboard, helping him with all the last-minute details. When everything seemed ready, when all the participants were finally in place, when Archie's coffin was resting solidly on a wooden bier, Carmela glanced at the cadre of mourners that had gathered near the wall and exhaled slowly. Then she dropped her eyes and opened her own program.

She'd designed it in haste, but the cathedral window image she'd selected for the front page was pretty near perfect. Inside, text in Bodoni bold listed the minister, various songs, and key persons who'd be delivering short eulogies. Visuals that punctuated these program listings included rubber stamp images of a single calla lily as well as one that depicted a Greek coin. Carmela hoped they served as a suitable, personalized tribute and that the green mulberry paper lent a touch of grace.

Pressing her back against a granite tombstone as the minister said his prayers, Carmela gazed at the crowd of mourners. She recognized several friends of Jekyl's, guests from his ill-fated Mardi Gras party. She studied each face carefully, wondering if she could discern any feelings of guilt or remorse behind their neutral expressions. No, not really. Mostly, these folks just looked restless. It was the thick of Mardi Gras, after all. There'd be craziness all over the city and nonstop parties raging for the next four days. This was one of those obligatory funerals that punctuated the revelry. They'd get going again soon enough.

But there were other mourners who looked downright despondent. Carmela recognized Miss Norma, the landlady, huddled near a set of antique wrought-iron gates that, maybe a hundred years ago, had been fashioned to represent the pearly gates. Margot Destrehan, Archie's museum friend, was standing a few feet from Jekyl, weeping silently.

Carmela's eyes sought out the back row of the crowd. There was the coin dealer, Robert Tallant, wearing dark glasses and looking slightly hungover. What a jerk he was. And his date hadn't exactly been a paradigm of grace, either.

A thought struck Carmela. Could the

Russian be here?

She glanced around quickly, a prickle of tension running through her. But she didn't see Vasiliy anywhere. Good. Don't need *him* complicating things. Earlier today, Carmela had filled Jekyl in on her encounter with the Russian. He'd listened studiously, taking it all in, then remarked that he didn't think the Russian was a serious suspect. Carmela decided to apply a bit of Napoleonic law when it came to Vasiliy: guilty until proven innocent.

The funeral continued with dignity. Poems were recited, hymns sung, eulogies given, tears shed. Carmela noticed that Lieutenant Edgar Babcock, standing in the back row, kept a watchful eye out as each segment unfolded. He was probably studying the mourners just as she was. Probably having just as much luck. Still, she decided, Babcock looked darned fine in his navy blazer and pleated dove-gray slacks. How did he manage such a classy wardrobe on a cop's salary?

Now, amid a great sniffling and dabbing of eyes, a small jazz group, which Jekyl had hired for a musical finale, did a quiet tune-up among themselves.

With a one-two-three count, they launched into a rousing instrumental version of what had been one of Archie's favorite songs, "The Battle of New Orleans."

In 1814 we took a little trip,
Along with Colonel Jackson down the
    mighty Mississip.
We took a little bacon and we took a little
    beans,
And we caught the bloody British in the
    town of New Orleans.

Carmela followed along with the lyrics in her head. It was a song made popular by Johnny Horton back in 1959, but it never failed to stir her and most other New Orleans folk, who burned with patriotic fervor for their city.

As the last notes of music hung on the wind, a group of six men shuffled forward and hefted Archie Baudier's coffin off the wooden bier. Marching in lockstep, they proceeded some thirty paces to one of the yellow brick wall crypts. Carefully, reverently, they slid his simple wooden casket into the gaping hole. With much effort, Jekyl and another mourner lifted a crumbling stone tablet, dropped it into place, then slammed the wrought-iron door shut. When Jekyl turned the key in the lock, there wasn't a dry eye in the house.

That was it, thought Carmela. Funeral over. Archie Baudier committed to the ages. Still, there was a murderer to catch, and she for one intended to keep fighting the good fight.

Margot Destrehan was one of the first people to approach Jekyl and compliment him on the service.

"Thank you," said Jekyl, looking bereft.

Carmela stepped in. "Excuse me, do you two know each other?"

Jekyl gave a small shake of his head.

"Margot is the curator at the Vieux Carré Historical Society," Carmela told him. "Where Archie did so much of his research."

"Oh, of *course*," said Jekyl. Now he was able to place Margot.

"Actually, I feel like I sort of know you," Margot told Jekyl. "Archie was always telling me about how you design those amazing floats. He said you were the best there was."

"I don't know about that," said Jekyl, clearly pleased.

Margot put on a more serious face. "Do you know, are the police any closer to . . . you know . . . catching someone?" It clearly pained her to talk about poor Archie.

"I can't say they are," said Jekyl, sounding bitter. "But I can tell you that Carmela has been looking into things, pursuing a few leads."

"The least I can do," murmured Carmela, embarrassed by Jekyl's confidence in her.

"And she's good," said Jekyl emphatically. "Clever. She's already uncovered a couple possible suspects."

"Good for you," said Margot, patting Carmela's arm. "Because from what I hear, all the police have accomplished so far is to be rather rude and ask nonsensical questions. I think they're more nervous about keeping order during Mardi Gras, what with all the tourists and the zooming crime rate."

"I think you might be right," said Jekyl.

As the mourners continued to clear out, Carmela remained with Jekyl, standing near the wall crypt. "You have two keys for two crypts?" she asked.

"Yes," said Jekyl. "Apparently, both were inherited from Archie's family."

"Have you learned anything more about his family?"

"Not really," said Jekyl. "I just know about the brother in prison. Even then, Archie was pretty closemouthed about him."

"Why did you put him in that particular wall crypt?" asked Carmela. "Versus the other one."

Jekyl gave her a sideways glance. "It was detailed in the instructions he left. In his will."

"Do you know who's in the other one?" Carmela asked in a low voice. She scratched at the stone with her index finger. It felt crumbly and dry. Old. As though you could almost pick it away.

"No idea," said Jekyl. "Maybe the bleached skeleton of a long-deceased relative? Or maybe it's empty, awaiting Archie's brother."

"Do you have the other key?" asked Carmela.

"Yes," said Jekyl, a little hesitant now. He held up the key ring, and Carmela could see there were two keys jangling together.

"Let's open the other vault," she said in a low voice.

"What?" exclaimed Jekyl, taking a step back. "Are you serious?"

Carmela nodded.

"But . . . why?" asked Jekyl, studying her.

"Indulge me?" she said.

"I need a better reason than that," said Jekyl.

"I figured you'd say that," said Carmela. "Okay." She thought for a moment. "Archie was brutally murdered, and the police still don't have a clue. *We* don't have a clue. The possibility exists that Archie *may* have had some sort of secret knowledge about treasure, and, obviously, a lot of people would like to figure out what, if any, information he had. We also know that Archie had developed a taste for absinthe, which means he was tangled up with unsavory people."

Jekyl hesitated, thinking about all the points Carmela had brought up. Finally, he gave a sharp nod. "We can take a quick peek, yes. But don't blame me if a moth-eaten skeleton comes rolling out!"

They did the smart thing: waited until everyone else had left. Then Carmela, Ava, and Jekyl crowded around the wall crypt.

"I can't believe you're really going to open it," said Ava, letting loose a little shiver. "There could be a real dead body in there."

"Probably is," said Jekyl. He gazed at Carmela, his expression serious. "You still want to go through with this?"

"Yes," she told him. "Absolutely."

"Spooky," said Ava. "Bring it on."

Jekyl jangled the keys in front of them, then inserted one into the lock. They held their collective breaths as he grasped it with both hands.

"Won't turn," he said. "Stuck."

"Wiggle it," suggested Ava.

"I'm trying," said Jekyl. "I'm wiggling like crazy, but nothing's happening."

"Can you pull the key back out?" asked Carmela.

Jekyl fought with it for a couple seconds, then gave a hard yank. "Yes." The key slid back out.

"Needs graphite," said Carmela, digging inside her purse.

"Whadya mean?" asked Ava.

Carmela pulled out a fat yellow pencil. One she used for sketching scrapbook layout ideas. "Lead," she told them. She stuck the tip of the pencil into the lock and jiggled it around inside, trying to transfer as much lead as possible to the inside of the lock. "Think of it as poor man's WD-40."

"Think it'll work?" asked Ava.

"Hope so," said Carmela. She gave the high sign to Jekyl. "Okay, now try it."

Jekyl stuck the key back in, hesitated, then turned it to the right. There was a slight hesitation, an audible click, and then the wrought-iron gate swung clear.

"Gracious," said Ava, putting a hand to her mouth. "It worked."

"The question now," said Carmela, "is what's in there?"

Jekyl hefted out a slab of stone, and they all peered in anxiously.

"Hm," said Ava, staring at dust. "No body."

"Nobody home," said Carmela.

"But look," said Jekyl. "There *is* something there."

Carmela reached in and withdrew a crumpled piece of paper.

"What is it?" asked Ava.

"Probably an advertisement," said Jekyl. "For stone carving or some nineteenth-century gravedigger's union."

Carmela gently smoothed the paper. "It's a map."

"Get out!" barked Ava.

Turned out the map depicted an earlier eighteenth-century Louisiana. *La Nouvelle Orleans* was clearly marked, along with rivers, bridges, and old city and fort names. All in French.

"What do you make of it?" Jekyl asked Carmela. "As our resident scrapbook maven, you're the one who's most familiar with old documents and such."

"It looks like a standard-issue map," she said. "But old."

"Where do you think he got it?" asked Ava.

"Search me," said Carmela.

Jekyl squinted at the map. "Archie was

always doing research, always visiting out-of-the-way historical societies and small-town museums, so there's no telling."

"The thing is," said Ava, "does the map tell *us* anything?"

Carmela studied the map. "Maybe. For one thing, small red flames have been painted near an area that's slightly upriver from New Orleans."

"What's that mean?" asked Ava. "Something burned down there?"

Carmela pursed her mouth. "I don't know." Tapping a finger where the flames were painted, she thought hard. She recognized the major rivers and topography just fine. Now she was trying to recall her history as well.

"What are you thinking, *cher?*" asked Ava. "Looks like something's percolating in your clever little brain."

"Could it be . . . ?" began Carmela trying to pull up the name. "Could it be Groomsbridge Plantation?" Groomsbridge Plantation was one of the places Jean Lafitte was reputed to have lived, along with its owner, an attractive widow. "Lafitte supposedly lived there," she said, "right after the Battle of New Orleans. When he was supposedly paid off and pardoned."

"I think you might be right!" said Ava

excitedly.

Jekyl was more than taken aback. "You think this is some sort of treasure map?" He gaped at the old piece of paper.

"It sure looks like it," enthused Ava.

Carmela was more realistic. "But if there was a treasure at Groomsbridge Plantation, wouldn't Archie have already located it? I mean . . . he obviously had this map." She thought some more. "Wouldn't *someone* have found it? People have been lusting after this treasure for a long, long time."

"Good point," said Ava.

"So why the map?" asked Jekyl. "Why here? Locked in this crypt?"

Carmela wasn't entirely sure. "There's always the possibility it could be fake. It does look a little like something you might buy in a souvenir store."

"Doesn't look fake," said Ava. "Then again, I'm no expert."

"On the other hand," said Carmela, "Archie could have thought it valuable and stashed it here for safekeeping."

Jekyl raised his eyebrows into twin arcs. "Or maybe Archie stuck it in the vault to keep someone from getting their hands on it? Or to throw someone off?"

"There's always that," said Carmela. "Still . . ."

"It's worth pursuing," said Ava.

They all stood around, staring at the map, until Jekyl's phone shrilled.

"Hello?" he said.

He listened for a few minutes, gave a couple of exaggerated eye rolls, and hung up.

"Problems?" asked Carmela.

"Brett Fowler," he told them. "From the Pluvius krewe. Giving me another screaming earful."

"What's wrong now?" asked Ava. She was well aware of his shaky relationship with that krewe.

"They want me at their den now," he said. "This instant. Ah dear." He shoved up his sleeve and looked at his watch. "Gotta run," he said, looking nervous and ragged. "Time is ticking away, and the floats are far from done." He shook his head, an expression of sublime sadness on his face. "Plus, we still haven't uncovered anything concrete that would lead to a real suspect in Archie's murder."

"Everything's circumstantial," said Ava.

"But we'll keep trying," promised Carmela.

"This map looks pretty authentic, huh, *cher?*" asked Ava. Carmela and Ava had gone back to Memory Mine to study the map. Gabby was up in front, waiting on a pair of customers, so Carmela and Ava spread the map out on the table in back.

"It does look old," allowed Carmela.

"Is it printed?" asked Ava. "Or some kind of etching?"

"Probably more like a copper engraving," said Carmela. Except for the hand-colored red flames, the map was black-and-white. Across the top ran the words, *"Carte le Louisiane by M. Bellin."* Small type at the bottom said, *"Issued Paris 1808."* To Carmela's trained eye, it looked like an authentic map that had been added to. The question was, who'd inked in those flames? Pirates, pranksters, or Archie?

"This could really be something," enthused Ava.

"What we're going to do first," said Carmela as she held her 8×-power magnifying loop to one eye, "is study the paper."

"What will that tell us?"

"Almost all paper from a century and a half ago was made by hand," explained Carmela, leaning over the map. "It was produced by pouring pulp into a wooden frame that had a bottom of crosshatched wire mesh. That mesh would ultimately leave its pattern on the paper."

"So does this paper have that kind of cross-hatching?" asked Ava.

Carmela studied the map for a few seconds more, then straightened up. "Yes, it does."

"So maybe this map really is authentic?" ventured Ava.

"Maybe," said Carmela. "Or the paper could just be . . . old."

"This flame thing," said Ava, tapping an index finger gently against the map. "You think it indicates something important."

"If the flames possibly represent Groomsbridge Plantation, that place is now a tourist attraction."

"Last I heard," said Ava, "that old plantation was offering guided tours. And I do believe they have a restaurant and six upstairs suites they rent out to visitors." She hesitated. "Maybe it wouldn't be a bad idea to drive up there and take a look around." Ava's questioning eyes met Carmela's.

"Maybe we should stay there tonight," said Carmela.

CHAPTER 18

Carmela made a fast phone call to Shamus, basically telling him this was his lucky day and that he was being awarded visitation privileges with the dogs. Actually, better than visitation privileges. Boo and Poobah were going to join him for an unprecedented overnight.

Shamus was so enthusiastic on the phone, Carmela figured he had to have been drinking. A fact that was confirmed when she and Ava stopped by Shamus's Garden District home to drop off Boo and Poobah. In fact, judging from the cars parked outside and the loud music spilling from his house, formerly *their* house, a fairly good-sized party seemed to be in progress.

Shamus came charging out to meet them on the front verandah, a loopy grin on his handsome face. "Come on in!" he enthused, grabbing for the dogs' leashes. "Have a little drink!"

"I see you're not exactly holding back," Carmela observed.

"It's Mardi Gras, babe," said Shamus. "Got to party hearty."

Party hearty, thought Carmela. Shamus still talked and acted like he was back in college. Come to think of it, his friends all acted that way, too. Chugging beer, whooping it up, always talking about the wild and crazy times they were going to have. It was all very time-warpy stuff, as though none of them really wanted to grow up and assume responsibilities, wanted to remain Peter Pan forever. Except Peter never lived off his family's money. Or cheated on his wife.

Inside, Shamus's house was jammed with friends as well as a gaggle of Meechum relatives. Carmela noted that the friends and the relatives weren't mixing particularly well. In fact, there seemed to be a sort of standoff, the friends having staked out the dining room and kitchen where the drinks were flowing freely, while the Meechums were seated sedately in the parlor, sending withering glances and telegraphing their trademark disapproval.

Shamus roved between each group, a goodwill ambassador in no-man's-land.

As the dogs tore off to meet and greet people, which in Boo's case meant sliming them, Carmela carried their food into the kitchen and plopped it on the counter.

"This is Boo's dry food," she told Shamus. "With half a Rimadyl tablet mixed in. Poobah, on the other hand, gets . . ."

"Have a drink, babe," said Shamus. He put one hand on the wall behind Carmela, forcing her to back up. Then he put the other arm up, successfully trapping her. "Stay and party with your old hubby, will you?" He sounded wistful and more than a little plaintive.

"You've got plenty of people here to party with," she told him.

"Not like you," he said, leaning close, trying to nuzzle the side of her face.

"Shamus," said Carmela, using her dog-training voice. "That's *enough*. Now back *off*." He backed off.

Sit, she wanted to tell him, while swatting him with a rolled-up newspaper. *Lie down. Bad dog.*

Instead she said, "We should probably be going."

"Well, look who's here," came a sarcastic female drawl. "Look who's *deigned* to join us."

"Hello, Glory," said Carmela, glancing past Shamus. Glory, of course, was Shamus's older sister: the one who sat on

235

several boards of directors, the one who controlled the family purse strings, the one who was nuttier than a fruitcake.

"Shamus tells me you're embroiled in yet another mesh . . . uh, mess," said Glory, her voice slurry and thunderous. As she shuffled further into the kitchen, most of Shamus's friends cast worried glances and carefully eased themselves away. Glory was two hundred pounds of trouble in a splotchy print housedress and gray helmeted hair. Sharp-tongued and mean to the core, she was also cursed with a touch of OCD, obsessive-compulsive disorder. Carmela would sooner tangle with a mountain lion.

"Nice to see you, Glory," said Carmela, determined not to lose her cool or flinch in the onslaught of Glory's vitriolic words.

Glory held up an empty glass and waggled it back and forth. "Shamus? Would you be so kind?"

"Of course." Shamus plucked the glass from Glory's plump hand and scampered to the makeshift bar. He filled Glory's glass halfway with bourbon, added a splash of charged water.

"Oh, that's helpful," said Carmela. "Do you think maybe the two of you could benefit from a few AA meetings?"

Glory's doughy face puckered into a

sneer. "It's Mardi Gras, in case you haven't noticed, Carmela. Always got to be a stick-in-the-mud. Never want to let your hair down."

Carmela abandoned all hope of counting to ten and was about to fire back, when Ava came breezing into the kitchen. "Whoa!" she exclaimed at the vision of Glory looming in front of her. She lifted an arm, as if to ward off a vampire. "Alert the villagers! Grab the torches and pitchforks!"

Glory spun fast, almost losing her balance. "Ava Gruiex," she spat out venomously. "Carmela *would* bring you along. Her trashy friend."

"That's me," grinned Ava. "Your typical deep-fried, grit-lovin' trailer trash gal. Got a four-ten shotgun stashed in my pickup and a little brother named Bubba. Come to think of it, I got a couple cousins named Bubba, too."

"You want a drink, Ava?" giggled Shamus. For some reason he seemed to think Ava's comeback was a real thigh-slapper.

"Sure," replied Ava. "Whatcha got?"

Shamus was beyond mellow. "Bar's stocked to the gills, honey. You name it, I'll pour it."

"Glass of champagne then," said Ava.

Shamus pulled open the refrigerator door

237

and dug around inside, past the pickles and the mayonnaise. Finally, he extracted a bottle of Perrier-Jouët.

"Look at that," exclaimed Ava. "You fancy folks keep your refrigerator *inside* the house. That's mighty handy."

"Skang," muttered Glory in a snorelike rumble. Carmela figured she was trying for either scag or skank.

Shamus undid the wire cage on the champagne bottle and haphazardly thumbed the cork. It popped like a firecracker and ratcheted off the ceiling, leaving a slight dent in the plaster. "Dang!" was all he said.

"Ava," said Carmela, knowing if they hung around too much longer, there'd really be trouble. "We should take off pretty soon."

"Just half a glass, okay?" said Ava as Shamus handed her a champagne flute, then filled it with bubbly. "After all, it's champagne. French champagne." She lifted her glass. "*Expensive* French champagne."

"Sure," said Carmela, reaching into the refrigerator for a Diet Coke. Why not stick around for the theatrics? In fact, stay long enough, and this place would end up being the *Masterpiece Theatre* of family melodrama.

Glory turned a cockeyed glance on Carmela. "I was at the historical society yesterday, and Margot Destrehan mentioned you'd stopped by." Glory took a long pull of her refreshed bourbon and smacked her lips. "Such a delightful woman. So studious and hardworking. I do believe I'll be funding her organization again this year."

"You're always so generous," said Shamus, beaming. "That's why everyone loves you."

Carmela almost choked on her Diet Coke. She felt the bubbles effervesce at the back of her throat and rise up to tickle the inside of her nose.

Ava did her own double take, then glared murderously at Glory. "Don't you think you should figure out a reasonable divorce settlement for Carmela *before* you start giving your money away? After all, Carmela's put up with your cretinous brother for quite a few years."

"Cretinous?" said Shamus, looking like a puppy dog who'd just been smacked with a rolled-up newspaper. "And I just gave you champagne!"

"Awright, awright," said Ava. "So maybe you're just ill-mannered."

"Don't you dare insult my brother!" roared Glory.

"Please," said Shamus, with a defeated sigh. "Can't we all just get along?"

This time Carmela, Ava, and Glory all

screamed in concert: *"No!"*

Five minutes later, Carmela and Ava were on the road, humming along.

"Well, that went well," said Carmela as fat raindrops suddenly splotched down on her windshield, smearing the glass. *Pat-pat-pat bloop.* She quickly turned on the wipers, adjusted the defroster.

Ava groaned. "I'm sorry, *cher.* But I just can't stand the thought of the Meechums cutting you out like that. Glory's as mean as a spitting cobra, and Shamus is just plain dense."

"There does seem to be a serious disconnect with that boy," agreed Carmela. "But I have faith. I know I'll get a settlement sooner or later."

"More later than sooner," said Ava.

"But thank you for rushing to my defense," said Carmela.

"I got your back, honey," said Ava. "You can take that to the bank, if nothing else."

Ava slid a CD into the car's music system, a Maroon 5 album, and they hummed and sang along all the way up Highway 44, also known as River Road. At the Highway 942 intersection, they zoomed past Houmas House, an old plantation that had served as the setting for the Southern Gothic thriller,

Hush, Hush, Sweet Charlotte.

"Cool place," said Carmela.

"Cool movie," replied Ava. "Always loved old Bette Davis with those crazy, googly eyes."

When they hit Tezcuco, they crossed over the Sunshine Bridge, so named because former Louisiana governor Jimmy Davis wrote the song, "You Are My Sunshine."

Now they were deep into plantation territory, where cotton, sugarcane, and rice had been big business back in the day. Fortunes made from these crops had spawned immense, elaborate plantation houses designed in grandiose styles that were often referred to as Louisiana classic and steamboat Gothic.

Carmela and Ava arrived at Groomsbridge Plantation without a reservation, received a somewhat chilly reception, and were shown to a small, somewhat chilly room.

"This is it?" exclaimed a disappointed Ava. "This is where we're supposed to *sleep?* I though we'd have four-poster feather beds with velvet coverlets and a big fancy room with flocked wallpaper. This place is minuscule and stuck in the rafters!" One side of the room did slope sharply, making it a pinched space for the two single beds. Although the room was decorated in cheery wallpaper and floral bedspreads, it was snug at best.

"Probably was a maid's room at one time," said Carmela.

"Well, they obviously didn't think much of the hired help," snorted Ava. "Is that supposed to be our *sink?*" She pointed a disdainful index finger at a large ceramic bowl that sat squarely on an antique wicker table. "And speaking of sinks, where's our bathroom?"

Carmela pulled open the only other door in the room and peered in. Five wire hangers hung from a metal rod. "Nope. Looks like the bath is down the hall."

"Yuck," said Ava, plopping down on one of the beds. "You don't know this about me, *cher,* but I have a phobia about sharing bathrooms. I mean, what if I'm puttin' on my eyeliner and some other guest comes knockin' on the door wanting to use the facilities? Worse yet, what if strange people have been spittin' in the sink before me?"

"Do you want to go down to the front desk and try to change rooms?" asked Carmela. "Maybe get one with a bathroom and a fireplace?"

Ava looked pained. "Let's just go down and get something to eat. Let me

242

fortify my body."

Dinner was a huge improvement. Succulent baked ham with sweet potatoes, grits, gravy, and chili cornbread, made all the cozier because it was served family style. Carmela had a generous helping; Ava had two.

"Feeling better?" asked Carmela as Ava scraped up the last bits of her pecan pie.

Ava nodded. "Lots." She pushed her chair back from the table and gave a quizzical look. "Now that I know I won't pass out from hunger, what exactly is on the evening agenda? A glass of sherry in the library? A rousing game of whist?"

"Now we do what we came here for," said Carmela. "Explore."

Even though it was dark outside, Groomsbridge Plantation was dramatically lit with floodlights. They showed off the dozen Gothic pillars that graced the front of the antebellum mansion and the two enormous wings that jutted out from the center of the house, each with its own large redbrick chimney. A *porte cochere,* or arched carriageway, sheltered visitors who were debarking from their car or carriage and led to the back of the property.

"Can you imagine living here? When this place was in its heyday?" asked Ava.

"It must have been amazing," replied Carmela. Great fortunes had certainly been realized here, the plantations and their owners enjoying enormous fortune right around the mid–eighteen hundreds.

They walked along the cobblestone drive, through the carriageway, and toward a dilapidated barn.

Ava nodded at the barn. "Place looks like it's falling down. Think it's even worth investigating?"

"We're here," said Carmela. "May as well check it out."

"Got to keep an eye out for those secret passageways," laughed Ava.

The gentle cluck of chickens and the dusty, vegetative scent of hay greeted them.

"No horses, cows, or pigs," said Ava. "Just chickens." She peered into a wire cage. "Pretty black chickens. Pretty black chickens with pom-poms on their heads."

"Black Silkies, I think," said Carmela.

"If we want omelets for breakfast tomorrow," said Carmela, "we're pretty much guaranteed the eggs are fresh."

"Unless they're just for show," laughed Ava. "Shill chickens out here and powdered eggs in the kitchen."

They continued to wander the grounds. Creeping into a few other buildings, they found only dust and cobwebs. They meandered through an old family cemetery surrounded by a black wrought-iron fence. In the center was an enormous live oak with gnarled aboveground roots that caused the tombstones to list dangerously.

"Amazing," said Carmela. "Some of these stone tablets date back to the late seventeen hundreds."

"Maybe the treasure's stashed in a coffin," suggested Ava. "Buried six feet under."

"Maybe our imagination is getting away from us," said Carmela.

The graveyard led to a well-landscaped rock garden that they decided would probably be spectacular in a few months when spring blooms began to appear.

The rain that had let up for the past couple hours began to fall again, and a cold breeze whispered through bare trees, then swooped down and battered at them.

"Rats," said Ava, clutching her jacket lapels. "And I'm wearing suede."

"Turn it inside out," advised Carmela.

"You're so smart, *cher*," said Ava, pulling her jacket off and quickly reversing it. "Oh, look over there! A wishing well." An old stone well with a pointed wooden cupola suddenly loomed in front of them.

"Maybe we should toss in a couple of

coins," said Carmela, digging in her pocket, "and make a wish." She thought for a minute. "Since coins were what started this whole wild-goose chase in the first place."

"So what are you gonna wish for?" asked Ava.

Carmela hefted a few coins in her right hand, then plunked them down the dark well. "I wish we knew what we were doing here," she said with a wry grin.

They stood there for a moment, listening, and finally heard a hollow clink.

"Deep," said Ava. She put one knee up on the side of the well, hoisted herself up, and peered over.

"Careful," warned Carmela. "Don't fall down that thing!" She plucked at Ava's jacket, trying to pull her back. For some reason she had a bad feeling about this.

Ava straightened up. "This well looks really old. Maybe Jean Lafitte tossed his treasure down here."

"Maybe," said Carmela. "But it doesn't jibe with the little red flames painted on the map." She thought for a minute. "If the treasure was down the well, wouldn't there have been some sort of water visual? Droplets of water maybe? Colored in blue?"

Ava stared at her. "Maybe we should look at that map again."

CHAPTER 19

Back in their room, the temperature seemed to have plummeted another ten degrees.

"It's *freezing* in here," complained Ava. "It's like a doggone meat locker."

"Or a wine cellar," said Carmela. She ran her fingers through her hair, trying to fix what she figured was a skinned rat look from wandering around outside in the rain. Then she stared at Ava, a crooked grin spreading across her face.

"What, *cher?* You look like you just got one of your crazy-but-brilliant ideas."

"That's it," said Carmela. "The cellar. We should go downstairs and check the cellar."

"You mean *this* cellar?"

Carmela nodded. "Sure. Maybe there's some kind of fireplace that, you know, corresponds to the flames on the map."

"We'll have to sneak down there."

"Nothing we haven't done before," said Carmela. "I figure we've earned PhD's in sneakology by now."

"It was awfully quiet downstairs when we came through," said Ava. "Just a couple of people having coffee in the library. And the desk clerk was nowhere in sight. I'm warming up to the idea, even if I am cold as an icicle."

Glancing about the room, Carmela saw a pink candle in a white ceramic holder. She snatched it up. Just in case.

"Okay then," said Ava.

They crept down the main stairway in their stocking feet. A few boards creaked here and there, but nobody popped up to ask what they were doing. So far, so good.

The lobby was dim; lights had been turned out. Only a small lamp glowed behind the front desk.

"We should still check this main floor first," whispered Carmela.

Ava nodded, gesturing toward the library. They tiptoed that way, hesitated at the doorway, then slid open a gigantic pocket door, relieved that it only gave off minimal creaks.

"Lots of books," marveled Carmela, admiring the shelves of books, swags of velvet draperies, and the large stone fireplace with its faintly dying red embers. She could see herself curled up here in one of the cushy, rump-sprung leather chairs, snuggled under an afghan, enjoying a cup of Darjeeling and an afternoon of quiet reading. "Shamus's uncle Henry would have loved this place," she told Ava. "He was quite a book lover and collector."

"He was the only Meechum relative you ever really got along with, huh?" asked Ava.

"Afraid so. And now, of course, he's gone," said Carmela, a wave of sadness sweeping over her. All the men in her life she'd truly loved — her dad, Uncle Henry, Shamus — were gone now. True, Shamus still trod among the living, but he was as good as gone from her life.

Ava ran her fingers lightly across an ornate wooden panel just to the left of the gigantic stone fireplace. "Maybe there's a secret panel here."

Carmela joined her. She pressed and thumped on the right-hand panel, testing each nook and cranny, looking for a hidden lever or button. But nothing sprang open to reveal a mysterious passageway. *Okay,* she decided. *Time to move on.*

They wandered through the rest of the main floor, peeking in rooms, spotting some marvelous antiques, giggling over some of the old portraits that hung in the hallway rogue's gallery, but found nothing.

At the rear of the mansion, just outside the dimly lit and now-deserted kitchen, Carmela eased open a heavy wooden door. When a musty smell assaulted her nostrils, she whispered, "Basement," to Ava.

"Got matches?" Ava whispered back.

Carmela shook her head, then slipped quietly into the kitchen. The place was still warm and filled with wonderful aromas. A pilot light on the stove glowed dimly. On the counter next to the industrial stove Carmela found a glass jelly jar filled with safety matches. She used one to light her pink candle and stuffed a few more in her pocket.

"Think it's safe to go down?" asked Ava.

But Carmela was already tiptoeing down the steps.

Judging from the junk piled in the basement, Groomsbridge Plantation had enjoyed a long string of owners. And each owner had seemingly amassed an enormous amount of junk, which they'd neglected to throw out. Over the decades, it had collected down here, a slag heap of debris that chronicled almost two centuries.

Holding the candle high, casting flickering shadows on the stone walls, Carmela and Ava gaped at the jumble spread out before them.

Spinning wheels covered with cobwebs so thick a pair of clever hands could probably spin them into ghastly skeins of yarn. Baby cradles of rotting wood and wicker. Moldering old English riding saddles. At least a half dozen dome-topped trunks filled with Lord knows what. Bolts of fabric covered in dark mildew were heaped on the floor. A sideboard stacked with chipped and cracked dishes stood listing against one wall.

Carmela decided that if you wanted to put together a gonzo garage or tag sale, this place would probably yield a veritable treasure trove. That is, if it didn't all turn to dust when you picked it up.

"Miss Haversham, where are you when we need you?" said Carmela in a low voice, making reference to the eerie character in *Great Expectations*.

"Exactly," replied Ava.

"Isn't it creepy?" remarked Carmela. "Ghostly remains of long-dead people." She reached down, grabbed a gnarled walking cane, and thrust it in front of her, swatting away a sheet of cobwebs.

"There better not be spiders," muttered Ava. "I have a phobia about spiders."

Carmela knew there had to be legions of spiders. Something had spun those enormous cobwebs. Was still spinning them.

Ava brushed at her hair nervously. "Maybe this wasn't such a good idea."

Breathing in dank air, wondering what lay ahead, Carmela peered through the gloom. At the far end of the basement, a dark form wavered before her eyes. What was it? She squinted harder, thinking it might be a doorway of some sort. Then her eyes focused, and it all came together for her. "There's a fireplace up ahead," she murmured.

"This is really old, huh, *cher?*" said Ava, reaching out gingerly to touch one of the rounded stones. "From like a hundred years ago?"

"More like a hundred and fifty," replied Carmela.

The stone fireplace took up almost an entire wall; giant pitted river rocks were stacked and chinked together, stained black from decades of soot and smoke. The fireplace opening was so enormous, a person could practically walk inside. Ancient wrought-iron utensils, smothered in soot and dust, hung from metal hooks. To the left of the fireplace was a built-in wooden cupboard.

"What did they cook in there?" asked Ava. "A whole cow?"

"Maybe," said Carmela. "Maybe in the

upstairs-downstairs scheme of things, this is where the downstairs folks cooked their food. Or baked their cornbread and pies." She thought for a moment. "This could have been the plantation bakery."

"The question is," said Ava, "is this the fireplace that corresponds to the flames on the map?"

They stood in silence for a few minutes.

"The map *seemed* to indicate Grooms-bridge Plantation," said Carmela. "If you hold with the legend that Jean Lafitte spent time here with the lady of the house, then . . . maybe. Maybe the flames are supposed to represent this fireplace."

"But it's just an enormous fireplace," said Ava. "Nothing special."

"You think," began Carmela, setting her candle on one of the cupboard's shelves, "we should try your press and tap system?"

"Didn't help upstairs," grumped Ava.

"Let's just give it the old one-two."

"Two minutes," said Ava. "After that I lose my good humor."

But two minutes of pressing and tapping, of looking for trapdoors and swinging doors, of searching cracks and crevices, turned up nothing.

"Crap," said Ava. "I ruined a perfectly good manicure for nothing. The only thing here is a wall of rocks and a basement full of junk. I think we should chalk this up to a wild-goose chase. Archie's map is a big, fat dud."

"No kidding," said Carmela. "Plus we shelled out way too much money for that crummy room." She grabbed for her candle, her hand brushing the edge of the shelf. There was a creak, then a small puff of air seemed to caress her face. "Huh?" said Carmela. Then her mouth dropped open, and she stared in disbelief as a panel behind the dusty cupboard swung inward. "Oh, Ava, darling," she called in a loud stage whisper. "I think there's something here after all."

"What?" said Ava, glancing over. She saw the gaping hole in the wall, gaped herself. "Shit! Carmela, baby, what'd you do?"

"Touched a spring or something," said Carmela.

"Clever girl," said Ava. "Now what do you suppose is back there?" She was so excited she was jittering in place.

Behind the fireplace was a low-ceilinged room. Maybe ten feet by twelve feet. Brick walls, wood beams, pounded earth floor, a fire pit in the center with a ring of rocks around it. Not unlike a campfire.

"What the heck is this place?" wondered Ava.

Carmela guessed a root cellar.

"Smells right," said Ava. "Musty. But what about that fire pit? What was that used for?"

"Roasting potatoes?" said Carmela. "Or corn? Provisions for the winter? Doesn't stuff last a lot longer when you cook it?"

"I dunno," said Ava. "After I cook something, I eat it." She nudged the ring of rock with her toe. "This sucker looks old."

"That's what I'm thinking," said Carmela. "Even though this house has been added on to over the years, this basement room had to be part of the original layout."

"This could be significant," said Ava. "Especially if this fire pit was meant to correspond to the flame visual on the map."

"So we search around," said Carmela. "See what we can see."

"Hoist up that candle, *cher,* and let's get to work."

They knelt on the floor, poking around in the old fire pit for a good ten minutes. Then they moved on to the brick walls, eager fingers searching for a single brick that might yield in their hands. That took another twenty minutes.

"Your candle's burning down," said Ava, pursing her lips and blowing strands of hair out of her face. "And we still haven't found anything."

Carmela held the sputtering candle at shoulder level, then slowly lifted her eyes. More spiderwebs. She lifted the candle a little higher, then blinked. Blinked again. On an ancient wooden beam, about ten inches above her head, was a strange carving. "Found something," she told Ava.

They both peered up at the old beam.

"Somebody carved an image," said Ava finally.

In the dim light, Carmela struggled to make out the letters or design or whatever it was. "Looks like a crown and what? The letter B?"

"What does that mean?" asked Ava. "King B? Do you understand that? Or is it some sort of code?"

Carmela reached up and touched the deeply grooved image with her fingertips. "Or Queen B," she said. "It could be Queen Bee."

"Okay then," said Ava. "Does Queen Bee mean anything to you?"

Carmela shook her head. "Nope."

"This is not finding treasure," said Ava, sounding more than a little frustrated. "This is discovering another clue."

"And I have a strange feeling," said Carmela, "that this might lead to another clue."

"And then the treasure?" asked Ava. "Wouldn't that be something?"

"I don't know," said Carmela. "Maybe."

"Pirate's treasure," said Ava, suddenly regaining her good humor and laughing softly. "Yarr, matey, we better grab ourselves a parrot and a bottle of rum!"

But Carmela followed up Ava's bit of whimsy with a sobering thought. "You realize," she said, "we might be following the same path Archie followed."

Ava let loose a sneeze, then scratched at her nose. "I wonder how far he got?"

Carmela grimaced. "He got himself murdered."

They tromped back upstairs, then locked the door to their room and sat on the bed, talking quietly about their strange discovery.

Ava snapped open her compact, gazed at herself in the mirror. "I look like I've got eye shadow *under* my eyes."

"Soot from that fireplace," said Carmela.

"When *Vogue* declared the sooty eye is back in style, I don't think they had this in mind," said Ava, dabbing away.

"You look gorgeous," said Carmela. "I'm the one who looks like a drowned rat."

"No, *cher,* you look like you've been

bound, gagged, and dragged by your heels through a pile of coal, too."

"Great," said Carmela. "And the shower's down the hall."

"What we really need," said Ava, wrapping a calico quilt around her shoulders, "is something to take the chill off. A nice hot toddy or even a cup of cocoa."

"We could go down to the kitchen and . . ."

Ava suddenly put an index finger to her lips. She mouthed the word "Footsteps," to Carmela, who nodded back. She'd heard something outside their door, too.

"Somebody's creeping around out there," said Carmela in a low voice, her hand poised on the brass doorknob.

But when they pulled the door open fast and gazed out into the hallway, it was deserted. Only shadows cast by brass wall sconces puddled on the carpet.

"I think we oughta get out of here," suggested Ava. "Even though it's almost the middle of the night. I'm cold, cranky, and feeling a might shaky."

"You think somebody might have been dogging our footsteps the whole time?" asked Carmela.

Ava nodded. "I don't have a strong feeling about it, but . . . yeah. It's possible."

"Then we're outa here," said Carmela, grabbing her sweater and stuffing it into her overnight bag.

Holding on to each other, they retraced their footsteps down the hallway, down the stairs, and out the front door. Gravel crunched underfoot as they hurried across the parking lot and jumped into Carmela's car.

And all the while, they never noticed the car that was parked nearby. Or the person who sat inside carefully watching them.

Chapter 20

A snarling Chinese dragon thrust its enormous snout in the air. An Egyptian sphinx, freshly gilded, stared somberly from its perch atop a float bed. Another dozen floats, looking like the seven wonders of the ancient world, were parked in the Pluvius krewe's cavernous barnlike building.

"Darlings!" exclaimed Jekyl, in the midst of this float-building chaos. "You made it! You actually came!"

Carmela and Ava exchanged air kisses with Jekyl. They'd promised to show up this Sunday morning to help him with the final push on decorating, and here they were, none the worse from last night's strange adventure.

"Holy moley," said Ava, looking around. "Looks like you got quite a party going on." Even though it was only noon, loud music blared from a pair of gigantic speakers, and a three-sided bar was set up in the center of the building. Krewe members were two-deep at the bar, clinking glasses, laughing, and boasting to each other. Definitely in party mode.

"I thought these people were here to help," said Carmela.

Jekyl gave his trademark eye roll. "Are you serious? These people are here to party. To toss as much whiskey and rum down their gullets as humanly possible and basically make my life a total misery."

"Oh, poor you," said Carmela, putting a hand lightly on Jekyl's shoulder. "And you go through this every year."

"So that makes me what?" asked Jekyl. "An idiot? A masochist?"

"It makes you *numero uno* float designer in New Orleans," laughed Carmela. "A float designer who's scored a major publishing contract to write a book."

"There is that," agreed Jekyl. He glanced around to make sure no one was listening, then dropped his voice to a conspiratorial whisper. "So, what's the deal?" he asked. "What's your take on that old map? Is it the real deal, or is the jury still out?"

"The jury's still out on a lot of things," said Carmela. "But we did a little follow-up last night and made a rather strange discovery."

She hurriedly filled Jekyl in on their hunch about Groomsbridge Plantation, their impromptu trip up there, and their foray into the plantation's subterranean basement. Jekyl's eyes widened when they told him about the crown and B symbol they'd found gouged on an old wooden rafter.

"Ladies," said Jekyl, "I am suitably impressed. A road trip and a basement creepycrawl. That's first-rate detective work in my book."

"We think so," said Ava.

"Problem is," said Carmela, "we don't know what the symbols mean."

"Do you think the crown might somehow relate to the Louisiana Purchase?" asked Jekyl. "You know, since this whole area once belonged to France? To the crown?"

"Good guess," said Ava.

"But if we stick with our Jean Lafitte theory," said Carmela, "then the idea of a crown or royalty doesn't really jibe. At least I don't think it does."

"Well, I'll leave you ladies to puzzle it out for now," said Jekyl. "In the meantime, I've got to deal with that idiot over there."

"Who dat?" asked Ava, glancing about.

"Brett Fowler," said Jekyl.

"The krewe captain," said Carmela in a

low voice. "Who happens to be heading this way."

Brett Fowler was a bandy rooster of a man. Bowlegged, red-haired, and a body gone soft from too much Jack Daniel's, fried catfish, and sweet potato pie. This was his first year as Pluvius krewe captain, and he meant to run a tight ship. With the hired help, anyway.

"Jekyl," said Brett Fowler in a high, reedy voice, "you got to move it along a whole lot faster." His florid face, which was as red as his hair, pushed close to Jekyl's, trying hard to invade his space. Fowler was obviously under the impression that he projected an aura of leadership. Unfortunately for him, he just looked like a posturing, scowling idiot.

"We've got the two Chinese-themed floats and the castle floats completely done," said Jekyl. "The sphinx and pirate ship will be finished tonight. That gives us all day Monday to put finishing touches on the Mayan ruins, coliseum, and plantation floats. And we're really only talking about lights, smoke machines, seating, and a little extra paint."

Brett Fowler pursed his lips and wrinkled his brow. "Not good enough, Jekyl."

Jekyl folded his arms and lifted one eye-

263

brow until it quivered. "I can assure you, if your krewe members pitched in, things would progress a lot faster," he told Fowler, his tone just this side of haughty. "Otherwise, my timetable stands."

Carmela and Ava glanced from Jekyl to Fowler. Things seemed to be getting pretty darned tense.

"Another thing," said Brett Fowler, coming right back at Jekyl, "we need a lot more color on that castle float. The thing's about as drab as a mud puddle."

"Now just a minute —" began Jekyl. But Fowler was closing in for the kill.

"I took the liberty of bringing in Jimmy Toups," said Fowler, a note of triumph slipping into his voice. "He can finish four floats, and you can finish four."

Jekyl took a step back. Jimmy Toups was Jekyl's big rival. They were forever competing against each other to win float contracts from the big krewes. Now, to have Jimmy slip in right under his nose was a tremendous slap in the face to Jekyl.

Carmela watched Jekyl carefully. This was the telling moment. The moment when Jekyl would either stomp off in a huff or stick it out because he needed the money.

Needed-the-money won. No surprise.

"Fine," said Jekyl, his face darkening, his

voice a tight rasp. "Whatever works."

Carmela studied Brett Fowler, who seemed to be reveling in his petty triumph. She noticed that his eyebrows were little individual tufts of red hair that moved up and down when he talked. And he had the same little tufts on his forearms, like a scrub brush.

Brett Fowler noticed her staring at him and smiled. His two front teeth were rimmed with a fine line of gold. Carmela looked away, then down at Fowler's shoes. They were brand-new, caramel-colored work boots laced tightly over khaki pants. But that wasn't what caught Carmela's attention. There were tiny gold flecks on the tips of Fowler's boots. Almost the same kind of material as the gold residue found on Archie Baudier's shoes.

"I can't believe you put up with that shit," said Ava, once Fowler had lumbered off.

"If I don't complete my contract," said Jekyl, "I don't get paid. And the last couple years have been pretty bleak for art and antique consulting in New Orleans."

"You did just fine," said Carmela, patting his arm. "Sometimes you have to just suck it up. Even if it tastes terrible."

"Look it," said Ava, tossing her head.

"That guy over there in the . . . holy shit . . . is that a white *jumpsuit?*"

"Good Lord," echoed Carmela. "He looks like he's in a Tyvek suit. The kind lab rats wear in Level Four containment centers for infectious diseases."

"He's a virus all right," snarled Jekyl. "That's Jimmy Toups."

They watched as Jimmy Toups strutted and pointed and bullied his workers, all the while pretending not to notice Jekyl standing twenty feet away.

"Fowler's trying to goad you into quitting," said Carmela. "And Toups is the bait."

"Absolutely he is," said Jekyl. "Asshole. Which is why I intend to stick it out."

"Bully for you, honey," said Ava. "You've got backbone. And you can count on us for whatever help you need."

"Thank you," said Jekyl, his shoulders suddenly drooping. "You've both been enormously supportive. Helping with the funeral arrangements, running your own brand of investigation into Archie's death . . . and now this." He sighed. "What can I say? I owe you big time."

"Don't think we won't collect," said Ava, grinning.

"Jekyl," said Carmela. Her mind had circled back to the gold flecks she'd noticed

266

on Fowler's shoes. "Are you by any chance using gold powder on these floats?"

"Hmm?" said Jekyl, distracted.

"Gold powder?" repeated Ava.

"No, not powder, per se," said Jekyl, his dark eyes still focused on Jimmy Toups. "But maybe a little paint and gold leaf here and there." He gestured toward the pirate ship float. "Face it, by the end of Mardi Gras, between the beads, foil, crepe paper, ink, and paint, this whole city will be dredged in gold."

Carmela and Ava were put to work on the plantation float. Their task was to artfully arrange silk magnolias on an enormous wire trellis.

"This sucks," said Ava, after she'd done her fiftieth magnolia.

"Float building ain't all it's cracked up to be," admitted Carmela.

"Nice float, though," said Ava, gazing up at a statue of a winged angel surrounded by plastic foam tombstones that had been spray painted silver. They were set against an enormous pair of wrought-iron gates that had a painted backdrop of a plantation house. The overall effect was highly atmospheric. Crumbling, frayed, a little dilapidated — like many parts of New Orleans.

Carmela studied the float. "Does that scene look at all familiar to you?"

Ava squinted upward. "Maybe a little bit like Groomsbridge Plantation?"

"Exactly my take," said Carmela. "I'm guessing Archie was the designer of this particular float."

"Jekyl said he came up with the whole Ruins and Doubloons theme," said Ava.

"Maybe we *were* on to something last night," said Carmela, her heart beating a little faster. She was anxious to leaf through the file she'd copied from the Vieux Carré Historical Society, take a second look to see if she couldn't somehow make better sense of the crown and B markings.

"Uh, don't look now," said Ava, "but your ex is over there."

Carmela didn't look. "Soon-to-be ex," she said, correcting Ava. "Let's not give Shamus any more status than he deserves."

"Whatever his marital standing, he's got a girl with him."

Carmela sighed. "What else is new?"

"I hate to tell you this," said Ava, "but she looks like she's about seventeen years old."

Now Carmela's curiosity was piqued. So of course she snuck a glance. And fervently wished she hadn't. Shamus was lounging at the bar, one arm draped possessively around the shoulders of a heartbreakingly beautiful young blond. Her long hair hung in gentle waves, her figure was ripe and lush, her eyes a piercing blue.

"A seventeen-year-old Aryan," said Carmela. "Great. Shamus has finally gone over to the dark side."

Shamus noticed Carmela noticing and lifted a hand. Carmela pretended not to see him. Didn't matter. Shamus bent down and whispered something in the girl's ear, then slid away from her.

"He's coming over here," said Ava, trying not to move her lips and sounding like a novice ventriloquist with metal braces.

"Crap," said Carmela.

"Hey there," said Shamus, sauntering up. "How was the trip?"

"Wonderful," lied Carmela. "Absolutely delightful."

"Pretty short notice," said Shamus. Now that he was sober, he was just this side of suspicious.

"Life's just one big impromptu bowl of cherries for us," said Carmela.

"The dogs missed you," said Shamus. "Boo had trouble going to sleep."

"Did you let her sleep on the bed?" asked Carmela.

Shamus nodded. "Mm-hm. Once Glory

was gone."

"Put a Milk Bone on her pillow?" asked Ava. "Read her a story?"

"Huh?" said Shamus.

"Come on, Shamus," laughed Ava. "You've got to read to her. She's at the fifth-grade level now." She laughed, then clapped a hand to her head. "Wait a minute, *you're* only at a fourth grade reading level. Silly me. Boo should've been reading to you!"

Shamus's face was suddenly rigid with anger. "You have a lot of fun at my expense, don't you Ava?" His skin had gone blotchy now, and a vein throbbed at his temple. Once that vein started to throb and turn an interesting shade of purple, that's when you knew you were getting to Shamus. Carmela had learned that lesson in their first month of marriage.

"Just have the dogs ready by six," Carmela told him. "I'm on a very tight schedule today."

Shamus lounged closer to her. "Baby's big party's tonight?"

Carmela nodded. "That's right."

"You used to take me along," he said. "I used to be your date." Now he sounded melancholy.

"You have a date," said Carmela in a matter-of-fact tone. "She's standing right over there."

"No she ain't," pointed out Ava. "Little Miss Muffet has abandoned her tuffet and is heading thisaway."

"Shamus?" came a tinkling, tentative voice. "What're you doing, honey? I miss you."

"The little woman beckons," snorted Ava.

"Shamus, honey, I need another drink," said the girl, drawing out her words and sounding whiny and more than a little needful.

"Your date is chitchattin' with his *wife*," Ava pointed out gleefully. "I think they might be tryin' to work something out."

"Wife?" squealed the blond girl, her voice rising at least ten decibels. She smacked an open hand hard against Shamus's upper arm. "You told me you were *divorced!*"

Now it was Shamus's turn to look flustered. "I'm sure I told you I was separated, honey. It's . . . it's really just a technicality. Heh-heh. No big deal."

"That's for sure," murmured Carmela.

"We're finished, Shamus!" exclaimed the girl. "I have no intention of hangin' out with a married man." She flounced off, calling over her shoulder, "I'm no home wrecker."

"Honey," chuckled Ava. "There weren't no home to wreck."

271

■ ■ ■ ■

By six thirty, Carmela was back in her French Quarter apartment, standing in front of her bathroom mirror, trying to decide between Lancôme's Couture Brown or Dior's Sky Blue eye shadow. Shrugging, she applied a little of both to her eyelids. She was attending a fancy party, after all. And wearing a costume. So, probably, a more dramatic eye was called for. At least she hoped it was. Otherwise she'd be the only raccoon at the party.

Once her makeup was finished, Carmela took a few minutes to feed the dogs. As usual, they acted like ravenous wolves, begging for another half scoop of food, cadging extra Milk Bones from the stash in her Felix the Cat cookie jar. Then, still dressed in a short silk slip, she padded into the bedroom and shimmied into her costume.

Since Baby had dictated a Riverboat Ramble theme for her party, Carmela had decided to go as a dance hall girl. Her dress, a short red shift that she'd rented from Grand Folly Costume Shop, was embroidered with sequins and spangles. Modeling it in front of a mirror, she cinched it with a wide black velvet belt, and decided it looked fairly cute.

So far so good. Feeling a burst of confidence, she plopped on the matching feather headpiece and adjusted one of the red ostrich feathers so it curled around the side of her face. Then she slipped into a pair of strappy red mules.

There. Perfect and very Miss Kitty.

Because Carmela had a few minutes to spare before Ava came by to pick her up, she grabbed her Jean Lafitte file and plopped down at her dining room table. She flipped through the sheets, scanning them for any reference she could find, however obscure, to Queen or the letter B.

Halfway through her file, she came across a map of the Barataria Bayou.

Barataria, she reminded herself, was a key landmark. Jean Lafitte's gang was sometimes referred to as the Baratarians, and that was one of the places they liked to hide out.

Smoothing her map, Carmela leaned over it and tried to pick out some of the more familiar aspects.

There was the small town of Baptiste Creek, of course. She was familiar with it because it served as the jumping-off point to get to the Meechum family's camp house. But the camp house was only a twenty-minute boat ride in through mangroves and bald cypress. And there were still thousands of acres of bayou she was unfamiliar with. Especially farther south in the Barataria Bay region.

So let's see. There was Leeville and Port Fourchon. And Grand Isle at the southernmost point. Carmela heard the door slam across the courtyard. Ava, no doubt. She was aware of high heels clacking across patio stones. And she was suddenly aware that she was staring at a tiny speck on the map that was labeled Queen Bess Island.

Could that be what she was looking for?

Sharp raps sounded on her front door.

"It's open," she called.

Ava came bouncing in, all gussied up in a rather sassy pirate's outfit. Tight red silk shirt cut down to there, tight black skirt, shiny black boots, and a tricorne hat emblazoned with a Jolly Roger emblem. A plush green parrot with beady button eyes bobbed from one shoulder. "Let's party!" she exclaimed.

Carmela smiled a cat-that-ate-the-canary smile. "I think I may have found the crown and B reference."

"What!" Ava scampered across the room, trying to dodge dogs, still getting whacked in the legs by friendly, wagging tails.

"Look." Carmela turned the map around

to show Ava. "Right here. Queen Bess Island." She tapped it with an index finger. "In the Barataria Bayou."

Ava let loose a low whistle as she eagerly studied the map. "*Cher,* I think you cracked the code." She slipped into the chair next to Carmela. "This is a great big wow!"

"You think?" asked Carmela. Suddenly she was flooded with doubts. "But we don't know what it means exactly. Or what's there."

"Then we should go explore," proclaimed Ava. "Rent a boat and check out this Queen Bess Island."

"What if it turns out to be another wild-goose chase?" asked Carmela, adjusting the ostrich feather that was tickling her cheek.

"Worth the risk," said Ava. She moved closer and patted Carmela on the back. "Good work, Miz Sherlock!"

"You think Jekyl will be at Baby's tonight?" Carmela wondered. He'd told her earlier that he might have to stay late at the Pluvius den to finish floats.

"Hope so," said Ava. " 'Cause I can't wait to tell him about your discovery! And I sure as heck want him to see our costumes, too." Her eyes wandered to Carmela's feather headpiece and her red spangled shift. "You're going as a flapper?" Her tone was just this side of skeptical.

"I'm a dance hall girl," said Carmela.

Ava wasn't convinced. "They had dance halls on riverboats?"

"They had dancing *girls,*" said Carmela. "You know, plinkety-plink piano music with girls who danced and strutted their stuff onstage? Besides, you're dressed as a pirate. When were pirates ever on riverboats?"

"Are you kidding? Pirates had to get their R & R jollies somewhere!" Ava jumped up and wiggled her curvaceous rear end. "Anyway, how's this for pirate booty!"

CHAPTER 21

Carmela needn't have worried about her costume. As she and Ava pushed their way through Baby's palatial living room, she encountered guests in all manner of dress. String ties and cigars seemed to serve as the main prop for the duded-up men, although a few affected a Rhett Butler–type costume. The ladies fared much better. There were tiered ruffle skirts with pantalets peeping out, off-the-shoulder dresses with wide hoop skirts, and even a couple Scarlett O'Hara costumes complete with green velvet gowns and gold cord belts and, of course, a sea of beaded bags and elaborate fans.

"See," Carmela pointed out as she spotted a few more feathers adorning heads, "I'm not the only dance hall girl at the party."

"But I'm the only pirate," laughed Ava, patting her little green parrot. "Yaaar!"

"Darlings!" exclaimed Baby as she flew across the room to embrace them. "You're here! Welcome!"

"Wow!" said Ava, gazing at Baby with open admiration. "I love your dress! It's like a wonderful, frothy bonbon!"

"Oh this," said Baby, smoothing the front of her ruffled floor-length gown. "It's really an old Dior piece I wore to the Art Institute gala a couple of years ago. I had my seamstress change the bodice and add a few bugle beads and geegaws."

"Wish my geegaws looked that good," said Ava.

"Oh honey," laughed Baby, "yours are so much bigger."

Carmela giggled at Baby's little joke as her eyes roved about her palatial home. Baby and her husband, Del, a prominent New Orleans attorney, had bought the house a dozen or so years ago and had never stopped decorating or adding adornment. As Baby pulled them into the living room, Carmela was struck by the high ceilings with their hand-carved cornices and not one but *three* crystal chandeliers. At the far end of the room stood a massive white marble fireplace flanked by matching Chippendale chests. French and Dutch landscape paintings graced the walls. A sixteen-foot

S-curved sofa in dusty pink brocade ran down the center of the room. Chinese-print club chairs formed conversation clusters in four other areas.

"Amazing," said Carmela. "You've completely redone this room. And, as usual, it's turned out gorgeous."

Baby smiled widely. "That sofa finally arrived two weeks ago. I absolutely adore it, but I wasn't sure what others would think. It *is* a little over-the-top."

"I'm sure they think it's absolutely perfect," said Carmela.

"Oh, you're always so sweet," said Baby, with a genteel wave of her hand. "Now why don't you darlings head into the dining room? Help yourself to some of our lovely food."

"Wonderful idea," said Ava. "I'm starving."

"And the bar's in there, too," said Baby, as she rushed off to greet more guests.

But it was the groaning buffet table that drew Carmela's and Ava's undivided attention.

"Oh my gosh," said Carmela, pointing to a mound of golden brown orbs that rested perfect and plump in a brass chafing dish. "Please tell me those are oysters."

"Pecan-breaded oysters," said the caterer,

looking pleased.

"Gotta try a couple," said Carmela, holding out her plate.

"Me, too," said Ava. "Oh, and you've got eggs New Orleans?" This was a variation on eggs Benedict: poached eggs on crabmeat with a spicy Hollandaise sauce. Decadent but so delicious.

The server, realizing he was in the presence of appreciative eaters, pointed out the rest of the offerings on the table. Gulf pompano, shrimp-stuffed merliton, oyster chowder, shrimp bouillabaisse, Vidalia onion casserole, blackened catfish, and fresh salmon topped with beurre blanc sauce.

"Maybe a little of each?" ventured Carmela.

"Maybe a lot of each," echoed Ava.

They filled up their plates, grabbed a glass of champagne, and headed for a seat in Baby's rear parlor. It was a smaller room, not quite as grand as the rest of the house, with elegant white wicker furniture and a fabulous view into the backyard garden. A painting of a curious blue dog with yellow eyes hung on the wall.

"That's what I'd like to own someday," said Carmela.

"Wonderful art," agreed Ava.

Ava was about to add something else,

when her words were suddenly drowned out by the raucous sounds of a zydeco band.

Situated in the solarium, they played three rousing, toe-tapping tunes, while Carmela and Ava happily enjoyed their food.

"Enough," said Ava, finally relinquishing her dish to a passing waiter and grabbing Carmela by the hand. "Time to pull out all the stops and really party!"

They weren't the only ones. They were soon lost in a mad swirl of revelers as the band, a group called the Catahoula Seven, played tunes like "Madeleine," "Baby, Please Don't Go," and "Danse de Mardi Gras." True to the zydeco style, they alternated their more rousing numbers with soulful, syncopated songs, and one musician even wore a traditional *vest frottoir* or rub board.

Carmela danced with a couple of men, one in a Confederate officer's uniform, while Ava changed partners after every song and showed no sign of stopping.

At the end of her third dance, Carmela pled exhaustion and stepped away from the mad frenzy. And ran right into Gabby and her husband, Stuart.

"Hey there!" exclaimed Carmela. "Good to see you." She hugged Gabby, accepted a polite kiss on the cheek from Stuart.

"Is Shamus here?" were the first words out of Gabby's mouth.

"Not this year," replied Carmela. Strangely enough, Gabby still had high hopes of the two of them getting back together. It was never gonna happen, of course. "I think Shamus has a big date tonight. In fact, I'm *positive* he does."

Jekyl Hardy suddenly appeared, and so did Tandy, and then it was a big love fest for a few minutes, while everybody hugged and kissed and admired each other's costumes.

Of all the male guests, Jekyl looked the most authentic, Carmela decided. Riverboat gambler hat, wing-collared shirt with ascot, cutaway coat, striped pants, narrow cheroot cigar in an ivory holder. Even a deck of cards. Trust Jekyl to be over-the-top theatrical.

A few minutes later, Carmela and Ava were able to guide Jekyl into a corner and tell him about Barataria Bayou and their discovery of a Queen Bess Island.

He was pleased and a little frightened. "You're not serious! This place really exists?"

"Isn't Carmela smart?" said Ava with a proprietary air.

"She's utterly brilliant," said Jekyl. "But,

truth be known, you ladies are beginning to scare me. What started out as a concerned inquiry seems to have turned into a full-on hunt."

"For treasure and for Archie's killer," said Carmela.

"We're even thinking of going out there," piped up Ava.

"To this Queen Bess Island?" asked Jekyl.

"We can't quit now," said Carmela. After all, they'd come much further than she ever thought they would. Lots of clues were piling up that were leading them to stranger and stranger places. Hopefully, they could home in on a suspect, too.

Jekyl placed his hands gently on Carmela's shoulders. "Kiss on the top of the head to you, my darling, but I think I pulled you into a very strange and sticky investigation."

"Agreed," said Carmela. "Still, I went in with my eyes wide open."

"We both did," said Ava.

"Considering there's safety in numbers," said Jekyl, "maybe we can all three go explore this island on Wednesday. Once Mardi Gras is over and done with for another year."

"We were thinking of driving down tomorrow," said Ava. "Maybe early afternoon."

"We were?" said Carmela. This was news to her.

"Gotta keep the pressure on," enthused Ava. "Don't want to lose the momentum."

Carmela knew Ava had a point.

"I hate the idea of you two exploring that bayou all by your lonesomes," said Jekyl, looking nervous. "But I'm gonna get fragged if I don't stay and finish those darned Pluvius floats." He glanced at his watch, gave a distracted frown. "In fact, I've got to get back there. I'm gonna scoot over to Napoleon Avenue first and do a quick check on the Bacchus parade, then head for the Pluvius den. I really just popped in for a quick hello."

"Finishing your floats is job one," agreed Carmela. "And please don't worry about us tomorrow. We'll be fine. We'll rent a boat and just do some basic scouting. Nothing dangerous. Campfire Girl 101." She fervently wanted to believe her own words.

Jekyl raised an eyebrow. "You sure about that?"

"Trust us," said Carmela, with more conviction this time. "We're not going to take any risks."

They bade good night to Jekyl then and, at Ava's urging, headed for the dessert table.

"All that dancing's given me an appetite

again," she confessed.

"I couldn't eat a thing," said Carmela.

"Sure you could," urged Ava. "Just let a notch out on that belt of yours."

"Is that what you do?"

"Not exactly. I just sorta burn it up. It's my —"

"I know," sighed Carmela, "it's your super metabolism."

"Back again?" said the caterer.

"Just for dessert," said Ava. "Whatcha got?"

Turns out there was a spectacular array of desserts, too. Banana walnut bread pudding, peach cobbler, mud pie, amaretto pear parfait, and, of course, Baby's lace cookies.

"A little slice of each?" the smiling caterer asked as he picked up a silver cake server.

This time only Ava nodded.

Settled in the library, Carmela was enjoying a quiet conversation with one of Baby's neighbors, a bachelor by the name of Joe Pickens, who'd just started a medical reporting software company. Ava was enjoying her dessert and flirting with Toby LaChaise, a young reporter who worked at the *Times-Picayune.*

"I'm just doing society stuff until I can get onto the police beat," he was telling her.

Gazing through a double door into the

living room, Carmela suddenly noticed a familiar face. Carmela eased her leg over and the toe of her bright red mule nudged Ava's leg. Ava looked up, noted the expression on Carmela's face, and glanced around quickly. It didn't take her long to pick out Vasiliy.

"The Russian," Ava said in a low voice.

The reporter looked at her. "Huh?"

"Excuse me?" said Carmela's companion.

Carmela turned to him. "Do you by any chance know that man?" She gestured discreetly toward Vasiliy.

Now both men turned to stare.

Joe finally nodded. "Not personally, but I know he came as a guest of the deGroonings." He gave a vague directional gesture. "Neighbors from across the alley."

"He came as a guest," said Carmela. "Interesting."

"Is there something I should — ?" began the reporter, but Carmela had already risen from her chair.

"Excuse me," she said sweetly.

"Excuse me, too," said Ava, standing up and following Carmela into the other room.

"Why do you think Vasiliy's really here?" asked Carmela.

Ava narrowed her eyes. "Come to spy on us?"

"He wouldn't have any way of knowing we were here. Besides, he's not that smart. At least, I don't think he is."

"Maybe he really did tag along with the neighbors," said Ava. "The . . . who were they? The deGroonings."

"Maybe," said Carmela. "Even though he's supposed to be renting a house in the neighborhood, it does seem like a weird coincidence."

They dogged the Russian as he moved through the crowd, following his moves, always keeping three or four people between them.

"I'm going to ask that artist to make a sketch of him," said Carmela.

Ava was curious. "Really?"

"I'm going to give it to Edgar Babcock and see if he can do some sort of investigation. I have a bad feeling about that guy."

"You mean like have Babcock run the drawing through Interpol or something?" asked Ava.

Carmela nodded. "Yeah, I guess that'd be one thing he could do."

"That's a great idea, *cher,*" replied Ava. "Very sophisticated thinking. Like international espionage." She hesitated. "You think Babcock will do it?"

"Probably not," said Carmela. "But at

least we've made a blip on his radar."

"I think Babcock would like to make a blip on *your* radar," laughed Ava.

"You think?" said Carmela. A low-level vibe had always existed between the two of them, but Carmela wasn't sure if it was because Babcock was always annoyed with her or because he was slightly interested in her. Or both.

"Oh man," said Ava. "Babcock's like a lovesick puppy when he's around you."

"I thought he was more like an unhappy Doberman," said Carmela. "Always got his guard up."

"Trust me," said Ava. "Babcock hasn't owned up to it yet, but he's completely head over heels for you."

"I don't think so," said Carmela. But she was still pleased and a little bit jazzed by Ava's words. Yes, more and more she found Edgar Babcock to be extremely attractive, possibly even her type. But the two of them always seemed out of sync when they were around each other. When Babcock was in his cordial mode, Shamus always seemed to be nosing around, trying to worm his way back into her heart. Maybe, just maybe, Carmela decided, she could do something to correct their lousy timing. A little remedial work.

Carmela eased over to the sketch artist and had a whispered conversation. A twenty dollar bill slid out of her evening bag and disappeared into the artist's hand. Barely five minutes later she had her sketch.

"Cool," said Ava. She managed a quick peek as Carmela was rolling it up. "Now we just have to avoid Vasiliy for the rest of the night."

"I'm thinking we should just take off."

Ava stifled a yawn. "You're probably right. Tomorrow's gonna be a huge day in the Quarter. Probably tons of customers. And we want to sneak in that bayou trip, too."

"Then let's find Baby and —" began Carmela.

"Oh rats," said Ava, stiffening.

The Russian had homed in on them and was bearing down like a heat-seeking missile. He slid to a halt, stared pointedly at Carmela. "You," he said. A light seemed to pop on behind his heavy-lidded eyes.

"Me," said Carmela, clutching her rolled-up sketch tightly.

"You asked the artist to make drawing of me, no?"

"No," said Carmela.

He tried to grab the sketch. Carmela jumped back.

"Hey, Boris!" yelled Ava. "Keep your

grabby hands to yourself. Do you really think a couple of hot babes like us would be interested in the likes of you? To put it in the vernacular, *nyet!*" She grabbed Carmela's arm and hauled her away.

"Boris?" said Carmela, when they were safely away.

"You know," said Ava, "like that little cartoon guy in *Rocky and His Friends.*"

Carmela shook her head. "Ava, you are so off the hook!"

Vasiliy Leonkov gazed after them, a crooked sneer on his rugged face. In his lifetime he'd butted heads with the KGB, the Russian Mafia, and the dreaded *Sluzhba Vneshney Razvedki* or Foreign Intelligence Service. He wasn't about to be made a fool of by these women. Or have his livelihood threatened.

CHAPTER 22

"Boris — that Vasiliy guy — is really freaky," said Ava, as they pushed their way into Carmela's apartment. "Too weird for words. And did you get a gander at his eyebrows? Why do guys let their eyebrows get all gnarly like that? Why can't they manage a little judicious trimming? Of course, he'd probably have to use a Weedwacker!" She slumped into a chair. "Gosh, I love a guy who's well-groomed."

"Shamus is well-groomed, and he still turned out to be a jerk," pointed out Carmela. She grabbed the two dogs, clipped lines to their collars, and pointed them in the direction of the courtyard. "He even enjoys pedicures."

"There's always an exception to the rule, *cher.*"

"Obviously," said Carmela.

"Now, take Edgar Babcock," said Ava, a wicked grin lighting her face. "There's a man who's well-groomed *and* stylish."

"How do you suppose he affords Armani and Brooks Brothers on a detective's salary?" asked Carmela.

"Maybe he's on the take," proposed Ava. But when she saw the startled expression on Carmela's face, she hastened to correct her words. "Hey, I was just kidding. Babcock's way too upstanding and Dudley Do-Right for that kind of thing."

Carmela pulled open the refrigerator and gazed inside. "You never know, though. Nothing surprises me anymore." She let out a sigh. "You want a drink? I've got enough Chardonnay for about a half glass each."

Ava sauntered over to the kitchen counter, leaned her backside against it. "I've got a better idea, *cher.*" She reached around and grabbed the bottle of absinthe. "When are we gonna crack open this baby?"

"Are you *serious?*"

"Hell, yes," said Ava. "It's supposed to be quite delicious."

"And illegal," said Carmela. "Frankly, the whole idea of drinking absinthe makes me more than a little nervous. I don't mean to be a stick-in-the-mud, but . . ." She suddenly closed her eyes, heard Glory's biting words echo in her head: *Carmela's always a stick-in-the-mud.* The dig gnawed at her.

Especially coming from a raving maniac like Glory. Still . . . maybe she could afford to loosen up. A little bit, anyway.

"Please?" said Ava in a wheedling tone. She held the bottle out in front of her, tipped it from side to side.

"All right," said Carmela. "Maybe just a *tiny* sip before we pour it down the drain."

"Excellent," said Ava. "You fix a nice pitcher of ice water; I'll do the rest. Oh, pop in a CD will you? A little mood music."

"How do you know what to do with absinthe?" asked Carmela.

"Checked it out on the Internet," said Ava knowingly. "You can find just about anything there, even far-out crazy stuff. You could probably get directions to build a thermonuclear bomb if you could locate some plutonium."

"Probably order *that* on the Internet," muttered Carmela.

Ava busied herself in the kitchen while Carmela retrieved the dogs and passed out treats. Finally, they were seated cross-legged on the floor in Carmela's living room in front of the glass coffee table. As Ava struck a match and lit two saint candles, Boo nuzzled the green parrot that drooped from Ava's shoulder. It had certainly seen better days.

"She's gonna chew that thing right off your shoulder if you're not careful," warned Carmela.

"Well, she can have it," said Ava, pulling the bedraggled little parrot free and tossing it across the room.

A mad scuffle ensued as Boo and Poobah raced across the floor and pounced on the parrot like stink on a piece of road kill.

"Rest in peace, little parrot," said Ava. She rubbed her hands together and said, "Let's do it."

"Okay," said Carmela somewhat dubiously.

Ava poured two inches of absinthe into each glass. In the flickering candlelight, it shimmered like liquid emeralds.

"I'm not used to drinking anything green," laughed Carmela.

"Not to worry," replied Ava. "Wait and see." She placed a sugar cube in the center of a slotted spoon and held it over one of the glasses. "Now you pour the water. Right onto the sugar cube. And slowly, please."

Carmela lifted the clinking pitcher of ice water and did as Ava had instructed. She poured out a tiny amount of water and let it trickle down onto the sugar cube. Amazingly, as the sugar cube dissolved and melted into the absinthe, the absinthe began to turn cloudy. "Wow. This is some kind of crazy."

"Keep pouring," said Ava.

Thirty seconds later the green absinthe had completely turned an opalescent white.

"That's called the absinthe louche," said Ava.

"You're making me a little nervous," laughed Carmela. "That you know so much about this."

"Hey," said Ava, placing a fresh sugar cube on the spoon and indicating for Carmela to trickle water into the second glass. "New Orleans used to be a hotbed of absinthe drinkers."

"I've heard a little about that," admitted Carmela.

"And in the Czech Republic you can walk into just about any bar and order absinthe. The real deal absinthe, not just the fake stuff like some liquor stores sell. I think in Canada and Spain, too."

"That's a comforting thought," said Carmela. Although it really wasn't.

"Now comes the true test," said Ava. She picked up her glass, held it to her lips, and took a tiny sip. She half closed her eyes, assessing it like a professional wine taster would. "Mmm," she finally said. "Tastes like . . ."

"Forbidden fruit," said Carmela.

"Like licorice," said Ava. "Those Twizzler things."

Carmela took a deep breath and a delicate sip, let the liqueur roll across her tongue. It was an interesting taste sensation. A little sweet with a strong hint of anise. Not bad at all. "When am I gonna start seeing double?" she asked.

"You're not," said Ava. "Because we're not going to drink that much."

"This is just an experiment," agreed Carmela, taking another sip.

"Research," said Ava.

"Part of our investigation."

"I can see how Archie got into this stuff," said Ava. She held up a hand, started to explain herself. "I mean, I wouldn't want to indulge every week, but . . ."

"But it is sort of nice," admitted Carmela.

"And I do feel a little floaty," said Ava. She reached a hand out, let it sway. "Makes the atmosphere seem so light and airy. Plus it *feels* like the music is all around us."

"Like the notes are flowing over our skin," agreed Carmela.

The loud ring of the nearby phone interrupted her thoughts.

Ava reared back and dropped her glass on the table, letting it hit with a loud crack.

"Mother of pearl, we're busted!"

"Take it easy," laughed Carmela. She reached a hand out to grab the ringing phone.

"Don't answer it," pleaded Ava. "What if it's Detective Babcock? He'll be able to guess what we're up to!"

"Stop being so paranoid," giggled Carmela. "It's a phone, not a closed-circuit camera." She held the receiver to her ear. "Hello?" For some reason, that single word seemed to take eons to spit out.

"Carmela?"

"Uh . . . Jekyl?" She recognized his voice, but something didn't sound quite right. Was she just reacting to the absinthe or . . . ?

"Jekyl? What's wrong?" asked Carmela, really focusing now.

"I'm sorry to bother you . . ." He sounded really stressed.

"What's wrong?" Carmela asked again, her heart suddenly doing a couple of extra thuds in her chest.

There was a low moan, and then Jekyl said, "Some idiot jumped me."

"What!" exclaimed Carmela.

"What?" asked Ava, looking worried.

"Outside my apartment."

"You mean in the hallway?" asked Carmela. "Or outside the building?"

"Front door of the building. As I was putting my key in the lock," said Jekyl. "They must have been . . . ah, I don't know . . . hiding in the bushes or something."

"Are you hurt?" asked Carmela.

"Oh no!" breathed Ava, her hand clapped to her chest.

"Banged up," admitted Jekyl. "Cut."

"We'll be right there," Carmela assured him.

Blood had congealed around Jekyl's nose and at the side of his face by the time the cab dropped them off and they raced upstairs.

"First aid kit," were Carmela's first words. In her haste, she'd forgotten to bring one.

Jekyl coughed and pointed. "Bathroom," he said hoarsely.

"I'll grab it," said Ava, dashing off.

"Tell me exactly what happened," said Carmela, leading him into the kitchen and pushing him down into a chair. "Someone mugged you? Tried to rob you?"

Jekyl grimaced and shook his head. "Not sure. All I know is one minute I was sticking my key in the lock, and the next minute my head was having a close encounter with the front door. Hundred-year-old oak, by the way."

"Then what?" asked Carmela. She went to the sink, squirted antibacterial soap into her palms, and began washing her hands.

Jekyl grimaced. "Not sure. Somebody sapped me on the head, then hit me from behind."

"What can you remember about your attacker?"

"It seemed like . . . maybe he wore a black outfit and ski mask?"

"Did he say anything? Give you a warning?"

"No."

"Do you have any idea who it might have been?" asked Carmela, drying her hands. A litany of names was running through her head: Robert Tallant, Vasiliy, Miguez the crazy Cajun. It could've been any one of them, or it could've been someone else completely. A random, bungled robbery. But somehow, she thought not.

Ava was back, fumbling with the first aid kit, spilling things. Finally, she thrust it at Carmela. "You do it. Your hands are steadier."

Carmela grabbed the white plastic box and pulled out a bottle of Betadine.

"Do you have to use that?" asked Jekyl, peering up at her.

"Not if you want to make a trip to the

emergency room," said Carmela.

"No thanks," said Jekyl.

Carmela poured a judicious amount of Betadine onto a cotton ball, swabbed at Jekyl's nose, then the side of his head.

"Ouch." He shifted unhappily in his chair.

"You were lucky," she told him, studying his wounds. "The nose is just a scrape. And the cut on the side of your head's not deep. Really just an abrasion."

"Then why did I bleed like a stuck pig?"

"All head wounds bleed," said Carmela. She'd picked up that nasty little piece of trivia somewhere. Probably not on *Jeopardy.*

"You want a Band-Aid?" asked Ava.

Carmela peered into the first aid kit. "Maybe a couple of those Steri-Strips."

"I'd like to get my hands on whoever did this," said Jekyl, wincing at Carmela's touch. "Make it a fair fight. None of this ambush-from-behind crap."

"Almost done," said Carmela as she placed a Steri-Strip above his ear. "And one more." She applied a second one. "Okay."

Jekyl was suddenly a whole lot better. Mad as a hornet and longing for retribution, he seemed to forget his cuts and scrapes. Jumping from his chair, he paced the small kitchen like a caged lion. "If I *ever* get my hands on that asshole!" he snarled.

"Do you think it could have been Jimmy Toups?" Ava asked mildly.

Jekyl stopped in his tracks and stared at her, clearly confused. "Why would Jimmy Toups want to hurt me? I mean, seriously? This is a guy who prances about in a white jumpsuit. His idea of great float design is an overblown piñata head stuck on the front of a flatbed truck." At least Jekyl hadn't lost his flair for drama or his sense of humor.

"Maybe Jimmy wanted to get you out of the way," suggested Carmela. "Keep you from completing your contract. Discredit you." Jimmy Toups seemed like a long shot to her, but you never know.

"Oh my gosh," said Ava, her eyes suddenly going wide. "Talk about connections. It never occurred to me until just this minute that maybe Jimmy Toups killed Archie."

Jekyl put a hand to his head, absently feeling the placement of the Steri-Strips. "Jeez." He frowned. "Are you serious?" He looked at Carmela. She shrugged.

Ava continued. "Maybe Jimmy figured that if Archie was out of the way, you'd go a little bonkers. Which would let him move in on your turf."

Jekyl sought out Carmela's eyes. "You think?" He was weighing in on Ava's theory.

"It's awfully far-fetched," Carmela admit-

301

ted. "But not completely out of the realm of possibility."

"Then I'm gonna knock that guy silly when I see him," said Jekyl. "Smack the truth out of him." For someone who prided himself on Southern gentility, Jekyl was acting awfully aggressive.

"No, you're not," Carmela told him firmly. "You're going to keep your cool and *report* this incident."

"You mean call Detective Babcock?" said Jekyl.

Carmela nodded. "Yes. Exactly."

"*You* call him," said Jekyl. "He likes you a whole lot more."

"He adores her," added Ava. "Throws her these long, smoldering looks."

"Tell you what," said Carmela. "You call tonight and make a police report, talk to whoever answers the phone at the Eighth District station. That's the closest one, at Royal and Conti. Then I'll follow up with Edgar Babcock in the morning. Have a conversation with him and try to get him to see that your getting jumped might possibly be tied to Archie's murder."

"You think he'll see it that way?" asked Ava.

Carmela raised an eyebrow. "No idea."

"You should get some sleep now," Ava told

302

Jekyl. "Give your body some downtime to recover."

"Not until we do a little carpentry," said Carmela.

"Huh?" said Ava.

Carmela stared at Jekyl. "You didn't board that passageway up the first time I asked you, did you?"

"No," said Jekyl in a meek tone. "I didn't see any reason to."

"Do you now?" she asked.

Jekyl shrugged.

"You have a hammer and nails?" asked Carmela.

"Sure," said Jekyl. "But I still —"

"We're going to take care of your secret passageway once and for all," Carmela told him. "There's always a chance someone could get to you that way."

"Sheesh," said Jekyl, still not convinced.

"Answer me this," said Carmela. "Has Miguez ever been to Archie's apartment?"

Jekyl's upper teeth worried his lower lip. "I suppose."

"Now for the grand prize question," said Carmela. "Does Miss Norma know about your passageway?"

Jekyl was shocked. "You can't *possibly* suspect her!"

"Just answer the question."

He drew a shaky breath, blew out. "Yeah, I'm pretty sure she does."

CHAPTER 23

Memory Mine was bustling with customers this Monday morning. Women were grabbing stickers, card stock, accordion books, ink pads, and scissors like they were going out of style. The scene was so gratifyingly normal to Carmela that she had a hard time believing that last night's craziness at Jekyl's had really happened.

Gabby was manning the cash register up front, ringing up sales as fast as she could, jamming merchandise into bags. When things finally settled down to a dull roar, Carmela headed back to the craft table where Tandy was waiting.

"Can you show me that frame technique you mentioned a couple of weeks ago?" Tandy asked Carmela. "You know, using stamped paper?"

"Did you bring a picture frame?" asked Carmela. She was a little in awe of Tandy's boundless enthusiasm for all things crafty.

Tandy bent down and pulled a six-by-ten-inch wooden picture frame from her craft bag. "Right here," she told Carmela.

Carmela studied the frame. It was an ordinary wooden picture frame, nothing special. The kind you could pick up for a few dollars in any discount or craft store. But when they were finished with it . . . well, that would be another story.

"Okay," said Carmela. "The big trick here is picking out a great rubber stamp that will let you create an overall motif."

"Got that," said Tandy. She showed Carmela her rubber stamp of a crane.

"A crane," said Carmela. "Did you know that in Japan cranes are considered very auspicious symbols?"

"No, I did not," said Tandy. "But it sounds like you might be headed somewhere."

"What if . . . ?" said Carmela, studying one of her floor-to-ceiling racks of paper. "What if we assumed a sort of Zen attitude?"

"Sure," said Tandy, peering over her bright red reading glasses.

Carmela fingered a pad of silver ink, then pulled out two sheets of thin, gold paper. "What I'm thinking is, you stamp your cranes using silver ink onto this gold paper. That will lend a very rich but subdued look.

Then, when the ink is dry, your stamped paper gets glued and molded to your picture frame."

"And voilà," said Tandy. "New life for an old frame. Well, not old, but ordinary, anyway."

"Go for it," said Carmela. Her eyes flicked to the front of the shop. Three women were just leaving, clutching plastic bags filled with pens, scissors, and albums. A man — a man who looked vaguely familiar — was holding the door open for them.

How nice, Carmela thought. Then she was jerked back to reality when she recognized the man: Miguez, the absinthe-dealing Cajun who'd lured them to that awful hospital basement.

Miguez saw Carmela and homed in on her immediately. "I want a word with you," he said, anger shading his voice.

Carmela tried to block him and force him back toward the front of the store. Hopefully back out the door and onto the street. It wasn't working. He was too big, too angry.

"Hey," said Miguez, fire blazing in his dark eyes now. "You didn't tell me that kid was *dead!*"

Carmela stared at him. "You mean Archie? You didn't know?"

"Yeah, I mean Archie," spat out Miguez. "I just found out. The question is, are you trying to pin that on me, too?"

Carmela held her ground. "I'm not trying to pin anything on you. But if you're willing to be a suspect, I'm sure we can work something out with the police. With Detective Babcock." She saw Miguez flinch and then said, "Wait a minute, how'd you find me, anyway?"

"Never mind," snarled Miguez. "I just wanted to let you know I got busted, thanks to *you*. The cops found out about a few of my absinthe deals!"

Carmela forced herself not to react, not to look guilty. After all, what had *she* been imbibing last night? "You got busted thanks to *you*," she told Miguez. "The cops were on to you all along."

"That's not what my lawyer says," said Miguez.

"Er, when exactly did you get out of jail?" asked Carmela.

Miguez fixed her with a resentful stare. "Yesterday afternoon."

Carmela grimaced. Miguez could have easily been the one who assaulted Jekyl last night. The question was — why? Jekyl wasn't into anything illegal, was he?

"The cops grilled me pretty hard about

Archie Baudier, too. Which I knew nothing about."

"You sure about that?" asked Carmela.

Miguez snorted disdainfully, then suddenly leaned in close to Carmela. "Has your friend been hanging around?"

"My friend?" It took her a couple seconds. "Oh, you mean Ava?"

Miguez nodded. "The looker."

The looker, thought Carmela. And what was she? Chopped liver?

"No, I haven't seen Ava for quite some time. Sorry."

"Yeah, I bet," said Miguez.

"But I'll tell her you asked about her," Carmela said sweetly.

As Miguez swaggered out the door, Carmela wondered if he could have murdered Archie over an absinthe deal. Miguez seemed tough enough, cold enough. Or had there been some sort of drug deal that had gone bad? Something they didn't know about? Had Archie been following in the footsteps of his incarcerated brother and gotten in over his head?

Then her shop got busy again, and Carmela blessedly forgot about murder and mayhem for a while. Two women came in looking for peel-and-stick fabric sheets. She showed them some new batik designs that had just come in. Another customer wanted chipboard designs to decorate. Carmela dug out an assortment of flowers, apples, leaves, and little houses.

Just before noon, Margot Destrehan walked in the front door of Memory Mine.

"Margot," said Carmela, glancing up from the counter where she was sorting through packets of glass beads and embellishments. "Hello."

"What a lovely shop!" Margot gushed as her eyes darted about eagerly. "You're just full of fun things, aren't you?" She fingered a piece of plum-colored sheer ribbon that curled down from its display rack. "Ever since you opened I promised myself I'd stop by."

"Glad you managed to squeeze in a visit," said Carmela.

Margot gave a tiny shrug matched with a slightly guilty expression. "You know how it is."

"That's okay," Carmela reassured her. "I wasn't exactly beating a path to your door, either."

"But now that you know about our little historical society . . ."

"I won't be a stranger," promised Carmela.

"I actually have an ulterior motive for

coming here today," said Margot, "besides being intrigued by all your lovely albums and papers and stamps." She opened her handbag and pulled out a crumpled piece of paper. "It's about this program you designed for Archie's funeral."

"Yes?" said Carmela.

"I'm so in love with the typeface and paper and everything about it." Margot hesitated. "And I'm guessing you do freelance design?"

"Whenever I can," said Carmela. Rents in the French Quarter were sky-high, and she did everything she could to help bolster her bottom line.

"Here's the thing," said Margot. "Our historical society is planning a two-day symposium on French Quarter architecture. In fact, I'm tentatively calling our gathering Lace and Grace. You know, lace referring to the wrought iron that's everywhere. And grace . . ."

Carmela nodded eagerly. "Because of old-world gentility."

"Exactly," said Margot. "Anyway, I was wondering if we could tap you for the program design. We don't have a huge budget, but I'm assuming we could work something out."

"Sounds like a fun project," said Carmela.

"Do you have a timetable?"

"I'm still putting together the program, waiting for confirmation from a couple of speakers, but I'll probably have all the details ironed out next week."

"Great," said Carmela. "We'll get together then, talk about the look and feel of your piece, maybe go over paper samples. You'd need what for your program? Maybe eight pages . . . two sheets folded?"

Margot thought for a few seconds. "That'd work."

Carmela continued. "We could even select a couple of photos from your archives to scan for the front cover."

"That's a wonderful idea," said Margot. She reached over, picked up a framed collage Carmela had created using old sheet music, a thirties-era sepia photo of her grandparents, an old Rudolph Valentino photo clipped from a magazine, and a vintage train ticket. "You know a lot about old documents, don't you?"

"Some," admitted Carmela. "Ephemera, that's the term everyone's using these days. Anyway, it's very popular. Lots of collectors are interested in it, as well as scrappers and journalers."

"Since you have so much knowledge and skill in this area," said Margot, "would you ever consider becoming a docent or volunteer with us?"

Carmela was flattered. It was always nice to have your talents acknowledged. And, of course, she was a big believer in giving back to the community. "I think I'd like that very much," said Carmela.

"Maybe we could even put our heads together and come up with some sort of fitting tribute to Archie. To honor his work as a volunteer," said Margot. She teared up a little upon mentioning his name. "I'm in the process of writing a letter to his brother in Angola prison. Trying to be as gentle as possible, of course. Tell him about the *good* things."

"Do you know, did they stay in touch?" asked Carmela.

"I think so. A little, anyway."

Carmela smiled at Margot, who seemed to be suddenly hesitant.

"There's something else I wanted to mention," said Margot. "Some pertinent information."

"What's that?" asked Carmela.

"A person came in a couple days ago looking for information on Jean Lafitte."

Carmela's antennae suddenly prickled. "When exactly was this? Do you remember?"

Margot scrunched her face and looked up to the left, trying to recall. "I guess it was Saturday. After the funeral."

"Do you know who it was?" asked Carmela. "Did you get a name?"

Margot knitted her brows together. "No, no. I'm afraid I wasn't even there. I was at lunch with the director. The only reason I know about this is because my assistant, Kimberly, mentioned it in passing. I think she was kind of surprised when I started to grill her about it."

"Did you ask her for a description?"

"I did," said Margot. "But Kimberly was awfully vague. Sorry. She's like that. A good worker, but a little . . . I don't know . . . indifferent at times."

"Wait a minute," said Carmela. She hurried back to her office, grabbed the sketch of Vasiliy from last night, and took it back to show Margot. "Do you think this could be the man?"

Margo shrugged. "No idea."

"What if I came over and showed this sketch to Kimberly?"

Margot shook her head. "She's off right now. In fact, we've closed the place down until next Monday."

"Hmm," said Carmela.

"Now you're worried, aren't you?" asked

314

Margot.

"A little," Carmela responded.

Margot gazed at Carmela, one side of her mouth twitching. "To be perfectly honest, since Archie's murder I've been nervous myself about being in the French Quarter. I remember Archie mentioned in passing once that he was thinking about taking Tae Kwon Do lessons." She sighed deeply. "In light of everything, I sure wish he had."

"Me, too," said Carmela.

"Hey, Carmela," said a voice as she stepped out the front door.

She wheeled and ran smack-dab into Edgar Babcock. "Detective," she said. There was, she realized, a note of pleasure in her voice.

"I heard about your friend."

"Jekyl called you?" She'd tried to reach Babcock earlier, had been told he was out.

"No, but the report came across my desk," said Babcock. "And so did that drawing you sent me."

"You got that?" said Carmela. When she couldn't reach Babcock, she'd scanned the sketch into her computer and e-mailed it to him. "I thought you were supposed to be out all day."

"I have people," he told her dryly. "I'm in

315

contact."

"Did you recognize the guy in the sketch?"

Babcock gazed at her. "Should I?"

"His name's Vasiliy," said Carmela. "I suspect he might be an international criminal. Guns and stuff."

"Guns and stuff," repeated Babcock. He looked a little bemused. "You live in a kind of *Terry and the Pirates* world, don't you?"

Carmela ignored his little stab at humor. "Rumor has it Vasiliy recently aced out Miguez in the local absinthe black market."

Babcock no longer looked bemused. Now he looked stunned. "Carmela, you need to start sharing information with me."

"What are you talking about? I just did."

"You obviously have some sort of inside line on this guy Vasiliy, as well as Miguez. You have to back off. Jekyl, too. He could have been hurt very badly last night."

Carmela stared into brown, liquid eyes. "Seriously, I don't *know* all that much."

Babcock still looked stunned. "Actually, it's beginning to look like you do. You just haven't put it together yet."

"And you'd be the man to jump in and do that?" she asked. She was flirting with him a little. Testing him, too.

"Archie Baudier's murder is an open and ongoing homicide investigation. Something

316

the NOPD takes very seriously."

"Hopefully, they take it seriously," said Carmela.

"Unfortunately, we haven't made much progress."

He stared down at her, and Carmela suddenly, desperately, wanted to fling her arms around Edgar Babcock's neck, bury her face in his cashmere jacket, and tell him all the bits and pieces she'd uncovered. Have him hold her, kiss her, and what? Make it all better? Sure, why not! She *wanted* to do all that, but something was holding her back. What? The fact that Shamus still loomed in her background like a bad recurring nightmare? Maybe.

"Carmela," said Babcock, studying her face. "What?"

She drew a shaky breath. His voice was gentle and, as he leaned forward, she could have sworn his lips brushed the top of her head. It was oh-so-subtle, almost imperceptible. But still, the feeling was there. A little sizzle of electricity jolting through her. Of chemistry building between the two of them.

Babcock remained close to her. She could feel his presence, wanted desperately for something to happen.

"Carmela," said Babcock softly. "I need to tell you something."

She gazed up at him. Their eyes locked. And just as he was about to open his mouth, the front door flew open with a loud crash, and Gabby came flying out.

"Carmela! Oh my goodness!" Gabby shouted, panting hard, as if she'd just run the fifty-yard dash. "I'm so glad I caught you. Shamus is on the line!"

CHAPTER 24

"You think Babcock was going to kiss you?" asked Ava. She was hunkered cross-legged in the front seat of Carmela's Mercedes convertible, hugging her knees, hanging on every word. Boo and Poobah were snuggled in the back compartment as they sped south on Highway 90, headed for the Barataria Bayou.

"Pretty sure," responded Carmela.

"And then your a-hole husband called?" said Ava, shaking her head. "Man, talk about rotten luck. Talk about an ill wind blowing your way. A real stinky poo of a wind."

"No kidding," said Carmela. She was still disappointed. She had a feeling there, just for a couple seconds, that Babcock might sweep her into his arms. And would that be a good thing? It sure *seemed* like a step in the right direction.

"What did Shamus want that was so

319

darned important?" asked Ava as she dug into a bag of corn chips.

"He wanted to know if the dogs could have another sleepover at his house."

"And there you were," laughed Ava, "hoping for your own little sleepover." She glanced sideways at Carmela. "Or would that be rushing things?"

Carmela squinted into the sun. "To tell you the truth, Ava, I'm not sure. I keep hoping I'll recognize the right guy when I see him. Like shopping for great shoes or picking out the perfect red lipstick."

"Men aren't that easy," said Ava. Then she suddenly let loose a hearty chortle. "On the other hand . . ."

Carmela laughed along with her. "Yeah, yeah, I know what you mean."

They cut over to Highway 1 and continued south, then cut back north and east just above Port Fourchon and bumped over a string of bridges until they reached Grand Isle. It was a village that had been slammed by Hurricane Katrina. A few buildings had been absolutely flattened. Luckily, many had been rebuilt.

"Colorful little place," remarked Ava as they rolled past the Catfish Café and Pie Eye's Bar. They pulled up in front of the

Blue Bayou Boat Rental and rocked to a stop.

"Now, hang tight to the dogs," warned Carmela, "until we get 'em loaded into the boat." The town dogs, a passel of curious, motley-coated, long-legged creatures, had come to stare at the new arrivals. Boo wagged her tail, thrilled. She was dying to run rough and tumble with these local tough guys.

Carmela approached a man with long, gray hair who was dressed in camo pants and a leather vest. "I'm Carmela Bertrand. I called about a boat?"

"For fishing?" he asked. One blue eye focused on her while the other wandered off to the left. Carmela saw he had some sort of tooth on a cord around his neck.

"That's right," said Carmela. "You're Garitty?"

"You don't have no equipment," Garitty observed.

Ava joined her with Boo and Poobah straining at their leashes. "Collapsible rods," she told him. "Very efficient."

Garitty snorted.

"Is that a shark's tooth?" Ava asked him.

He touched it with rough fingers. "Barracuda." Then he turned and lumbered down the narrow wooden dock where boats bobbed and clunked at their tethers. "You're not gonna go and get yourself lost, are you?"

"No problem," said Carmela.

Garitty hooked a thumb backward over his shoulder. "That way's the Gulf of Mexico. Big." He waited a beat. "T'other way's bayou." His good eye fixed on Carmela again. "If you come back after five, just tie up at the dock. If you're not back by tomorrow morning, I'll give the Coast Guard a toot."

"Do that," said Carmela, as Ava clambered into the boat, and the dogs followed suit.

Fifteen minutes later they'd lost sight of Grand Isle and were skimming across sparkling water. The sun shone down brilliantly, kaleidoscoping into a million points of light.

"Fun," shouted Ava above the roar of the outboard motor. She'd wrapped a red kerchief around her head and, with her hair billowing out around her gold hoop earrings, looked once again like a sexy female pirate.

Carmela studied her map and adjusted course. They headed for a spit of land studded with saw palmetto and tupelo gum trees. They'd be entering one of the Barataria Bayou's waterways now, and she wanted to be dead on course.

They zigged, then zagged, slowing even

322

more. Large rough-shelled turtles peeked at them, pitcher plants littered the nearby banks.

"You love it down here, don't you," said Ava.

Carmela nodded. Most people were afraid of bayous. They were terrified of snakes and alligators and the twisty-turny waterways among the mangroves where a person could get lost. But Carmela felt a kinship with this still, dark water and the tall trees draped in canopies of vegetation. As long as you took precautions, creatures wouldn't bother you. As for getting lost . . .

"We're not gonna get lost, are we?" begged Ava. "I don't fancy spending the night out here. Although then we might meet some of those hunky Coast Guard fellas."

"Don't worry," said Carmela. She had her map and her trusty Brunton orienteering compass. And, if either of those failed, there was always the sun. As long as she kept that giant yellow orb just over her left shoulder for the next hour or so, she'd know precisely where west was.

Puttering along, they spotted an old cabin hidden in the woods.

"People live out here?" asked Ava.

"Sure," said Carmela. "A few. Some of these places are camp houses where folks from town come to hunt and fish. But there are a few local denizens who live out here, hidden away. Sell their pelts or fish for cash and completely dodge the IRS and everything else federal."

"That's good to know," said Ava. "In case we're ever on the lam or something."

"When I was looking through that file I got from the historical society, I found a newspaper account about a guy who lived in this neck of the woods," said Carmela. "Name of Billy Bowlegs."

"Sounds like a real cutie," said Ava. "Who was he?" She was leaning against the bow of the boat, trailing one hand in the water, leaving her own miniature wake.

"An old pirate," said Carmela. "He served with Lafitte for a while and finished out his days in a small cabin somewhere right around here. He's reputed to have died in 1888 at the ripe old age of ninety-five."

"So Billy Bowlegs almost peeked into the next century," said Ava. "That's really something."

"I came across another strange story," Carmela told her. "Don't know how true it is, but one of the more colorful legends associated with Jean Lafitte's treasure is that he left a gang of skeletons to guard it."

Ava hunched forward, looking startled.

"You never mentioned *that* before."

"Because I didn't know about it. I just read it this morning before we headed out here."

"Were the guys dead or alive when he left them?"

"Good question," said Carmela.

"Man," said Ava, looking nervous. "I wish you wouldn't tell me stuff like that. Gives me the willies."

Carmela was dumbfounded. "Ava, you've got skulls and skeletons and shrunken heads hanging all over your shop! You, of all people!"

"But those are plastic," said Ava. "Not real clackety-clack skulls and bones. *Big difference.*"

Carmela consulted her map and adjusted her direction again. Just below Madison Canal was a stream called Bayou La Cache. *Cache,* of course, literally translating to a cache of treasure. It was supposedly the area where Lafitte had hung out right before the Battle of New Orleans.

She slowed the boat, eyeing the contour of the land, measuring it against the outline on her map. When she spotted the stream, she checked her speed even more and gently turned in.

325

"This is gorgeous," declared Ava as they swept upriver. Ferns and water hyacinth lined verdant banks. Ospreys and ibises screamed from trees; speckled trout darted beneath their boat. The scene was almost primordial in its beauty.

"Whoa!" exclaimed Ava. "Did you see that?" She pointed toward one of the banks.

"What?"

"It was white, only a slip of a white shadow. But it looked . . . almost ghostlike."

"Nutria," said Carmela.

"Huh?"

"It was probably one of the rare white nutria that live out here. You were lucky to spot one; they're very elusive."

"Don't people wear nutria coats?" asked Ava.

"I think so," said Carmela. "But I'm pretty sure these critters are protected. Besides, you might not see another one for five years. Take a long while to put together a coat."

"That little guy was actually pretty cool," remarked Ava as the banks continued to close in on them.

"Keep your eye out for two key landmarks," advised Carmela. "Devil's Point and Arch Rock."

"How do you *know* about this?" asked Ava.

"I just kept poring through those documents and then coupled it all together."

"So which comes first?"

"Devil's Point," said Carmela.

"And that would be . . . what? Some sort of hill?"

"Or high point," said Carmela.

They motored along slowly, both women scanning the banks and up ahead.

"What about that?" Ava pointed toward an elevation of land. It wasn't exactly a hill, but it stuck up maybe ten or fifteen feet.

"Looks good," said Carmela. "Now if we can find Arch Rock . . ."

That appeared a few minutes later. A red rock that literally formed a small archway.

"And there's a dock," said Ava, excited.

Carmela pointed the boat toward a large dock that was half sunken in the water and overgrown with bright yellow cow lilies.

"Careful . . . careful," said Ava as they swung in.

"Looks rickety," said Carmela, as Ava placed one foot on the bow of the boat, ready to jump. "Be careful."

Tentatively, Ava set one foot on the dock. "No way is this thing solid," she warned. "It's all spongy and rotted through."

"Then let me maneuver us closer to shore."

"Okay," said Ava, grabbing a line while

the boat sputtered in toward a clump of reeds. "I think I can jump now."

She made it by just inches, but she made it.

"Okay if the dogs come?" asked Ava. No sooner had the words escaped her mouth than Boo and Poobah rocketed off the boat like a couple of flying squirrels. "Okay," said Ava, making a hand-dusting gesture. "That went well."

Carmela made the jump and landed badly, the heel of her shoe sinking into muck.

"Good thing you wore Keds and not Manolos," remarked Ava. She looked around. "Now what?"

Carmela studied the surrounding landscape, trying to visualize how it might have been a hundred or more years ago. Finally she said, "Why is there a dock there?"

Ava thought for a minute. "Don't know, but I bet if we hunt around, we might figure it out."

Loud barking up ahead told Carmela her dogs had already discovered something.

Thirty yards in, they stumbled upon ruins. A scatter of bricks here, a fallen-down pile there.

"What is this?" Ava wondered aloud.

They pushed on through underbrush, came across a giant black cauldron, pitted and rusted through, lying on its side.

"That's some kettle," said Ava. "Somebody made a heckuva pot of jambalaya."

A large, rusted, square-shaped contraption lay a few feet away.

"Okay," said Ava. "I'm not mechanically inclined, but I know that's not a carburetor."

"It's some sort of press," said Carmela. "If I had to guess, I'd say we stumbled upon the ruins of an old sugar plantation."

"I get it," said Ava. "The cauldron was once the melting pot."

"It's cool, isn't it," said Carmela, gazing around. "I mean this place."

"Like discovering King Tut's tomb," said Ava. "Really old. Think any buildings are left?"

"Let's find out."

"Hey, there's one," said Ava, pushing ahead and pointing through the trees. "Well, actually it's just a single brick wall. Pretty dilapidated, but still standing." She dug in her oversized purse, pulled out her camera phone, and handed it to Carmela. "Take a picture of me, will you? I'll stand in that doorway and pretend like I'm holding the whole thing up. You know, like a trick picture?"

Carmela backed up a few feet while Ava

posed in the open doorway, her arms stretched overhead as if struggling to hold up the wall.

"Be careful," said Carmela as she focused.

"No problem," said Ava, stretching her arms higher and pressing them into the wooden doorframe. "I think this —"

Creak!

"Ava! Watch out!" shouted Carmela.

Ava dropped to her knees and had only enough time to cover her head with her hands as the entire brick wall collapsed slowly around her. "Oh my Lord!" she screeched as dust billowed up and a loud, metallic clang rang out. "Help!"

When the last brick finally settled, only the wooden doorframe was left standing.

Ava peeked out from behind one hand. "I thought I saw dead people." Then she gazed around in awe. "It's a goner."

"I thought *you* were a goner," said Carmela, running to her and brushing her off. "Man, I should have known better. You could have been seriously hurt. The dogs could have been hurt —"

"What was that loud clang?" asked Ava.

"What?"

"Somethin' metal landed right behind me. Heavy metal. Almost took my head off." She turned around, squinting.

They poked in the rubble.

"There it is," said Ava. "Sticking up a little. Looks like maybe . . . a bell?"

Carmela grabbed a hunk of wood and worked to unearth it. Ava knelt down, her bizarre brush with death, or at least serious injury, momentarily forgotten.

"This is pretty cool," said Ava, scooping away dirt and rubble, unearthing a large, seriously tarnished bell. "Maybe it's worth something. You think it's made of gold?"

"Probably more like brass," said Carmela.

"Still . . ." said Ava. "It'd make a great souvenir." She brushed away more dirt, trying her best to clean it.

"It looks a little like a ship's bell," mused Carmela.

"You mean like, 'two bells and all is well'?"

"Yeah, but it's really crusted," said Carmela. "Wonder if we can tell who the maker is."

"Is that important?" asked Ava.

Carmela shrugged. "Maybe. Jekyl might be able to look it up in an antique guide. That thing was probably hanging there for a long time. Maybe a hundred years. Even two hundred."

"You know what?" said Ava, still on her hands and knees. "This bell has an inscription inside."

"No kidding."

"Take a look."

Carmela knelt down and studied the inside of the bell. There seemed to be letters or numbers or something etched on the inside rim. "Hard to read, it's so crusted," she said, trying to trace the etchings with her fingertips. "We need a heavy-duty metal cleaner. Like acetone or something."

"Hold everything," said Ava, digging in her purse.

"You don't really . . ." said Carmela.

Looking triumphant, Ava held up a small bottle of nail polish remover. "Will this work?"

It worked just fine. Rust, grime, and even some of the corrosion scuffed off.

"Can you see what it says?" asked Ava, excited now.

"Not letters," said Carmela, "but numbers. Let's see . . . two, eight, three, six, ten, sixteen, seventeen, and eleven."

"Yeah, but what do they mean?" asked Ava. "I have the feeling that's not a telephone number or somebody's Internet password."

Carmela thought for a minute. "Something to do with the maker?" she ventured.

"Maybe," said Ava.

"How about compass points?" Carmela

offered. "Or latitude and longitude? Or even an important date in history?" She thought some more. None of it seemed to track.

"Probably just one of history's mysteries," said Ava. "Except that . . ." she gazed earnestly at Carmela. "Archie's map led to Groomsbridge Plantation, where the inscription above the fireplace seemed to indicate this island."

"So we're still talking . . ."

"Pirates?" said Ava.

"Then there's another possibility," said Carmela slowly. "What if these numbers are some kind of cipher?"

Ava squinted at her. "A cipher? You mean like a one-eyed monster? Wait, that's a Cyclops."

"A cipher is an intricate puzzle. You know, numbers that correspond to letters and the letters spell something out."

"Sure," said Ava, "like a cryptoquip. In the same section of the newspaper where they have the daily horoscope."

"Sort of like that," said Carmela. "Problem is, to decode a cipher requires an encoding algorithm. You know, some kind of document."

"A document? Like what?" asked Ava.

"The Declaration of Independence, the Bible, *Betty Crocker's Cookbook.* You name it. Could be anything."

"Should we try to haul the bell back with us?" asked Ava.

"Not a bad idea," said Carmela.

They both grasped the bell and pulled. It barely budged.

"Okay then," said Carmela. "Let's just copy down those numbers."

They were back at Blue Bayou Boat Rental with plenty time to spare.

"Hey," said Ava, as she clambered out of the boat, "you know anything about that old sugar plantation on Queen Bess Island?"

Garitty squinted at her. "That's where you went?"

"Had ourselves a little picnic," said Ava.

"I thought you girls was fishing."

"Weren't biting today," said Carmela.

Garitty scratched at his three-day beard. "Place is old. More'n a hundred years. Maybe a hundred and fifty. I figured those ruins got flattened when Katrina blew through."

"Sounds like you know something about that place," said Carmela.

Garitty shook his head. "No more than most. It supposedly was part of the old Drouet Plantation." He gave a slow wink. "Pirate's lair, don't ya know."

"You know anything about Lafitte's treasure?" asked Ava.

He grinned, showing two prominent gold teeth. "Sure do."

"Like what?" asked Carmela.

"I know thousands of people have searched for it, but nobody's come close to finding it."

CHAPTER 25

It was just after four when Carmela dropped off Ava and the two dogs.

"C'mon *cher,* hang it up for the day," urged Ava as she gathered up her bag and leather jacket. "I'll come over to your place and cook us somethin' real tasty."

"Sounds good, but I have to make a quick run to Memory Mine," Carmela told her. "To make sure Bobby LeClerq strung that cyclone fence across my front windows." The one year she hadn't put sturdy fencing up was the year a lurching drunk was shoved clean through her window. Oh happy day.

Carmela also wanted to pick up the day's receipts from Gabby. Tomorrow, Fat Tuesday, was not a great day to have money just sitting around in her cash register.

Cruising Royal Street, Carmela was about to turn down her alley when she noticed a familiar form.

Who is that?

It was Miss Norma, Jekyl's Miss Norma. And she was standing at the front door of Royal Coin and Curios, ringing their bell!

Now wasn't *that* interesting?

Stunned, Carmela watched a few moments longer, saw the door open and Miss Norma's ample form disappear inside. Her curiosity burning, Carmela wondered what the heck Miss Norma's business was with the scummy Mr. Tallant.

Was she buying coins, selling coins, or did she have something else going on? If they were in collusion together, that wasn't good, either. In fact, it would mark them as serious suspects in Archie Baudier's murder.

As Carmela bumped down the alley and parked behind Memory Mine, she wondered if Miss Norma was still strong enough, muscled enough from her dancing days, to get the jump on someone. She decided she just might be.

Pushing through the back door, Carmela found that Gabby was just closing up.

"Oh, hi," said Gabby. "I didn't think you'd be back."

"Busy day?" Carmela gave a slight grimace. She felt supremely guilty about being gone.

But Gabby looked calm and unruffled. "Not too bad. Tandy was in for a few hours and helped out. Restocked paper and organized a couple shelves of albums."

"Have to put her on staff," said Carmela.

"Just keep gifting her with paper, ink pads, and rubber stamps; she's plenty satisfied being paid that way. And I know she really enjoys hanging out here."

"You're probably right," said Carmela. "Hey, tomorrow's the big day. Am I gonna see you and Stuart at the parade?"

Gabby grinned from ear to ear. "Are you kidding? We wouldn't miss seeing you and Ava riding your float for anything in the world. Just be sure to toss us some beads!"

Alone now, Carmela wandered into her office, poured herself a half cup of coffee — the dregs from what was left in the pot — and thought about the discovery today on Queen Bess Island.

Could the numbers on the bell actually mean something? Could they, in fact, be a cipher?

Ava was fairly convinced the bell was another clue. If so, that meant the bell's inscription pointed to yet *another* clue. So where did it end? Or did it?

Twenty minutes of Internet research gave Carmela a basic overview on ciphers. They'd been extremely popular a hundred, two hundred years ago to encrypt important messages. In the last century, ciphers had fallen out of favor. And today, there were computer programs capable of cracking them in a matter of seconds.

So . . . okay. What did it all add up to? If anything? Miss Norma and Robert Tallant, the possible cipher on the bell, Vasiliy with his guns and absinthe, wacky Miguez, Archie's dogged hunt for Lafitte's treasure, and, of course, Archie's murder?

Carmela stuck the envelope filled with the day's receipts into her purse and decided to see if Jekyl had any ideas. He'd be at the Pluvius den, of course, all lathered up and in a mad rush, putting the final finishing touches on his floats.

"Can you stand it?" hissed Jekyl. "Jimmy Toups has completely redone the Mayan ruins float! Moved the pyramid to the front, painted the outside of it with garish gold hieroglyphics, and hung a pair of bizarrely ugly snake heads on the back. What kind of nightmare is that? *Snake* heads!"

"It's a monstrosity," agreed Carmela. Actually, she didn't think the float looked all that bad. The snake heads were strange, but who was going to see them in back?

"Why do I endure this indignity year after year?" asked Jekyl, throwing his hands in the air. "Why do I put myself through such gut-wrenching pain?"

"Because it's your passion," Carmela reminded him "It's what you do."

"And I've got that book contract," said Jekyl, fidgeting and pulling down the sleeves of his tight-fitting black leather jacket.

"With a deadline approaching," said Carmela. "And you probably already spent the advance they paid you."

"Oh, thanks so much for reminding me," snapped Jekyl.

"Listen," said Carmela, putting a hand on his arm, hoping to calm him down. "I need to talk to you about a couple of things." She pulled him into a corner, quickly told him about their afternoon in the bayou, the discovery of the bell and inscription, and how she'd seen Miss Norma entering Tallant's shop. Jekyl was mildly interested in their finding the bell and troubled by the Miss Norma sighting.

"Miss Norma?" said Jekyl. "Now *that's* a puzzle."

"Could she have stolen some coins from Archie?" asked Carmela. "And is now trying to sell them to Tallant?"

"I'd be more inclined to think that maybe

Archie *gave* her some coins," said Jekyl. "And now she's trying to cash them in. It could be purely innocent, you know."

"Maybe," said Carmela.

Jekyl thought for a moment. "The other possibility is that Tallant knew she had some coins and simply contacted her. He's certainly been bugging *me* right along. Wanting to buy Archie's coins."

"Are they for sale?" asked Carmela.

Jekyl shrugged. "His estate has to go through probate first."

"Who's honchoing that?"

"Apparently the police turned it over to a lawyer Archie had done business with. He's going to handle the estate and see what, if anything, passes on to the brother."

"Are inmates allowed to inherit things?" asked Carmela.

"Search me," said Jekyl. "No pun intended."

On her way out of the Pluvius den, Carmela ran into Melody Mayfeldt. Melody and her husband, Garth, owned Fire and Ice Jewelers, an upscale shop in the French Quarter that specialized in antique and estate jewelry. Garth belonged to the Pluvius krewe, and Melody was in the newly organized Demilune krewe with Carmela.

"Can you stand it?" exclaimed Melody. "Just one more day!" Melody was slim and petite with long, dark hair and a pert nose. She had a thing for Dior suits and looked like she should be organizing golf scrambles and silent auctions for the Junior League. But Melody had a killer instinct when it came to fine jewelry. Melody knew an old mine–cut diamond from a European cut, could divine Edwardian from Victorian in a heartbeat. And she was a virtual shark when she hit the auctions at Sotheby's and Christie's in New York.

"How does our float look?" asked Carmela. The Demilune float was being constructed across town in the Rigadoon krewe's den.

"Gorgeous," said Melody. "I only wish we had some sort of special throw."

"We do," said Carmela. "Our star and moon beads are spectacular."

Melody shook her head. "I'm talking about something really special."

"Like . . . ?" said Carmela.

"Oh, you know," said Melody. "The Zulu krewe tosses the requisite strands of beads, but then they hand out painted coconuts to a chosen few. It's a *huge* honor to get one."

"I see what you mean," said Carmela. She decided it *would* be neat if they had a unique handout that, over the years, acquired a special cachet and became a real treasure for die-hard collectors of Mardi Gras paraphernalia.

"And the Marquis krewe gives out scepters," continued Melody.

"You know," Carmela told her, "I just might have an idea."

The first thing that hit Carmela as she walked through her own front door was the aroma of cinnamon, apples, and hot grease.

"It smells like a carnival midway in here," said Carmela. "Where are the Pronto Pups and funnel cakes? More to the point, what on *earth* are you cooking?"

Ava turned to greet her. She was wearing a frilly red apron over a pair of black slacks and a black turtleneck. "You're just in time; everything's ready."

"That apron looks like it came from one of those sexy French maid outfits they sell at the Funky Love Shop on Rampart Street," remarked Carmela.

"Oh, it is," said Ava. "Fourteen ninety-nine with a cute little cap and panties to match. Here, sit down. Boo, Poobah, move your furry little tushes, and let your momma rest her weary bones." Ava turned back to the stove, grabbed a frying pan, and hurried back to the table where Carmela had taken a seat. "Here, taste." She plopped a half-dozen golden-brown, puffy apple rounds on Carmela's plate, then added a liberal sprinkling of cinnamon and sugar.

"I didn't know you could cook," said Carmela, unfurling her napkin.

"I can't," laughed Ava. "I could barely manage these."

Carmela took a tentative nibble. They were steaming hot but delicious. Unbelievably delicious.

"These are wonderful!" exclaimed Carmela. "They're . . . what? Fritters?"

"Slap Yo Momma Apple Fritters," said Ava. "An old family recipe."

"Uh . . . pardon?" said Carmela.

"It's a recipe I got from my grandma, Sweet Momma Pam. It was passed down to her from her great-grandma, Momma Nedra."

"I kind of get that part," said Carmela. "But what's with the slap yo momma bit? What's that *mean?*"

Ava dumped a couple more fritters on Carmela's plate for good measure. "I think," she said, laughing, "it's just my crazy family's way of saying finger lickin' good."

CHAPTER 26

Fat Tuesday dawned warm, sunny, and crazy. The Zulu parade, which had been scheduled to roll in the morning, was still sitting in its den. They were three hours late, headed for a probable four-hour delay. Which meant the Rex parade would also be colossally jammed up and starting way late.

Even so, the French Quarter was thronged with revelers. Almost half a million out-of-town visitors were expected this year, along with pretty much the whole of New Orleans and half of Louisiana proper.

As they did every year, the costumes seemed to get more and more elaborate. A geisha with a white-powdered face held hands with King Arthur. Batman and Minnie Mouse waved as they snapped pictures of passersby. A throng of Venetian lords and ladies in velvet costumes and gilded carnival masks pushed their way past vampires, a Civil War general, a man in a deep sea diver's suit, and a former president.

Beads were hurled as music blasted from bars that had remained open all night, and everyone sipped drinks from the ubiquitous plastic *geaux* cups.

Carmela was working away inside Memory Mine. She'd slipped through the crowds around ten this morning, as police began to cordon off key streets with black-and-yellow barricades.

Sitting at her computer, she scanned in an old map of the French Quarter, one she'd found in a book at home. She studied it for a moment, then added a few faint touches of color. *Good, perfect,* she decided. Carmela stood up and stretched her arms languidly above her head while her map printed out onto white paper. Then she grabbed it and walked out to appraise her selection of antique and vintage-looking paper.

She eyed the faded blue. That had a nice look of age to it. No, the antiqued gold parchment was even better. Classy-looking. Plus they had tons in inventory.

A sudden knock on the window interrupted her thoughts.

"We're closed," she yelled without looking over. She had no intention of making eye contact with whatever visitor wanted in.

A more insistent knock followed.

"What?" said Carmela, annoyed. Then she finally glanced up. "Oh." The visitor tippy-tapping at her front door was Lieutenant Edgar Babcock. She realized she wasn't entirely displeased at his unannounced arrival.

"What's up?" she asked as she unlatched the door.

"It's crazy out there," he said, shaking his head and hustling inside, slamming the door behind him.

"And you're a cop," said Carmela, a smile on her face. "You're used to craziness."

"Well, we like to think we can remain calm in the fray of things."

"Yeah, right," said Carmela.

"I just came from Ava's shop," said Babcock.

Carmela tried to read the look on his face. Nope, nothing doing. He was managing a great stone-face impression. "What's up with Ava?" she finally asked.

Now Babcock looked askance at her. "I'm happy to say your friend Ava spilled the beans a little."

Carmela feigned innocence. "Whatever are you talking about?"

"Come on now," said Babcock. "You two have been running all over hell and gone, hunting for treasure."

"No, we haven't," protested Carmela. "We've been trying to figure out who killed Archie. The treasure is really incidental."

"Are you serious?"

"Yes. We've truly been . . . investigating."

Babcock took a step closer to her. "That's what you call it?"

Carmela grinned up at him. "Works for me."

Babcock put his arms around her and pulled her close. "I wish you wouldn't put yourself in harm's way like that. I worry about you."

"I . . ." began Carmela; then Babcock's lips closed gently on hers. She swayed slightly, then leaned against him, enjoying the closeness, enjoying the moment. Time hung suspended for a good long couple of minutes as they nuzzled each other, testing, tasting, giving pleasure.

And then . . . talk about bad timing . . . his cell phone rang!

"Don't," she said, nuzzling him again.

He pulled away from her reluctantly. "I have to." Grabbing his phone from his belt, he quickly flipped it open. "Babcock." He was slightly flushed, and his voice sounded a little hoarse. Carmela was thrilled she could still have that effect on a guy.

Babcock mumbled into his phone. Said, "Yes, no, yes," then hung up. Then he looked at her, a little hungrily, she thought. "I'll call you later; we need to talk."

She touched his arm. "I'd like that."

He was about to say something more, when he glanced down at the map still clutched in her hand. "Treasure maps," he murmured. "Why is everybody so worked up over treasure maps?" He pulled her close to him again. "Please, Carmela, I know you don't want to hear this, but you need to quit this crazy hunt. Anyone who's searching for Lafitte's treasure is probably quite dangerous and determined."

She kissed him again on the cheek. "I know that."

"And *X* does not necessarily mark the spot!" he added.

Then Carmela watched as he slipped out the door and disappeared in the human wave that flowed by.

Oh really? she thought to herself, a little amused, a little flustered.

Back at her computer, she studied her map and recalled a little French Quarter history. William Faulkner had been a resident here for a short time. In fact, he'd written his first novel, *Soldier's Pay,* while living in a humble little apartment in Pirate's Alley.

Hah. Pirate's Alley. Perfect.

Smiling to herself, Carmela hit a key and made a giant *X* on her map, right at Pirate's Alley.

Then she loaded her paper tray, pressed Print, and watched with satisfaction as her laser printer spat out fifty copies of her newly created map. She gathered up the stack of paper and tapped it hard on the table to align all the sheets, all the while humming, thinking about Edgar Babcock.

Applying a little bronze-colored paint to a sponge, she dabbed paint on the edges of the maps to give them an aged look. Then she began rolling up each map and tying it with a piece of cord.

As she worked, Carmela was more than pleased. Her "treasure maps" looked darned authentic. They'd make a particularly nice giveaway when her Demilune krewe rolled tonight.

And after that . . . well, she hoped she'd be meeting up with Edgar Babcock.

"Over here!" called Ava. She waved a hand wildly, and when Carmela didn't catch sight of her right away, wove through the crowd at Mumbo Gumbo on four-inch red stilet-

350

tos to grab her.

"Oh, hiya," said Carmela, whirling around. "Sorry I didn't . . ."

"What's *wrong?*" asked Ava. Her bright lipstick matched her heels.

"Wrong?" Carmela was taken aback. "Nothing's wrong."

But Ava was suspicious. "You've got an awfully funny look on your face. Like something . . . Oh, *he* stopped by, didn't he?"

"Huh?" said Carmela. Was it that apparent?

Ava's eyes lit up, and she adjusted her sheer polka-dot blouse the better to show off her cleavage. "*Cher,* something happened, didn't it?"

A silly grin flooded Carmela's face. "Well, maybe a little something."

"Come on over and tell me all about it!" She plucked at Carmela's sleeve.

Carmela gestured at the table where Jekyl, a few of his antique dealer friends, and some women from the Demilune krewe sat. "Not in front of everybody," Carmela protested.

"Then let's go in the ladies' room," said Ava. "And I want to hear every juicy, saccharine detail!"

By late afternoon Jackson Square was a

madhouse. Jugglers, fortune-tellers, mimes, and Mardi Gras revelers all competed for space and attention. Sated from food and wine, Carmela and Ava pushed their way through the crowd, headed for Carmela's shop. They planned to change into their midnight-blue Demilune costumes, primp a little, then wander over to their float.

"Hold up a minute, *cher,*" said Ava. "I want to get a Lucky Dog."

"You just ate," marveled Carmela. "Jambalaya, red beans and rice, soft-shelled crab. *Four* soft-shelled crabs."

"Yeah," said Ava. "But that was a couple hours ago."

"Barely an hour," said Carmela.

"Can I help it if my metabolism's jumped into overdrive?" asked Ava. "I'm just so hyped about tonight." She pulled a couple dollars from her wallet. "You want one, too?"

"Okay," said Carmela.

While Ava was buying Lucky Dogs from one of the familiar hot dog–shaped carts with the red-and-white umbrella on top, Carmela glanced at the statue of Andrew Jackson sitting atop his rearing steed. It was a major landmark and the first statue ever designed where a horse had more than one leg off its base. As she stared at it, Carmela experienced a slight ping in her head. Which usually meant she'd made some sort of connection. Edging closer to the statue, Carmela studied the inscription: "The Union must and shall be preserved."

Could this be the phrase that decoded the cipher? she wondered. She turned the idea over in her mind. It was of the same era. On the other hand . . . it seemed like a long shot.

Suddenly, the music and babble of conversation around her was overshadowed by the chiming of the bells in St. Louis Cathedral, just a half block away. And this time something stirred deep within Carmela. Another germ of an idea. She frowned, glanced up at the triple steepled church that jutted high above the French Quarter.

"Here's your Lucky Dog, *cher.*"

Carmela continued to stare at the cathedral steeples. "Oh my goodness!" she suddenly exclaimed. "Listen! Do you hear those bells? They're the most famous bells in all of New Orleans!"

Ava glanced up, a little mystified. "Okay."

"Those are the very same bells that rang out like crazy the day the British were defeated!"

"So you're thinking . . . what?" asked Ava, taking a bite of her hot dog.

"Maybe those bells are somehow connected to the bell we found on Queen Bess Island," said Carmela, her words tumbling out now. "You know, from the same maker or something."

"Ya think so?"

"Could be," said Carmela, warming up to the idea. "If they date back to the same era, they can maybe tell us something."

"Then maybe we should go take a look," said Ava agreeably.

They switched direction, cutting diagonally across Jackson Square.

"You still want your hot dog?" asked Ava.

"You eat it," said Carmela. She was jazzed and anxious to take a look at those bells. If they could even get up there!

Pushing their way through a contingent of revelers who were all dressed in Peking Opera costumes, a familiar face suddenly loomed in front of them. A face that, when recognition finally dawned, pulled into a nasty sneer.

"Vasiliy!" exclaimed Ava, recognizing him.

He stared at her, hate radiating off him like heat waves. "You've got a smart mouth, girl. You should be careful; you could get your teeth knocked out!"

Ava cocked her arm back and made a fist. "Are you threatening me, you dumb goomba? 'Cause if you are, I'll knock your block off!" She turned to Carmela. "Carmela, do you know how to say *pepper spray* in Russian?"

Carmela pulled out her cell phone, held it up in Vasiliy's face. "Back off, or we call the police!"

Ava grabbed the silver chain she wore around her neck and pulled it out for him to see. "See this?" She dangled her red evil eye charm in front of his face. "It's a genuine evil eye that can put a nasty curse on your head. And don't think I won't use it!"

Vasiliy shrank back like a vampire confronted with a bouquet of garlic. "What do you know about such superstitions?" he snarled.

"Honey, I'm the queen of superstition," bragged Ava. "I own a voodoo shop!"

"C'mon, Ava." Carmela grabbed her friend's arm and pulled her away from Vasiliy. "He's drunk, weird, and dangerous," she cautioned. "Let's just get away from him!" Together they ducked into the Blind Tiger jazz bar and ran the length of the bar, heading toward the back door. Popping out into the alley, they circled back around to St. Louis Cathedral.

■ ■ ■ ■

The inside of the cathedral was a sharp contrast to the craziness happening outside. The interior of the great church was dark, cool, and serene. Candles flickered, the stained glass windows offered a kaleidoscope of colors, the elaborate wall murals glowed dramatically.

"Lovely," breathed Ava. "This place really touches my soul."

Carmela raised an eyebrow. "Seriously?"

"Oh yeah," said Ava. "Everybody thinks I'm this irreverent sort of person, but I'm actually very religious. I have a huge collection of saint medals and rosaries and holy cards." She gazed around the cathedral, noticed a couple of old women dressed in black kneeling in the back pews, reached down, and buttoned a button on her blouse.

"So you're okay with this?" asked Carmela. If Ava was so devout, she might not approve of scrambling around in the church.

"Oh sure," said Ava. "Just as long as we don't run into any ghosts."

"Ghosts?"

Ava nodded vehemently as she did up another button for good measure. "There's three or four that supposedly hang out here.

Although my favorite by far is Père Antoine." Père Antoine was the pastor for the newly built cathedral who ministered to the poor and infirm and was beloved by the entire city until his death in 1829.

"Will I know him if I see him?" asked Carmela.

"Long robe, sandals, sharp nose, white beard," said Ava. "Lots of people have seen his apparition."

But they didn't run into the good père, even when they snicked open the door to the central bell tower and wound their way up the narrow, wooden stairway. It was tough going in the dim light. The stairs were much steeper than normal stairs, and space was limited. Because of the design, they were forced to climb four stairs, turn, climb another four, then turn again. It was a dizzying exercise.

"My thighs are burning," whispered Ava. "And we're only halfway there."

Carmela nodded. "Not enough time on the old Thighmaster."

"Just this old-fashioned stair climber," muttered Ava. She let loose a high-pitched sneeze. "And, phew, is it dusty up here. Seems to me they could benefit from a few cans of Endust."

"Smells like they rubbed down these walls

with turpentine," remarked Carmela. "No wonder this place has burned down twice already."

The staircase got smaller and more cramped as they neared the top.

"I'm dying," gasped Ava.

"Couple more turns, and we've got it made," said a hopeful Carmela.

And they did make it, finally reaching the small bell tower room that housed the great brass bells and offered a dizzying view.

Ava shrank against the wooden interior wall with a panicked look on her face. "I neglected to tell you I'm afraid of heights."

"You could have fooled me," said Carmela. "Tottering around in those four-inch stilettos."

"Different paradigm," said Ava.

"Just focus on the bells," said Carmela.

"What if they start ringing?"

"Cover your ears," said Carmela. She glanced at her watch. "We should be okay, they're not scheduled to ring for another ten minutes."

"Gotta hurry then," said Ava.

They scrunched and hunched their way around the swinging bells, searching for something, anything, that might connect them to the old bell they'd found on Queen Bess Island.

"You see a maker's mark or anything?" asked Ava.

"All I see is an inscription," said Carmela, peering at incised French wording around the bottom of the largest bell. "It says: *'Braves Louisianais, cette cloche dont le nom est Victoire a ete fondue en memoire de la glorieuse joumee du 8 Janvier 1815.'*"

"What if this is the . . . what did you call it before, *cher* . . . the encoding rhythm?"

"Encoding algorithm," said Carmela.

"Yeah," said Ava. "The phrase that decodes the cipher. Wouldn't that be cool?"

Carmela shrugged. "Let's copy it down and give it a try. We don't have anything else going for us at the moment."

"I think I've got a pen and paper in here," said Ava, digging in her oversized bag.

Brrrring!

Startled by the shrill noise, they both jumped.

"Jeez, *cher,* your cell phone scared me half to death!"

Carmela thumbed the On button. "Hello?"

"Carmela," came Edgar Babcock's familiar voice.

"Hi there," she said, trying to sound chatty and innocent.

Obviously, she didn't sound all that innocent. "Where are you?" he asked, a note of suspicion creeping into his voice.

"Over . . . uh . . . near St. Louis Cathedral," she answered.

"Can we get together?" Babcock asked.

Carmela covered the phone. "He wants to get together," she whispered happily.

"Tell him by all means yes," Ava whispered back.

"Uh, I can't meet right now," said Carmela.

"Wrong answer," muttered Ava.

"We need to change into our costumes then hustle over to our float," Carmela explained to him. "So . . . later?" She let a hopeful note creep into her voice.

"I've got something I have to cover," said Babcock. "But how about we try to bump into each other . . . let's say the corner of St. Peter and Dauphine Street? Say around nine? There's a quiet café there, the Déjà Vieux. Well, hopefully quiet."

"St. Peter and Dauphine," she repeated. "At nine."

"We'll be in the parade then," hissed Ava. "Probably running really late."

Carmela covered the phone with her hand. "The parade goes right by there. Maybe I can . . . you know . . . jump off or something."

Ava peered at her. "Mmm, you got it bad, *cher.*"

"Are you still there?" asked Babcock.

"Absolutely," said Carmela.

"See you then," said Babcock.

"You'll be there?" asked Carmela, suddenly sounding worried. Shamus was always saying he'd be someplace, and then he never was. It made it difficult for Carmela to rekindle her trust.

"I'll be there," promised Babcock.

CHAPTER 27

"Do you think my costume's too tight, *cher?*" asked Ava. She had shucked out of her slacks and blouse and shimmied into her Demilune tunic. It was silky blue and skimmed her body. It was also so short it didn't leave much to the imagination.

"It looks fine," said Carmela. They'd be up on the float, after all, tossing beads. The crowds below wouldn't see all that much of their costumes.

"No, *cher,* I *want* it to be tight," said Ava, wiggling her hips. "I like the idea of being . . . uh . . ."

"On display?"

"Now that you mention it." Ava grinned.

"It's particularly snazzy with the red stilettos," remarked Carmela.

"That's what I thought, too," said Ava as she poufed her hair into an outsized mound, then sprayed it with super-hold hair spray.

"That stuff looks like lacquer," commented Carmela, who was trying to coax a little life into her do.

"That's the general idea," said Ava. She snapped the top back on the can. "Okay now, let's take a look at that inscription. You've still got the numbers we copied down yesterday?"

"Got 'em right here," said Carmela as they pulled out chairs and seated themselves at the table in back.

"What's the first number?" asked Ava.

"Two," said Carmela.

"Okay," said Ava. "The second word in the bell's inscription is *Louisianais,* so that's an *L.* What are the next two numbers?"

"Eight and three," said Carmela.

"So that's *est* and *cette* which gives us an *E* and a *C.*"

"Right."

Ava and Carmela continued to work quickly. When they'd finally finished, Ava frowned at the letters she'd scrawled on a piece of paper and said, "What's Lec La Ige? Maybe some kind of Native American word?"

Carmela studied it for a few seconds. "It's LeClaige!" she exclaimed. "As in the old LeClaige House over on Toulouse Street!"

"What!" screeched Ava. "We did it?"

"I think we did!" exclaimed Carmela.

Ava held her hands in the air as if asking for calm. "Wait a minute," she said in hushed tones. "What exactly did we do here?"

Carmela stared at her, her excitement continuing to build. "Solved it?"

Ava slapped a palm hard against the table. "Holy shitski! Are you telling me we might have found the treasure?"

"Looks like we're a step closer," said Carmela.

"And it might be somewhere in the Le-Claige House?"

"Maybe," said Carmela.

"That place is a dump!" said Ava. "It calls itself a tavern and an oyster house now, but it's really a rat trap."

"Sure," said Carmela. "But it's a historic rat trap."

"Decrepit," said Ava.

"Almost two centuries decrepit," agreed Carmela.

"So that puts it in the realm," said Ava.

"You mean the realm of possibility?"

"No," squealed Ava. "The realm of Jean Lafitte!"

"Just hearing you say that scares the crap out of me," said Carmela.

"Don't tell me you've got a bad feeling about this?"

"Maybe just a tingle," admitted Carmela.

Ava reined in her enthusiasm a notch. "You get serious tingles, *cher.* I gotta respect your tingles."

"Still . . ." said Carmela.

"We gotta go look," said Ava. "The sooner the better."

"I think the parade route winds past there," said Carmela.

"Have to make a little detour then," Ava said, giggling. "Wait. You think the place will be open?"

"It's a bar," said Carmela. "Trust me; it'll be open."

"So we're just gonna cowboy our way in?"

"You know a better way?"

Ava thought for a moment. "It's gotta be downstairs. We're gonna need to snoop around the basement, don't you think?"

"I think you're probably right," said Carmela.

"Could be dirty," said Ava.

"Could be dangerous," said Carmela.

That thought slowed them down for half a second.

Ava cackled wickedly. "Let's go do it. Jump on our float and then bail out when we get to the LeClaige House."

"Sounds like a plan."

Ava was headed for the door when Carmela called out, "Wait!"

Ava stopped in her tracks. "What?"

"Can't forget the special handouts I made this morning." Carmela quickly unrolled one and handed it to Ava. She stuffed the rest of the maps in a large plastic tote bag.

Ava was delighted. "This is great work! People are gonna fight to get one of these maps. How many did you make?"

"A limited run of about fifty."

"Collector's items then," said Ava, carefully rolling the map back up. She slipped the ribbon on and stashed it in her oversized handbag. "In fact, this one *I'm* collecting."

"You want to sit up top on the throne?" Melody asked Ava. Carmela and Ava had arrived at Louis Armstrong Park and were milling about excitedly with the rest of the Demilune krewe.

"It would be an honor," said Ava. "Course, halfway through I'd be happy to give somebody else the chance to perch up there." She gave a slow wink to Carmela.

"Great," said Melody. "And Carmela, I simply adore these treasure maps you did. You're just so darned creative!"

"Thank you, Melody," said Carmela.

Melody took the tote bag filled with maps.

"So everybody gets three or four to pass out?"

"Sounds good," said Carmela. She winked back at Ava, who was now perched on a blue throne set in front of a gigantic silver moon. "You look like you should be holding a scepter or something."

"Kid, this is such an enormous rush I can barely stand it," Ava said, giggling. "Climb on up here as close as you can."

Carmela tugged her costume down in back, then scaled the float until she reached the tier that was second to the top. She settled in behind a slightly wobbly railing and a bucket filled with beads that was hidden behind a gigantic painted cloud.

And then they were rolling!

"Wowee!" yelled Ava. "Fantastic!"

In fact, all the members of the Demilune krewe were hooting and hollering as the float lumbered slowly down North Rampart Street toward the parade starting point at Ursuline Street.

When they pulled in behind the Pluvius krewe's float lineup, Melody jumped down from the float and waved her arms. "Okay now," she yelled above a sea of voices. "Everybody look sharp and hang on tight. If you run out of beads, just yell for Gloria. She's sequestered on the inside of the float and can get another bucket up to you." She grinned. "Ready, ladies?"

"Ready!" screamed Carmela and Ava along with the other women as Melody swung back up onto the float.

And then, two minutes later they were rolling for real!

Marching bands blared, flambeaus with their flaming torches went whirling by them, police officers on horseback clopped past. And everywhere they looked was a sea of excited faces. Because they followed the Pluvius krewe, one of the super krewes, throngs of onlookers lined the streets. Hundreds perched on stepladders along the way; others hung from lampposts, leaned down from balconies, and hung precariously from windows. The atmosphere was raucous, it was wild, it was darned near intimidating.

"I love this!" shrieked Ava as she tossed a handful of beads into the crowd.

Carmela tossed a handful of her own, then leaned forward and slipped two strings of beads into a plastic bucket someone held up to her on the end of a bamboo pole.

"I wish I could see Jekyl's finished floats," Carmela said to Ava above the din. Those floats were just ahead of them in line, and Carmela knew Shamus was up there, too, tossing his own strands of beads. Probably tossing down a few drinks, too.

"Have to catch them at the end of the night," Ava shouted back.

Carmela nodded. But she was secretly hoping that the end of the night for her would mean a rendezvous with Edgar Babcock.

Then Carmela let herself relax and enjoy the total experience. The frenzied crowds screaming and waving at her, begging for beads. The bright lights of the floats contrasting against the dark night sky. The colorful neon of the French Quarter and the soft yellow of the gaslights that seemed so welcome and familiar as they rolled past them. The old brick buildings that stood shoulder to sagging shoulder with ancient wooden Creole cottages.

And then, sooner than she would have thought, Ava was tapping her on the shoulder, reminding her they'd just turned onto Bourbon Street and were within a couple blocks of the LeClaige House. Another Demilune krewe member had already climbed up and now occupied the exalted throne position.

"How are we going to get down?" asked Carmela.

Ava crooked a finger, and Carmela followed. They edged down a narrow walkway to the back of the float, ducked through a small opening, then descended a short ladder. Now they were in the guts of the float where volunteers slashed open bunches of beads and stuffed them into buckets.

"Back here?" asked Carmela, pointing toward the rear of the float.

Ava nodded. "That's it. I already asked Melody about hopping off. She said when we turn the corner at St. Peter, the tractor that's pulling us will slow way down. That's when we can just sort of jump down. Of course, we gotta make it quick, since there's another float right behind us. Then we hotfoot it through the crowd."

"You make it sound so easy," said Carmela. "Remember, there could be a few thousand people blocking our way."

"C'mon, *cher*," laughed Ava. "Where's your sense of adventure?"

They rolled along, hanging off the back of the float, ready to jump. When they felt a shudder and a downshift run through the wagon, Ava nodded. "This is it."

Then it was just a matter of jumping down and scurrying across the street.

"Not too bad," yelled Carmela as she pounded across the pavement, wondering

370

how on earth Ava could run in her high heels.

"Here we are!" cried Ava as she elbowed through a crowd that was maybe ten deep and headed for the front door of the Le-Claige House.

"So how are we going to get downstairs?" worried Carmela. "We can't just go clumping in and demand access to their basement."

"Leave it to me, *cher*," said Ava, as they careened through the front door and into the darkened bar. The smell of stale beer, hot oil, and cigar smoke assaulted their nostrils. Customers were lined up at the bar five deep; an aging pool table had a scrum of pool players clustered around it.

"Try to look sick," instructed Ava. "Pretend you're gonna barf!"

Carmela cupped a hand over her mouth and squeezed her face into a grim mask, trying to project an air of nausea. Which wasn't all that difficult, considering the overpowering smell in the bar.

"The ladies' room!" screamed Ava, her voice rising to an almost hysterical pitch. "Quick! Quick! Where's the ladies' room?"

A dozen fingers pointed toward a dim hallway, then looked away, embarrassed.

"Thisaway," called Ava, plucking at Carmela's sleeve.

They ducked down the hallway, never pausing at the door that said Dames.

At the end of the hallway was a narrow flight of stairs. Dark, wobbly, crooked. Carmela and Ava hesitated for just a split second, then plunged downward.

CHAPTER 28

Downstairs was truly the basement from hell: small, dark, and gloomy, with a pounded earth floor and filmy white sweeps of cobwebs hanging everywhere.

"This is awful!" lamented Ava, brushing nervously at her hair and shoulders. "What is this place? A chamber of horrors?"

Carmela gazed around. A single strand of dim lightbulbs, offering just a modicum of illumination, ran along the top of the low-beamed ceiling. Cartons of whiskey and scotch were stacked to either side of them. "It's just a basement storeroom," she said. "For booze."

"That's it?" asked Ava. "This is how our search ends?" She sounded supremely disappointed. "There's *nothing* here!"

"You were maybe expecting casks full of treasure?" asked Carmela.

"Not casks exactly," said Ava. "But *something* for our trouble."

"Give it a chance," suggested Carmela as they edged past crates of liquor. "You didn't think this was going to be easy, did you?"

They moved stealthily through the first room into a second, smaller room.

"More booze," said Ava, studying the labels. "Good thing they're pouring eighty proof upstairs. Kill some of the germs."

That second room connected to a smaller third room.

"This setup reminds me of railroad cars," said Ava. "Or a shotgun-style house. Or . . . hey, did you ever see that movie, *Silence of the Lambs*?"

Of course she had. "I don't want to hear any analogies!" warned Carmela.

"Well, it just reminded me," muttered Ava. "All creepy-like."

Dampness hung in the air; the temperature was definitely chilly. "It's very creepy," admitted Carmela.

They poked along slowly, one room leading to another. The wooden ceiling seemed to press down on them as the rooms got narrower, the lightbulbs fewer and farther between.

"Still nothing here," said Ava. "Although I think I hear water dripping somewhere."

"Keep looking," said Carmela. "There's gotta be *something* here. And if it was easy to find, the liquor delivery guy would have found it."

"Maybe he did," said Ava. "Maybe he's living like some royal potentate in the Bahamas. Drinkin' banana daiquiris and eatin' grilled lobster for breakfast. Got all his money stashed in one of those tricky offshore banks. If I was gonna . . ."

Carmela suddenly stiffened. "Shush!"

"What?" whispered Ava.

"I heard something," Carmela muttered under her breath.

"Probably the bartender coming down to grab a couple more liters of rum," grumped Ava. "Did you see how sloshed those guys at the bar were? One of 'em was —" She suddenly stopped midsentence.

Carmela cocked her head at Ava, raised her eyebrows.

Ava nodded slowly. She'd definitely heard something, too.

Carmela held her breath and listened. Now she heard a slight rustle, detected a disturbance in the air. "I think . . . somebody's following us," she whispered.

Ava cringed. "What if it's that miserable Russian?" she whispered back. "You think he could have trailed us here?"

"Maybe," Carmela said, under her breath. "But I've always had a bad feeling about

Robert Tallant." At the same time, she was trying to figure out what to do, where to hide. There weren't a lot of options.

"What are we going to do?" whispered Ava as they crowded together and slid behind a stack of wooden crates.

Carmela nodded at the crates, carefully eased the top off one, then reached in and grabbed a bottle to use as a weapon. Ava quickly followed suit.

Gathering her courage, Carmela yelled out, "We know you're there!"

Footsteps shuffled, something clunked woodenly, and then a figure appeared in the dim light.

Carmela strained to see. It looked like . . . no, it couldn't be, could it?

Margot Destrehan emerged from the shadows, a revolver clutched in her right hand.

"Margot?" said Carmela. Her voice sounded small and deflated, as if she couldn't believe what she was seeing.

"*That's* Margot Destrehan?" said Ava, startled.

Margot didn't waste any time with niceties. She turned steely eyes on Carmela. "You know where the treasure is." Her voice was harsh and accusing.

"No," said Carmela suddenly. "We really

don't. Cross our hearts."

Ava kissed the tip of her thumb and hastily crossed her heart for emphasis. "Really. We're as clueless as you are."

Margot was not so easily dissuaded. "You've been following clues and searching for that treasure for almost a week. Now I want to know what you know! It was obvious that Archie was close, that he'd found some sort of map, but he played his cards very close to the vest. *Too* close for his own good."

Staring at Margot Destrehan in this damp, dark basement, Carmela wanted to kick herself. She'd misjudged Margot entirely. Margot had been the one leaning over Archie Baudier's shoulder as he spent hours researching Jean Lafitte's treasure. Margot had been doing book repairs with gold leaf and leaving a clue of powdered gold paint. Margot toiled in a job that probably paid low to desultory wages. Was forced to grovel to donors, like Shamus's sister Glory, and act grateful for every single contribution that came their way.

"And now," said Margot, "you're going to tell me exactly what you know. Exactly what you've found!"

"Are you not listening, Margot?" yelled Carmela. "We don't know anything!"

"What part of no, or not know, don't you understand?" chimed in a petulant Ava.

Margot lifted the revolver and waggled it at Carmela, then at Ava. "What *you* don't seem to understand," said Margot in a nasty tone, "is that *I'm* the one giving the orders!"

"You're crazy!" shrilled Carmela. "Cracked!"

Margot's face constricted, and her pupils shrank to pinpricks. Her index finger twitched spasmodically and a loud blast rocked the basement.

"Holy shit!" cried Ava as wood splinters exploded near her head.

Margot grimaced and shot again. This time Carmela felt chips of something, plaster or rock, sting the side of her face.

"*Cher,* you're bleeding!" cried Ava.

Carmela held up both palms in a gesture of supplication. "Okay, that's it, Margot. No more shooting. We give up. We'll give you exactly what you want."

Margot narrowed her eyes as she lowered her gun slightly.

Carmela hung her head, trying to appear whipped. "Ava," she told her friend in a dejected tone, "Margot's got us. We're going to have to hand it over."

Ava's head whipped toward Carmela and fixed her with a blank stare. "Huh?"

"The map," said Carmela.

"Map?"

"It's no use," said Carmela, nudging Ava's shoulder gently. "Give her the one in your purse."

"Oh," said Ava, letting out a long breath. "*That* map. Yeah, I guess." She gave a resigned nod. "Looks like you win after all, Margot."

Margot held out her hand. "Give it here," she demanded, her lips curling in an unsavory manner, her eyes as flat and hard as a reptile's.

Ava pulled the map from her bag and reluctantly held it out, letting loose an exaggerated sigh.

Greedily, Margot reached out and snatched the map from Ava's hands. Then she jammed it deep down inside her own purse.

Carmela watched nervously as Margot's hand continued to feel around inside, then slowly drew out a small red-and-white metal can. Carmela recognized it immediately: lighter fluid.

Ava was no slouch either. "Whoa!" she cried.

"You don't need to do that, Margot," said Carmela, fighting to keep her voice even. "You won. You've got the map. You hold all the cards."

"I really don't like messy endings," hissed Margot. "Which is why I have a little plan for you ladies. A good plan, really."

"Margot," pleaded Carmela. "Don't do this. You don't want our blood on your hands. You're going to get caught, and there's the death penalty to consider. Louisiana isn't shy about leveling the death penalty when it comes to first-degree murder. Lethal injection, in case you've forgotten."

"Or, best-case scenario," warned Ava, "they'll send your sorry ass down to the women's prison in San Gabriel. Life's not too pleasant near those swamps. It's hotter than Hades, and your hair will frizz in perpetuity. Plus the place is a breeding ground for wood ticks and mosquitoes. You might even contract malaria."

"Shut up!" snarled Margot as she pulled the red plastic top off the can and squirted streams of lighter fluid toward them. "You're over, you're through!"

Carmela and Ava jumped back. Quick as a snake, Margot flung the can at them and flicked her thumb against a red plastic lighter. She tossed the lighter and, instantly, like a hellish nightmare scenario, flames roared to life.

"Get back!" Carmela warned Ava.

"I am!" Ava screamed back.

Through bright, licking flames, Carmela caught a glimpse of Margot's face; then Margot retreated, and they were trapped by the roaring fire.

"Oh Lordy!" yelped Ava. She grabbed a hunk of loose cardboard and started fanning.

"Don't!" yelled Carmela. "You're literally fanning the flames!"

"Sorry!" cried Ava as they retreated farther into the recess of the last room.

Terrified now, images of Boo and Poobah flashed before Carmela's eyes. And her momma, too. What would happen to all of them if she perished down here? And what of Edgar Babcock? Hadn't they been close to finally declaring their love for each other?

"Let's try to flatten ourselves against the back wall!" shrilled Ava. She grabbed Carmela's arm, tried to tow her along. But she got tripped up on something, pitched forward awkwardly, and landed flat on her face.

"Ava, honey!" cried Carmela.

Ava writhed in pain, coughing from the smoke and heat. "Dang," she said, "my toe's hooked on something!" Ava let loose a series of wretched coughs as the room continued to billow with smoke.

Carmela dropped to her knees and flailed around. Her fingertips dug into soft mud and skittered across . . . what? An iron ring? Her brain struggled to work overtime. Could there be some sort of trapdoor here?

"Ava, quick!" Carmela yelled above the roar of fire. "Help me clear some of this mud and gunk!"

Their fingers dug frantically. Fifteen seconds later they'd cleared away enough mud to reveal a round, wooden trapdoor.

"Pull!" instructed Carmela.

Together they half pulled, half pried it open. A terrible smell, like rotting eggs, poured out.

"No way!" cried Ava. "We'd need gas masks!"

"Ava," cried Carmela. "Listen."

Above the crackle and pop of flames was the distinct sound of running water.

"It could be a way out," said Carmela.

"Could be a death trap," protested Ava. She peered down into the dark, secret passageway. "We can't climb down, it's pitch-black!"

Wrenching a piece of wood from an overhead beam, Carmela stuck it in the fire, then raised her makeshift torch above her head. "Now go!"

Ava had a leg halfway in when a look of

panic crossed her face. "What if there are alligators down there? Like the sewers of New York! Blind, *albino* alligators?"

Carmela shot a nervous glance at the advancing wall of flames. She felt the tiny hairs on her arms being singed. "If they're blind, they won't even notice us! Now jump!"

Ava plunged down the rabbit hole. Carmela followed in a mad scramble.

CHAPTER 29

"It's a sewer!" cried Ava, one hand pinching her nose. They'd tumbled down a ten-foot iron ladder, dangled from the bottom rung, and been forced to drop another five feet. Carmela clung hard to her torch, burning her arm in the process. Now, as they stood in ankle-deep water, gaping about, their sputtering torch revealed a low, round-ceilinged tunnel.

"At least we can breathe the air," Carmela said nervously. They'd escaped a roaring inferno only to drop down into a nasty, damp, underground cavern.

"Let's try to climb back up," pleaded Ava. "Maybe the fire's burned out by now."

Carmela tapped a finger against the bottom rung of the ladder. It was hot to the touch. "There's no going back," she told her friend. "Probably the entire bar is on fire by now."

"What do we do?" asked Ava. "Ooh . . .

try your cell phone!"

Carmela tried. "Nothing. Doesn't work down here."

"What is this place?" asked a terrified Ava. "Sewer? How come it's not full of water?"

"Maybe most of the time it is," said Carmela.

"I hear water dripping now," said Ava. They both went silent, listening to an insistent drip, drip, drip.

Carmela held her sputtering torch over her head, studying the barrel-shaped tunnel, peering down a length of impenetrable darkness. "So we go . . . that way?"

"Yech," complained Ava, lifting a foot out of the water. "My heels are completely trashed. And these are Steve Maddens!"

"Sorry," said Carmela.

"Fifty-nine bucks. Big investment for a gal like me."

"I hear you," said Carmela as they slogged along.

"And now they're probably covered in rat poop, too," complained Ava.

"Try not to think about it," said Carmela. "Try not to *envision* it."

"Jeez," shuddered Ava, "is it just me or does this tunnel seem to be getting smaller?"

"I thought it was just my whacked-out perception," said Carmela, her teeth chattering in the chill air, "since I clunked my head back there. But I think you're right."

"What if this just dead-ends?" asked Ava. Her breathing was shallow and labored. She was nervous edging toward scared silly.

"Don't even think it," warned Carmela.

"Nasty phrase, huh, *dead* end?" breathed Ava.

"Ava . . ."

"Oh man," said Ava, and now Carmela could see shiny tears streaking Ava's cheeks. "Your torch is getting low. I think it's gonna burn out!"

"Got to find something else," murmured Carmela. "Hunk of wood or something. Piece of cloth." She looked around frantically. Ava was right; the torch was suddenly hissing and sputtering. It would only last a few more seconds.

"There's nothing!" wailed Ava.

Carmela took a few steps down the tunnel, held the torch out to her side, and spun around quickly, searching for something, anything, that might be combustible.

"*Cher,* do something!" pleaded Ava.

Just as the stave of wood was down to a final, glowing ember, just as darkness was closing in, Carmela glimpsed a shred of something out of the corner of her eye.

A rag? Yes, has to be.

She pulled hard, grappling with it. It was some kind of fabric, attached to a stick. She hastily touched the glowing embers of her failing torch to the flimsy material, hoping she wasn't too late or the fabric too damp.

"Is it gonna catch?" asked Ava, miserably.

"It's . . ." began Carmela, then snapped her mouth shut, held her breath, watching.

Slowly, inexorably, small flames licked tentatively, then caught hold. And, slowly, her new jerry-rigged torch began to glow.

"Thank heavens!" said Ava, throwing her arms up in jubilation. Then as the new torch burned brighter, Ava clapped a hand to her mouth in horror.

"What?" said a puzzled Carmela. She looked up, suddenly realizing that the burning rag wasn't wrapped around a piece of wood at all but a long, knobby bone!

Stunned, Carmela held her grisly torch higher and was shocked to see a strange, ghostly tableau of six human skeletons leaning against the wall. Crumbled and corroded, the dust on the rib bones looked like gray felt, a half inch thick.

"Oh my God!" screamed Ava. "Who are they? *What* are they?"

Carmela let loose a strangled cry. "I think they're . . . what's left of Lafitte's men!"

All the old legends she'd heard as a kid

came flooding back to her. The courageous pirate, Jean Lafitte, sailing into the port of New Orleans, his ship's sails billowing in the hot winds of battle. Arriving just in the nick of time to throw in his lot with Andrew Jackson. Pirates feeling a sense of duty to defend this proud city as they stood heel to toe with the army, the citizens of New Orleans, and the Native Americans.

"Don't you get it?" murmured Carmela, a catch in her voice. "They're the guardians of the treasure. The last of Lafitte's men!"

Ava gasped in amazement. "It wasn't just a myth?"

"This is incredible!" marveled Carmela. "After all these years!"

"Why weren't they washed away in the flood?" asked Ava.

"Look," said Carmela, pointing at the wrist of one skeleton. "Shackles."

Ava blanched in horror. "While they were alive?"

"No," said Carmela. "I think this place served as some sort of . . . burial vault."

"But no treasure," said Ava. Now she sounded disappointed.

"You're right," said Carmela. "It's gone."

"All for nothing," muttered Ava. "Archie would have come up empty, too. After all his years of research."

Carmela held the torch closer, studying the skeleton in the center. Around its neck hung a small leather bag. She reached out and snapped it free. "Gotta keep moving," she told Ava.

They slogged along for what seemed like another fifty yards.

"Listen," said Ava. "Do you hear something? Besides water dripping and my heart pitter-pattering in fear?"

Carmela listened. There did seem to be a dull roar. Coming from . . . above?

"Whoa!" exclaimed Ava. "Look here. A ladder!"

It was a metal ladder, similar to the one they'd come down at the other end of the tunnel.

Carmela handed the torch to Ava. "Hang on to this, I'm going to climb up."

She climbed up the metal ladder, poked tentatively at the ceiling of the tunnel. After prodding and scratching, her fingers finally traced a circular outline. An opening? Had to be!

Carmela climbed up another rung, wedged herself, and jammed a shoulder against what she hoped was the opening. Pushed as hard as she could. Nothing.

"Ava, you gotta climb up here and push with me. This thing is like sealed in concrete or something."

"Hang on, *cher.*" Ava kicked off her shoes and climbed up barefoot. She wedged herself in next to Carmela, and together they grunted and groaned and pushed with all their might.

"Did it move?" asked Ava hopefully.

"Not sure. Try again."

They pushed with renewed effort, straining together.

"It might have moved a tiny bit," said Carmela.

"Optimistic, aren't you," muttered Ava. "Okay, one more time!"

They leaned into it like a couple of determined Sherpas, intent on pushing their cargo up Mount Everest. Suddenly, there was a loud whoosh and a clatter of metal. And then they were struck with a glut of cool, fresh air.

Their heads popped out of the hole like a couple of manic gophers.

"Holy shit!" cried Ava as she took in the scene aboveground. Sirens blasted, two nearby buildings were engulfed in flames, fire trucks were parked everywhere, gigantic hoses snaked across the street, firemen scrambled in all directions.

"You think," said Ava in a snide tone,

"that Margot's gonna have to pay for all this?"

"She better hope she gets that money from Glory," said Carmela.

"Whoa! Incoming!" whooped Ava. They were suddenly right in the glaring headlights of an onrushing police cruiser.

"How are we gonna explain this to the cops?" wondered Ava as a bright spotlight suddenly flashed at them.

Then the cruiser's door opened, and a pair of feet scrambled out.

"Carmela?" called a familiar voice. A voice that carried over and above the roar of the fire and the clamor of the crowds and rescue workers. "Is that *you?*"

Then Edgar Babcock was reaching down and lifting her up with such strength and energy that Carmela literally flew through the air for a couple of seconds. Two more police officers rushed over and hauled Ava out.

"Dang!" exclaimed Ava. "Thank you, boys." As she brushed herself off, her head spun around, searching for Carmela. "*Cher, cher,* are you okay?"

Carmela stood in the flickering light, looking a little forlorn, staring up at Edgar Babcock with a questioning look on her face. A single tear trickled down her sooty cheek.

Edgar Babcock spread his arms wide, then wrapped them gently around her. "Carmela," he murmured, pulling her closer to him.

"You're here," she said. "You said you'd be here, and you're actually here."

"Darling," he whispered in her ear.

CHAPTER 30

"We got her," Babcock told them. "A squad just picked up Margot Destrehan. Kicking and screaming like a lunatic, I might add." His cell phone was pressed to his ear, even as he carried on a running conversation with the group of four police officers that hovered outside his cruiser. Carmela was tucked in the passenger side, while Ava sprawled in the backseat.

"Of course, you got her." Carmela smiled. "All you had to do was follow the X."

Babcock gave a low chuckle. "You got me. In this case X really did mark the spot."

"It did for Margot, anyway," said Carmela.

"We gotta call Jekyl," said Ava. "Fill him in. Hey, you think Margot was the one who mugged him the other night?"

"Had to be," said Carmela. "She must have thought he had the map. Margot probably hung around at the cemetery, spying on us."

"And all along I thought it was the Russian who murdered Archie," said Ava. "Now I feel kind of bad, being so mean to him."

"You two probably put U.S.–Soviet relations back a full ten years," observed Babcock.

"No," said Carmela. "Vasiliy *threatened* us. He's dealing guns and, I'm pretty sure, drugs."

"I know, I know," said Babcock mildly. "We're watching him."

"Better get the FBI on his ass," warned Ava. "And if that doesn't work, well . . . here." She slipped the chain from around her throat, passed it forward to Babcock.

"What have we here?" he asked.

"An evil eye charm from my shop," said Ava. "It really works!"

"Of course it does," said Babcock, stuffing it into his jacket pocket.

"Here I was," said Carmela, "thinking Tallant and Miss Norma were in collusion, when I should have figured out Margot's involvement earlier."

"You didn't know, *cher*," said Ava. "Nobody did."

"When I stopped by to see her last Friday, she was doing bookbinding." Carmela shook her head. "The gold leaf was sitting right there on the table."

"Probably the same gold leaf we found on Archie's shoes," murmured Babcock.

"You can't beat yourself up over it," said Ava, patting Carmela's shoulder.

"We all missed it," said Babcock. "There just wasn't that much evidence."

"Excuse me," said Ava. "But haven't we forgotten something in all this excitement?"

"What's that?" asked Babcock.

"Carmela told you our fantastical story about finding the skeletons and all that," said Ava. "But nobody's peeked inside that leather bag yet. The one she grabbed from around that one skeleton's neck."

"Carmela mugged a skeleton?" asked Babcock.

Ava nodded happily. "You could probably arrest her, but you're about a hundred and sixty years too late."

"Maybe house arrest then," murmured Babcock, turning to smile at Carmela.

Carmela pulled the bag from her pocket and plucked at the leather. The cord was so stiff and ancient, it crumbled in her hands.

"This is so exciting!" exclaimed Ava, leaning over the backseat.

Digging inside the small bag, Carmela's fingers touched metal.

Could it be gold coins? she wondered. *A gold bar?*

As she poked at it further, a satisfied smile flickered across her face.

Maybe this is a talisman. A portent of things to come.

Carmela closed her fist around her prize and withdrew it from the leather sack.

"Whatcha got, *cher?*" asked Ava.

"Hold out your hand," Carmela told Babcock. As he did, she passed her find to him, then closed his fingers around it.

"Come on, you two," chided Ava. "Quit playing games. And quit looking at each other like that."

"Like what?" asked Babcock.

"Like you're ready to slip off to the boudoir." Ava laughed.

Slowly, Edgar Babcock opened his hand. In his palm lay a slender gold key. "Looks like pure gold," he said, clearly impressed. "But what's the key for? Since you never actually found any treasure."

"Don't be so sure," whispered Carmela. Smiling shyly, she snuggled against Edgar Babcock and rested her head on his shoulder. For the first time in a long time she looked completely happy and at peace.

"If you ask me," said a grinning Ava, "I'd say it's the key to her heart."

SCRAPBOOK, STAMPING, AND CRAFT TIPS FROM LAURA CHILDS

Add Punch to Black-and-White

Your black-and-white photos deserve a scrapbook page, too. But to really make them pop, mat them using scarlet or purple card stock, then arrange them against a background paper that color-coordinates with your mat. The effect will be stunning.

Making Memory Boxes

It's amazing how many small household containers we simply just throw away. Think Altoid tins, Brie cheese containers, cardboard jewelry boxes, and tea tins! But these humble containers can be painted, decoupaged, embellished, and bejeweled to gain a second life as elegant little memory boxes.

Stamp Paper not Grapes!

Wine is always a perfect hostess gift. But think about making your own stamped and decorated wine labels. For example, an Italian wine brings to mind rubber stamps that carry motifs of opera, grapes, Venetian masks, Tuscan vistas, and domed churches. Use papers and inks that evoke a rich, warm feel and tie raffia around the wine bottle to complete your Italian motif. You could even add an Italian saying or two, such as *Buona sera, Buon appetito,* or *Salute!* Since you're covering the vintner's label, be sure to add a small line that details exactly what type of wine it is.

Trifold Album

Make your own trifold album by cutting out three equal-sized panels of red chipboard. Punch holes down one side of the two side panels, punch holes down both sides of your center panel. Decorate and embellish using a red-and-gold theme, then add your photos. Burnish all edges of your panels with gold paint, then lace the panels together using thin brass wire.

Under the Asian Influence

Add elements of the Far East to your cards and scrapbook pages. Rubber stamps of cranes, rice paper, calligraphy, Chinese seals, blue-and-white beads, miniature fans, and red-and-gold tassels all work well. Or you could try your hand at origami, the Japanese art of paper folding. If you didn't find time for Christmas cards or left a few folks off your list, consider sending out Chinese New Year cards.

Scrapbook a Vintage Necklace

Do you have old skeleton-type keys lying around? String two or three on a piece of thin velvet ribbon and embellish it with antique buttons, bits of lace, and a few brass charms. Tie loose knots, twist in a second piece of ribbon, and even add a tiny metal picture frame; the quirkier your necklace, the better. Chances are you have many of the materials you need right there in your scrapbook corner or tote bag!

Get an Antiqued Look

Black-and-white photos look elegant when set against cream- or pearl-colored paper. Add snippets of lace, vintage ribbon, and old buttons. Using a sepia-colored pen to write a few words enhances your antique look. For color photos, just place a piece of vellum atop your photos to tone down colors and "ghost" your image.

Foam from Home
You can make elegant ornaments or small treasures using polystyrene foam apples and orbs from the craft store. Slice foam in half, then cover the outside with gilded paint or gold spackle. Then cover the inside with bits of paper and embellish these with stamped images. Add a small brass hinge and clasp so your creation easily opens and closes, then tie on a sprig of ribbon.

FAVORITE NEW ORLEANS RECIPES

PURPLE HAZE

1 1/2 oz. vodka
1/2 oz. black raspberry liqueur
Cranberry juice

Pour vodka into highball glass filled with ice. Add black raspberry liqueur, fill with cranberry juice, and stir.

VAMPIRE BAT WINGS

4 Tbsp. ketchup
3 Tbsp. soy sauce
3 Tbsp. chili sauce
2 Tbsp. honey
2 Tbsp. vinegar (regular or balsamic)
2 Tbsp. sugar

1/2 Tbsp. ground black pepper
12 chicken wings, cut into 2 pieces

Mix together ketchup, soy sauce, chili sauce, honey, vinegar, sugar, and pepper. Add chicken wings to marinade, cover, and set aside for at least 30 minutes. Put a metal rack in a roasting pan and places wings on top. Bake in oven at 250° for approximately 15 minutes. Now turn oven to broil, move pan to about 4 inches from broiler, and broil for 5 or 6 minutes, until wings turn dark and crispy (but not overly crispy). These are great for picnics, parties, or as a game-day treat.

CHEWY COCONUT-CRANBERRY BARS
1/2 cup all-purpose flour
1 tsp. cinnamon
1/4 tsp. baking soda
1/2 tsp. salt
1/2 cup butter
1/2 cup brown sugar
1 egg
1 1/2 cups sweetened shredded coconut
1/2 cup dried cranberries

Combine flour, cinnamon, baking soda, and salt in a bowl. Mix and set aside. In a separate bowl, cream butter and brown sugar until smooth. Add egg to the creamed mixture and continue blending. Now add flour mixture and blend. Stir in coconut and cranberries until well mixed. Spread evenly into an ungreased 8-inch square baking pan. Bake at 350° for approximately 20 minutes. Slice bars when cooled.

GULF SHRIMP FETTUCCINE

1/2 cup butter
1/2 tsp. fresh ground black pepper
1 lb. small shrimp, cooked in seasoned water
1 lb. fettuccine noodles, cooked and drained
1/2 cup heavy cream
1/4 Parmesan cheese, grated

Melt butter in large saucepan and add pepper. Split shrimp lengthwise and sauté in the butter for 2 to 3 minutes. Add cooked fettuccine and gently toss together. Add cream and Parmesan cheese and toss again. Serve immediately in shallow bowls with plenty of crusty French bread. Serves 4.

BIG EASY BREAD PUDDING

8 slices of bread (broken into small pieces)
1 stick melted butter
6 eggs, beaten
1 1/2 cups sugar
1 can evaporated milk (16 oz.)

1 1/2 tsp. vanilla
1 tsp. ground cinnamon
1/2 cup raisins (optional)

Mix all ingredients together in a large bowl. Pour into a glass pan and place that pan in a shallow dish of water. Bake at 350° for approximately one hour.

EVEN EASIER SAUCE FOR BREAD PUDDING

1/2 cup sugar
1/2 cup brown sugar
1/2 cup whipping cream
1/2 cup melted butter
1 tsp. vanilla

Combine sugar, brown sugar, whipping cream, and butter in a saucepan. Stir over medium heat for 6 to 8 minutes until mixture boils. Stir in vanilla and serve over bread pudding.

CRAB CAKES CARMELA

3 Tbsp. butter
2 Tbsp. diced onion
1/3 cup diced celery
1/2 cup bread crumbs
2 beaten eggs
1/2 cup milk

2 cups cooked, flaked crabmeat
1/2 tsp. prepared mustard
1 tsp. lemon juice
1/2 tsp. salt
1/2 tsp. paprika
Flour
Olive oil

Melt butter in saucepan and sauté onion, celery, and bread crumbs for 3 minutes over medium heat. Add in the eggs, milk, crab, mustard, lemon juice, salt, and paprika. Mix well and chill for about 2 hours. When ready to cook, shape mixture into 8 crab cakes and dredge in flour. Fry in olive oil over medium heat for about 4 minutes or until brown. Carefully turn crab cakes and fry an additional 4 minutes. Enjoy with your favorite tartar or aioli sauce.

SOUTHERN PEACH COBBLER

1/2 cup butter
2 cups sugar
3/4 cup all-purpose flour
2 tsp. baking powder
Salt, pinch
3/4 cup milk
2 cups sliced peaches

Melt butter and pour into 2-quart baking

dish. In separate bowl, combine 1 cup sugar, flour, baking powder, and salt. Now add milk and stir until mixed. Pour this batter into the baking dish, but don't stir. Combine remaining cup of sugar with sliced peaches and mix. Spoon over batter, but don't stir. Bake at 350° for one hour.

AUNT LAILA'S LACE COOKIES

2 sticks butter
3 cups brown sugar, packed
1 medium egg
1/4 tsp. salt
1 tsp. vanilla
4 cups quick rolled oats
1/2 cup pecans, chopped

Blend butter and sugar in mixer. Add egg, salt, and vanilla, then blend again. Now blend in the rolled oats and chopped pecans. Lightly grease a baking sheet. Using a melon baller, make small balls and drop onto sheet, about two inches apart. Bake at 325° for about 8 minutes. (Note: Cookies will melt, spread out, and become lacy. Let cool completely before removing them, and handle gently.)

CHILI CORN BREAD

2 15-oz. cans chili or 4 cups homemade chili
1/2 cup milk
1 egg, slightly beaten
2 Tbsp. vegetable oil
1 cup yellow cornmeal
1 to 1 1/2 tsp. baking powder
1/2 tsp. salt
1 cup cheddar cheese, shredded

Pour chili into lightly greased 8-inch square baking dish. In saucepan, combine milk, beaten egg, vegetable oil, cornmeal, baking powder, salt, and 1/2 cup cheese over medium heat. Stir until smooth, then pour gently over chili. Sprinkle remaining 1/2 cup of cheddar cheese evenly over chili batter. Bake at 400° for 30 to 35 minutes. Cool for about 5 minutes before serving.

VIDALIA ONION CASSEROLE

1/2 cup butter
1/2 cup self-rising flour
Salt and pepper to taste
3 Vidalia onions
1 cup medium to sharp cheddar cheese, shredded

Melt butter, then gently stir in flour, salt, and pepper. Peel and slice onions into rings, then dip each ring into the flour and butter mixture and place in a 9-inch-by-12-inch greased casserole dish. Stack in the rest of the onions, then top with shredded cheese. Bake in a 375° oven for 45 minutes or until brown and crispy on top. Serve hot. (Note: For variation, add a jar of pimientos, drained.) Makes a great side dish.

No-Cook Amaretto Pear Parfait

3 or 4 juicy pears, peeled and chopped
2 Tbsp. sugar
2 Tbsp. amaretto liqueur
1 cup gingersnap crumbs
2 cups vanilla ice cream
4 Tbsp. crumbled pecans

Combine pears, sugar, and amaretto, then cover and chill for one hour. To prepare parfaits, spoon gingersnap crumbs into parfait glass, add a dab of pear mixture, then a spoonful of ice cream. Repeat layers, then top with pecans. Chill until serving time. Makes 4 parfaits.

Slap Yo Momma Apple Fritters

1 egg, beaten
2/3 cup milk
1 Tbsp. melted butter
1 1/2 cups flour

2 tsp. baking powder
1 Tbsp. sugar
1/8 tsp. salt
3 apples (tart or Granny Smith)
1 lemon (juice only)
2 to 3 cups cooking oil

Whisk together egg, milk, and butter. Stir in flour, baking powder, sugar, and salt. Blend well and set aside. Peel and core apples, slice into 1/3-inch rounds, and toss with the lemon juice. Heat oil in deep skillet over medium-high heat. Gently dip apple slices into batter and drop into hot oil. Fry until golden brown and puffy on both sides, approximately 5 minutes. Remove using slotted spoon and drain on paper towels. Keep warm in oven until all apple slices are cooked. To serve, place fritters in dish and top with a little cinnamon and sugar. Or pull out all the stops and serve with ice cream or whipped cream.

ABOUT THE AUTHOR

Laura Childs is the bestselling author of the Tea Shop Mysteries and the Scrapbooking Mysteries. She is a consummate tea drinker, scrapbooker, and dog lover, and travels frequently to China and Japan with Dr. Bob, her professor husband. In her past life she was a Clio Award-winning advertising writer and CEO of her own marketing firm.

We hope you have enjoyed this Large Print book. Other Thorndike, Wheeler, Kennebec, and Chivers Press Large Print books are available at your library or directly from the publishers.

For information about current and upcoming titles, please call or write, without obligation, to:

Publisher
Thorndike Press
295 Kennedy Memorial Drive
Waterville, ME 04901
Tel. (800) 223-1244

or visit our Web site at:

http://gale.cengage.com/thorndike

OR

Chivers Large Print
published by BBC Audiobooks Ltd
St James House, The Square
Lower Bristol Road
Bath BA2 3SB
England
Tel. +44(0) 800 136919
email: bbcaudiobooks@bbc.co.uk
www.bbcaudiobooks.co.uk

All our Large Print titles are designed for easy reading, and all our books are made to last.